THE OLD GALS' BUCKET LIST

KAREN KING

B

Boldwood

First published in Great Britain in 2025 by Boldwood Books Ltd.

Cover Design by Head Design Ltd.

Cover Images: Shutterstock

Interior images: Boldwood Books and Shutterstock

A CIP catalogue record for this book is available from the British Library.

Paperback ISBN 978-1-83617-615-2

Large Print ISBN 978-1-83617-616-9

Hardback ISBN 978-1-83617-614-5

Trade Paperback ISBN 978-1-80656-021-9

Ebook ISBN 978-1-83617-617-6

Kindle ISBN 978-1-83617-618-3

Audio CD ISBN 978-1-83617-609-1

MP3 CD ISBN 978-1-83617-610-7

Digital audio download ISBN 978-1-83617-611-4

This book is printed on certified sustainable paper. Boldwood Books is dedicated to putting sustainability at the heart of our business. For more information please visit https://www.boldwoodbooks.com/about-us/sustainability/

Boldwood Books Ltd, 23 Bowerdean Street, London, SW6 3TN

www.boldwoodbooks.com

For Ann and Jen, with love and thanks for all the friendship and fun.

PROLOGUE
SANDRA

June

'Slow down for goodness' sake! You'll crash!' Sandra shouted, gripping onto the side of the speedboat for dear life. Patti was speeding along the coast of Fuengirola as if she hadn't got a care in the world.

'Hold tight and you'll be fine.' Mary laughed.

What on earth was she doing here? Sandra played it safe, always had, and now look at her! Oh heck, they were heading straight towards another boat, they were going to collide! She closed her eyes and gripped tighter.

'It's okay, she's turned in time!' Mary shouted.

Sandra opened her eyes and breathed out a sigh of relief when she saw that they really had turned around and were heading back to the shore. Adrenaline suddenly flooded through her as she relaxed and watched the foamy waves licking the sides of the boat. She had to admit it was exhilarating. She couldn't believe the things she'd done in the past few weeks. And it was all because of Patti. And Mary.

'You three are incredible!' Rob, the instructor, said, when they were all back on land again. 'You're real daredevils.'

'We're just three old gals living our best lives,' Sandra said, her eyes sparkling.

And that, she realised, was exactly what she was doing.

1

SANDRA

Two months earlier

'We're selling up and moving to Cambridge,' Don continued, his deep brown eyes – so like Brian's – gazing solemnly at her. 'I can't afford to turn down this promotion, Mum, it's a big increase in salary. It will make a huge difference to our lives.' He was leaning forward, elbows on the table, waiting for her response.

Sandra stared at him wordlessly. She felt like she'd been punched in the solar plexus, she was completely winded. This was the last thing she'd expected. When Don said that he was popping in on Saturday morning for a chat, she thought he might need a loan; she knew things had been a bit tight for them since Laila's hours at work had been reduced to four days a week. Of course she would help them. She wasn't flush, but she still had a bit of money in the bank, although not as much as she would have had if Brian hadn't forgotten to renew his life insurance when the mortgage had been paid off a few years ago. She wasn't going to dwell on that though, she could manage. She hadn't expected her son to tell her that his company were opening a new branch in Cambridge – a couple of hours drive away – and he'd been asked to manage it.

'You do see that I have to go, don't you, Mum? You know how we've been struggling financially. I can't afford to turn down this promotion.' Dressed as he was today in black T-shirt and jeans, his thick brown-with-a-bit-of-grey hair tousled – instead of the suit and gelled hair look he wore for work – he reminded her of when he was a teenager, confessing that he'd run into the car with his bike. She could see that he felt awful about moving away and leaving her.

She nodded, thoughts tumbling around in her mind as if they were on the last spin of a washing cycle. How would she manage without them? Don, his wife Laila and their two children Kali and Rana, lived a short drive away and were always popping in, inviting her over for dinner, asking her to babysit the children. She loved being involved in their life and couldn't imagine not having them nearby. Since her husband Brian had died eight months ago, they had been her lifeline. She didn't know how she would have got through the days without them.

'Of course. I understand.' Tears were pricking her eyes but she refused to let them drop. She was being selfish, Don and Laila had their own lives. They had to put their family first. She could manage. Of course she could. It wasn't the same as actually seeing them but she could Facetime regularly, like she did with Becky, her eldest, who lived in Australia with her husband Hogan and teenage children Zac and Honey. Martin, her middle child, had died before he had a family. It saddened her that he hadn't left a little version of himself behind.

She missed him terribly, and losing Brian had left another big hole in her life. Don, Laila and the children had helped fill that hole. And now they were leaving. A lump formed in her throat as she thought how much she would miss the hugs from six-year-old Kali and eight-year-old Rana's jokes, having them overnight for sleepovers, sharing Sunday lunch with them all.

She could still have her grandchildren to stay in the holidays, she told herself. And she could visit.

'What about Laila's job?' she asked, although what she wanted to ask was 'What about me? What am I going to do?' Laila was a project manager for a large healthcare company, she worked from home a couple of days a week but had to go into the office for the remaining two days. It would be a long drive for her from Cambridge.

'Her company said she can work from home completely, as long as she attends a meeting once a month. This is perfect for all of us, Mum. I can't turn this down.'

'Then I'm pleased for you, darling. Congratulations.' Her mouth said the words while her mind was still reeling. 'I'll miss you all, but you must do what is best for you,' she added, hoping he hadn't noticed the quiver in her voice.

Don reached out and took her hand. 'We'll miss you too, Mum, which is why we want you to come along too. Sell this house and move to Cambridge with us.'

She startled as if she'd been shot. Sell up? She'd lived in this house for forty-five years. She and Brian had worked hard, saved hard to put down the deposit needed to buy it and had been so proud when they'd moved out of the flat they were renting into their very own home. Becky, Martin and Don had grown up here. The walls sang with cherished family memories. She didn't want to move. And was he suggesting that she lived with them? Give up her independence?

'It's not good for you to be rattling around in this old house by yourself, Mum. I worry about you so much. You selling up and moving with us is the perfect solution.'

He said it as if it was decided. Cut and dried. They were moving, so she was too.

'This is a big step, Don. I have to think about it.' Her voice faltered.

'I know it's come as a shock, Mum, but seriously what's there to think about? You don't want to stay here by yourself, do you?'

No she didn't. But she didn't want to up sticks and move a couple of hundred miles away either. 'I'm settled here. It's been my home for years. I don't think I can face a move.' She couldn't believe this was happening.

'I know it's a lot for you to get your head around, but we'll help you tidy up the house ready to put it on the market. I think you'd get a tidy sum for it.'

Panic welled up inside her. This was moving too fast. 'I don't want to sell up, Don. Maybe I can come and stay with you at weekends? Or the children can stay over with me sometimes?'

Don looked exasperated. 'It will be too tiring for you to travel every weekend, Mum, and we'll be too busy to drive over here very often. You'll be here on your own. And what about the kids? They will miss you so much.'

Sandra would miss the children terribly too. The days were long and empty enough as it was now that Brian was gone. She would be so lonely without them, but she didn't think she could cope with moving. She'd barely recovered from losing Brian, she couldn't give up their home.

She twisted her wedding ring around on her finger. 'When are you leaving? Are you waiting until you sell your house first?'

'I have to start work at the new office next month. The company are going to provide me with a flat until our house is sold, and Laila and the kids will stay here until then. I'll return home weekends, or they'll come to me. We're hoping that we can time the move with the summer holidays so that they can start their new schools at the beginning of the new school year.'

A few months and they'd be gone. She couldn't get her head around it. She had never dreamt that Don and Laila would move away, they seemed so settled here. And she'd come to rely on them so much. Now, without any warning, it was about to change.

'Look, we're putting our house on the market next week,' Don continued. 'If you put yours on too then they might sell at the same time. I know it's all a bit sudden, Mum, but I can't afford to turn this promotion down.'

'I realise that. Of course you must accept the job. It's just a bit of a shock, that's all. Cambridge is such a long way away.' She'd never even been there before, not even for a quick visit. Her gaze swept around the kitchen. 'And the thought of leaving here... I assumed I'd be living here for the rest of my life.'

'You'll soon settle, we'll help you.' He reached for her hand and she raised her eyes to meet his and saw the guilt and worry in them. He was a good son and only trying to look out for her. She knew that.

Don had always been her rock. Martin had died in a paragliding accident fifteen years ago, and Becky lived the other side of the world, so it was Don who had always looked out for her and Brian. When Brian had died, Don was by her side immediately. In his usual calm and determined way he had stepped into his dad's shoes and started organising things, starting with the funeral and then moving on to her finances while Sandra reeled from this sudden explosion of her world. She and Brian had been teenage sweethearts, married at twenty-one, and it would have been their fiftieth wedding anniversary this year if Brian hadn't suddenly dropped dead one evening as he was making the hot chocolate they always had before retiring to bed. A burst aneurysm apparently, that had been growing silently inside him for goodness knows how long, before it ruptured, taking Brian's life instantly. The doctor had assured her he wouldn't have felt any pain. She was glad about that, but she wished she'd had warning, had chance to say goodbye, to hug him one last time. She'd been devastated, broken-hearted, barely able to function. She had been glad of Don – and Laila's – support in the dark months after Brian's death, but if she was honest, she had recently started to feel a little suffocated by her son's constant 'advice'.

Don glanced at his watch. 'I must go but please have a think about it, Mum. We're going to take a drive over to Cambridge tomorrow, so I'll pick you up about eleven and you can see for yourself what a lovely area it is.' He kissed her on the cheek and was gone.

Leaving Sandra feeling blindsided. What should she do? She didn't want to leave. But did she want to be stuck here alone without Don, Laila and the girls dropping in?

She wished she had someone to talk to, but over the years the neighbours they knew had moved on or died, and since she'd retired she'd lost touch with her work colleagues. It hadn't mattered, as she and Brian had done everything together. But now there was no Brian. And no friends to have a cup of coffee with and talk things over. Sometimes she bumped into someone she knew and stopped to say hello, they asked how she was, but she wasn't close to any of them enough to confide in.

When Brian had died, she'd felt as if a bomb had gone off in her life. Now, it felt like another one was about to explode.

She needed to get out, not sit here maudlin. She'd take a trip into the town centre and have a walk around, clear her head a bit. She'd go on the bus, she decided. It was chilly but dry, and she didn't fancy driving, she hated parking in that multi-storey car park. She'd been confident once, but when Brian had retired he'd done all the driving and she was out of practice.

She pulled on her coat and boots, picked up her handbag and set off for the bus stop, her mind a tumble of thoughts. Was it time to move on? There was nothing to keep her here really. Only memories.

2

PATTI

'I'll pop in later to see how you've got on, Gran. And remember to get some healing cream from Paul, you'll need to keep the tattoo moisturised.'

'I will, dear.' Patti's eyes swivelled to the clock on the wall. She'd already missed the earlier bus that she hoped to catch so she'd have to get the next one. She'd been about to go out when Kit had phoned and they'd been chatting for ages now. It was nice that she got on so well with her granddaughter. Strange how different your relationship with your grandchildren was to that with your children. 'You were never that patient with me' was her daughter Amanda's constant refrain, which Patti had to admit was true. She and Amanda had always had a strained relationship. Still did. 'I must go, Kit, or I'll miss the bus,' she said.

'Okay, Gran. See you later. Good luck!'

Patti grabbed her coat and bag, pulling the coat on as she hurtled out the front door, closing it behind her, and down the front path. The bus would be here any moment. It's a good job she only lived around the corner. She raced to the stop, already gasping for breath, just as the bus was pulling up. Thank goodness another woman had been there to stop it, otherwise she would have had to wait half an hour for the next one.

'Tell him to hang on!' Patti yelled, as she dashed over.

The woman turned and raised her hand in acknowledgement. She took her time stepping on and getting her pass out of her bag, giving Patti chance to jump on the bus before it set off. That was kind of her.

'Thank you,' Patti puffed as the bus doors closed.

'You're welcome,' the woman replied, then made her way down the bus, her purple three-quarter-length coat swinging, dark denims tucked into brown leather boots. She sat down on a vacant seat near the window, opened her bag and dropped her purse back inside. Patti followed her, holding on to the bars for support as the bus turned a corner. She frowned as she got nearer to the woman and took in the short white, chin-length hair framing her elfin face, high cheekbones, pink lipstick. There was something familiar about her, but she couldn't place her. As if sensing her stare, the woman glanced over, her pale blue eyes meeting Patti's, and they both recognised each other at the same time.

'Patti Jordan!'

'Sandra Wheeler!'

'Goodness me, it's been years!' Sandra exclaimed. She moved her handbag off the empty seat beside her for Patti to sit down.

'Twenty at least.' They'd worked at the local supermarket together many years ago, before Patti had moved to Nottingham. Sandra had long dark hair then, and her eyes – which Patti noticed were now tinged with sadness – used to twinkle with a quiet humour.

'It must be. How are you, Patti?'

'I'm good. How are you? Do you still live around here?'

Sandra nodded. 'Have you moved back or are you visiting?'

Patti's ex-husband's company had relocated him to Nottingham years ago. 'I live here. Adrian and I divorced a few years ago, we managed to keep it amicable though. When I retired, I started to feel at a bit of a loose end, so I moved back a couple of months ago. I've always loved Worcester, and my granddaughter Kit – Amanda's daughter – lives in student accommodation here.'

'I love Worcester too,' Sandra agreed. 'Where are you living now? Obviously not St Johns, unless you've been visiting someone.' Patti used to live the other side of the river.

'No, I'm just a couple of blocks away from you. That is, if you're still in the same house,' Patti replied. 'I expect you are. I remember you and Brian loved that house.' Brian was a proper DIY enthusiast and had spent his spare time doing up their home. He'd built a conservatory and a patio in the time Patti had known them. He'd probably done a loft extension and all sorts by now. 'How is he? And the kids?' Sandra had three children, she remembered, a girl and two boys. 'You're probably a grannie, like me, now.'

Sandra's eyes misted over. 'Brian died eight months ago, and Martin was killed in a paragliding accident fifteen years ago.' She took a breath before continuing. 'But yes, I am a grannie, both Becky and Don have children. And I'm still in the house. For now.'

'Oh, I'm so sorry, love. That's awful.' Patti reached over and patted Sandra's hand comfortingly. Martin was a nice lad but had always been a bit of a daredevil, tearing around on his motorbike and going off to remote places for weeks on end. It was sad that he'd died so tragically. And Brian too. She remembered how close Sandra and Brian had been and could see that she was still grieving. 'So, you're thinking of moving then?' she asked, remembering Sandra's 'for now'. Maybe she wanted to get away from the memories. Losing someone dear affected some people that way, while others wanted to stay put and cling onto everything.

Sandra sighed. 'I'm not sure. Don and his wife and children live in Malvern at the moment, but he's been offered a job in Cambridge. They want me to move there too.'

'That's a bit of a way. Do you like it there?'

Sandra turned to her. 'I don't know, I've never been. I really don't want to move from my home but I'll miss them so much. Becky still lives in Australia so they're my only close family.'

Patti could see that her old friend was conflicted. She had met Don a few times when he'd popped into the supermarket to see his mum, he was a serious looking lad and did well at school. She could imagine that he'd been very protective of Sandra when Brian died. 'It's not an easy decision to make, is it? But be sure to make the right one for you, don't be talked into anything you don't want to do,' she said softly.

'Right now. I'm not sure what's right for me,' Sandra confessed. 'How about you and your family? Do you have a partner or are you living on your own now?'

'I live by myself, although Kit often pops in on me. Amanda still lives in Nottingham.'

The two women chatted away, sharing news about what had happened since they last met and chuckling over anecdotes about the old days at work.

Patti was so pleased she'd bumped into Sandra again. She'd wondered if Sandra still lived in the area and had thought about looking her up a couple of times, thinking it would be good to see a friendly face, but hadn't got around to it. If she'd known about Brian she would have popped around and offered her condolences right away. Poor Sandra, that must have been a hard blow for her. Life could be cruel and something could come along to knock you off your feet when you were least expecting it. When Patti had been diagnosed with breast cancer three years ago it had completely devastated her. At first, she thought she was going to die and had been so angry at having her life cut short but luckily the treatment had worked. It had been debilitating though and there were days she could barely drag herself out of bed. Life had felt like one long struggle for survival. She thought she'd never feel well again, but gradually she had started to feel stronger. She'd promised herself that if she beat the bloody Big C she was going to look ahead to the future and get every ounce of enjoyment out of her life that she could. And here she was, cancer free and back in Worcester, where she was happiest. And how lovely that she'd bumped into Sandra again. They'd got on so well when they worked together. She was glad that she hadn't caught the earlier bus now, she would have missed her former friend. Thank goodness Kit had phoned her.

They chatted away, so engrossed in their conversation that they didn't realise they were at the bus depot until the driver stood in front of them and asked, 'Are you ladies getting off or are you staying on for a tour of Worcester?'

'Ooops! Sorry, yes!' Patti said, and they both scooped up their bags and got up, giggling. It was just like old times.

3

SANDRA

It was so good to see Patti again, Sandra thought as they both dismounted. It was a wonder they hadn't bumped into each other before as Patti only lived a few minutes away. Sandra hadn't been out much since Brian died though, had she? And she might not have recognised Patti with her short cropped red hair. She used to have long fair hair and she'd lost so much weight. She looked great though, in that red jacket she was wearing over a grey knitted dress and knee-high black boots.

'Do you have shopping to get or are you just having a wander around?' she asked, thinking that if Patti wasn't in a rush maybe she could suggest that they go for a coffee.

'I'm having my first tattoo today,' Patti replied, an impish grin on her face. 'I've got an appointment in ten minutes.'

'A tattoo?' Sandra tried to hide her surprise. Not that she had anything against tattoos, but wasn't it usually something the youngsters did?

'Yes. I know most people might think I'm a bit old at sixty-eight to have my first tattoo but,' Patti paused before continuing, 'I've finished all my treatment and been clear from breast cancer for a year now, so I want to mark the occasion.' She pointed to her red spiky hair. 'Hence the cropped hair. It's growing back now but it's taking its time, so I thought I'd dye it.' She patted it with her hand.

Oh, my goodness, that's why she'd lost so much weight, poor Patti, that was awful. 'I'm so sorry that you had to go through all that, it must have been dreadful. But how wonderful that you're now cancer free. And I love your hair, it really suits you.' Sandra moved aside a little, aware that they were blocking people from getting onto the bus.

Patti moved over too. 'It's been a bit of a tough ride, but I'm over it now and focusing on the future.'

'Good for you.' She had to ask. 'What tattoo are you having?'

Patti opened her bag and took out her phone, opening up the phone case she made a couple of taps on the screen. 'This,' she said, turning the phone to show Sandra a fine line image of two elongated bull's horns with 'Grab life by the horns' written above them in cursive script. 'I know it's a bit ballsy but that's how I feel!'

'It's fun and feisty,' Sandra told her. 'And a wonderful sentiment.'

'I promised myself that if I survived, I'd live my life to the full, no fear, no excuses, I want to make every single day count.' Patti closed the case and put the phone back in her bag. 'And I've always wanted a tattoo, so I'm going for it.'

'Good for you. Where are you having it?' Sandra asked. They were both walking side by side out of the bus depot now.

'My upper right arm, loud and proud! So that I can see it and remind myself every time I waver. Although, truthfully, I'm wavering a bit now,' she confessed. 'But I really want to do this, and it can't hurt more than all the treatment I've had, can it?'

'I'm sure it won't. I can understand you feeling nervous though. Would you like me to come with you for a bit of moral support?' Sandra asked impulsively, then wondered if she was being pushy. Patti might not want an audience.

'Would you?' She could hear the relief in Patti's voice. 'That would be amazing, but only if you have time.'

'I've got plenty of time,' Sandra told her, glad that she'd made the offer now. It was only a small thing, after everything Patti had gone through, but she wanted to support her brave friend, who she could see was a bit apprehensive. Who wouldn't be?

'Thank you, I appreciate it,' Patti said. She glanced at her watch. 'We'll have to dash though.'

* * *

'Hello, ladies. I'm presuming one of you is Kit's gran come for your first tattoo?' A tall, burly man with close cropped hair, wearing jeans and a black vest top revealing tattoos covering his arms and neck, greeted them as they both walked in.

'That's me.' Patti half raised her hand. 'My friend has come with me for moral support. Are you Paul?'

'I am and I have strict instructions to look after you.' He grinned. 'I have to say that I don't get many ladies your age having tattoos.'

'I like to be a trendsetter,' Patti told him flippantly, taking off her coat and sitting in the chair Paul indicated. Sandra sat beside her and watched, fascinated, as Paul took out his phone and pulled up a picture of the design Patti wanted. 'Kit said this is what you want.'

Patti peered at the screen then nodded. 'That's the one.' She turned her head so she could see the top of her right arm and pointed just below her shoulder. 'I want it here.'

He nodded and indicated the black leather reclining seat. 'Make yourself comfy.'

Paul pulled on disposable gloves, sterilised the working area, prepared the ink then set to work. Sandra talked to Patti throughout the process to distract her as she watched, fascinated.

'Does it hurt?' she whispered.

'Not really. It's like a hot scratch,' Patti told her but Sandra noticed that she winced a few times.

When the tattoo was finished Paul showed it to Patti in a mirror. 'What do you think?'

It looked so neat, Sandra thought in surprise, as if Paul had drawn the design on with a pen rather than injected ink through Patti's skin. The area around it was red and a bit raised.

Patti nodded approvingly. 'Perfect. Thank you. When will the redness go?'

'In a few days.' Paul put a dressing over the tattoo and handed Patti a small tub of cream. 'Leave the dressing on for at least two hours, then apply a thin layer of this cream several times a day for the first few days. It's important to keep the tattoo hydrated,' he instructed. 'Any problems, come back to see me.'

'I will,' she promised.

Sandra helped her on with her coat and they left.

'You were very brave. Didn't it hurt at all?' Sandra asked.

'Not really, it was a bit uncomfortable, like a scratching sensation. Thanks so much for coming with me. I'm so pleased we bumped into each other again,' Patti said with a smile. 'I don't suppose you fancy a cup of tea and cake to celebrate? My treat.'

'I do!' Sandra replied. 'But it's my treat!'

'Absolutely not, you gave me much needed moral support,' Patti insisted.

As they sat down, over a slice of fruit cake and two pots of tea, they chatted away and it was like they couldn't stop, there was so much to catch up on.

'Do you remember how we used to chat so much in our lunch break we had to put the timer on our watches to remind us when we had to go back to work?' Patti laughed loudly at the memory and Sandra smiled. How she remembered that laugh! Many a time she'd heard that laugh as Patti talked to a customer at the till and everyone would turn around to see who it was. It was a laugh that filled the room.

Patti told her how her granddaughter Kit was studying art and design. 'She's a lovely girl, kind, full of energy. She pops in on me a few times a week. She recommended Paul to me, she's got a few tattoos herself. I'm meeting her when she's finished uni, she wants to check everything went okay.' She took a bite out of her cake and chewed it before asking. 'When are your son and his family moving away?'

'Don's moving next month but Laila and the children are remaining here until the house is sold. They want me to put my house up for sale now too so we can all move at the same time. They're hoping it will all be sorted out by the summer holidays,' she added.

'It's nice to be wanted. It's a big move though. Are they expecting you to move into their new house with them?'

Sandra paused as she was about to take another sip from her cup. 'You know, I did wonder about that myself, Don wasn't specific but I presumed he meant for me to get my own place.'

'Would you want to move in with them?'

'Absolutely not. I want to keep my independence.' Goodness, she loved her son and grandchildren but she didn't want to live with them.

'It might be best to establish that right away then.' Patti finished her mouthful of cake then asked, 'So you've never been to Cambridge?'

Sandra shook her head. 'No, but Don is taking some stuff for his flat tomorrow and I'm going with them so I can have a look around.' She finished her drink. 'I'm just not sure I want to move though, Patti. It's such a big upheaval and I love living in Worcester. But I'll miss them so much if I don't go with them.'

'Well good luck. How about we meet up again on Monday and you can tell me all about it?' Patti suggested.

'Deal.'

'Great. Then let's swap phone numbers and we can message each other.' Patti took out her phone again. 'Read your number out to me and I'll send you a text.'

Sandra read her number out and Patti keyed it in using her index finger, one digit at a time, like Sandra did. The youngsters always used two thumbs and were so fast. A minute or so later a text pinged in from Patti. She opened it to see a hand waving emoji. She saved the number in her contacts.

'Got it.'

The two friends chatted away then a text pinged in Patti's phone. She glanced at the screen. 'Goodness, it's Kit. I didn't realise it was that late. I'd better go.' She grabbed her bag and stood up. 'Enjoy your weekend.'

'You too. See you on Monday.' Sandra waved cheerily as Patti dashed off.

* * *

Sandra arrived home feeling a lot lighter than when she'd left. It had been good to get out today. She'd shut herself away far too long.

Later that evening a text arrived from Patti with a photo of her tattoo, it still looked red and raised but the design was clear. She wrote:

PATTI

All healing well, and it got the thumbs up from Kit.
Thanks for your company again.

Sandra messaged back.

SANDRA

A pleasure.

She smiled as she put down the phone. Patti had cheered her up no end. She needed to stop fretting and see what she thought of Cambridge tomorrow. It was kind of Don and Laila to ask her to move with them. She was fortunate to have such a loving son, she reminded herself, some people didn't have family who cared about them.

4

Cambridge was a beautiful city, Sandra thought. She'd been surprised how many green spaces there were, and bikes! So many people cycling. Don parked up and they had a walk around the city centre, stopping for lunch in a pub overlooking the river. The children ran off to play on the swings in the pub grounds.

'The area we're going to live is on the outskirts,' Don told Sandra. 'It's out of the bustle, but not far to drive – or cycle – into the city centre. There's regular public transport too.'

'And there's a very good school for the girls only a few minutes away,' Laila added. 'We'll show you after lunch.'

Remembering what Patti had said about whether they were expecting her to move in with them Sandra decided to clarify just what they had in mind. 'It seems quite expensive here but hopefully I'll find a little bungalow not far from you if I do decide to move.'

Don and Sandra exchanged a look.

Then Don leaned forward, rested his elbows on the table and steepled his fingers. *Uh-oh, she knew that look.* 'Laila and I, we've been talking, and we think that you'd be comfier, and safer, to live in a retirement apartment, Mum. There's a lovely one in the area we're hoping to be in, you'd only be a short drive from us. It's part of a big development called Orchard House, with communal gardens, a communal hall, and an on-site warden. You'll be warm and will have company whenever you want it. And as luck would have it, a one bedroomed apartment has just become available.'

'You want me to go into a home?' Sandra was stunned. She hadn't expected this.

'It isn't a home, Mum. It's a retirement complex,' Don patiently explained. 'You'll have your own apartment and can come and go as you please. If you don't fancy cooking, you can eat in the communal hall, and they have all kinds of activities for the residents.'

'It's got very high ratings, Sandra,' Laila added. 'It's clean and modern with lots of facilities.'

'Of course, you can come and visit whenever you want,' Don added. 'And hopefully we'll have a spare room so you can stay over if you babysit, or if not, we can put the girls in together for the night.'

Sandra looked wordlessly at them both. She didn't know what to say. She had never considered moving to a retirement complex. Never dreamed that Don would suggest it. How long had he been planning this? It was almost as if he wanted to know she was being looked after, so he wouldn't have to bother. She'd be tucked away in her little apartment and he could come and visit at weekends.

Don't be silly, he just wants to know you're safe. Especially as you'll be in a strange city and won't have friends nearby.

That's if I move with them.

'We've gone ahead and booked an appointment so we can have a look around this afternoon. See what you think, Mum. It really is too good an opportunity to miss. And you should have a decent amount left from the sale of your house to keep you in comfort for a few years.'

They really had thought this through, hadn't they? 'I don't think it's for me, love, but I guess there's no harm in looking,' she said.

'I think you'll be pleasantly surprised,' Don told her.

* * *

It looked like a nice development, modern and clean, and Marilyn, the warden, was warm and friendly. 'Hello, Mr and Mrs Wheeler, and you must be Sandra.' She focused her attention on Sandra. 'I'm delighted that you're interested in living in Orchard House. Let me tell you about it, then I'll show you all around.'

Marilyn explained that all the apartments were one or two bed, each with a wet shower room and a lounge/kitchen. 'We cater for all your needs here. There is a wide range of activities you can join in if you want to.' She reeled off a list of activities then took them to see the apartment that had just become available. It looked modern, clean but a little bare, Sandra noticed.

'Obviously you can furnish it however you want, add your own personal knickknacks and make it homely,' Marilyn said.

'What do you think, Mum? It looks perfect for you, doesn't it? And you're so lucky that it's available.' Don was beaming.

Sandra didn't think it was perfect for her. It was too new, too modern, too compact, too... bland. And although there were the communal gardens to sit outside in, she had no plot of her own where she could tinker about. She loved being out in the garden, potting plants, pruning, doing a bit of weeding. It cheered her up and took her mind off things. She understood why Don wanted her to live here, the apartment would be easy to clean and keep warm, there were lots of available facilities and healthcare; she would be looked after. He wouldn't have to worry about her. He'd probably planned it, that this would be her home from now on. That she could grow old here, her ever increasing care needs would be met by the staff. She would be safe.

And miserable. She couldn't see this apartment ever feeling like home. She loved her house: it might be a bit shabby, the furniture and carpet a little weathered, but it was home. It held lots of wonderful memories – and some not so wonderful, but that's life, you get your ups and downs. Becky had only been three when they moved to Worcester, the boys had followed later and they had all grown up in the house. What would she do in this apartment? There was hardly room to put anything. It seemed soulless. And there was no room for the grandchildren to have a sleepover, like they did now. Although Don had said she could sleep over at their house if she was babysitting, so obviously he'd thought of everything. But she enjoyed having the girls to stay overnight, they had such fun and didn't have to worry about creating a mess in her house, like she did at Don and Laila's.

'There's the alarm to pull if you have an accident or need help,' Laila said. 'And there's a sit-in shower, we won't have to worry about you falling and lying injured for hours.'

Goodness, how old did they think she was? To hear them talk, she had one foot in the grave! You're seventy-one, she reminded herself. And Brian died so suddenly at the same age you are now. No wonder they're worried.

Even so, she didn't feel old. She cast her mind back to Patti yesterday. She was only a little younger than Sandra and look at her overcoming cancer and getting her first tattoo to celebrate. Seventies wasn't old any longer, there was plenty of life left in her yet. And she couldn't help wondering why the apartment was suddenly available.

'What happened to the person who lived here?' she asked.

'They've moved out, gone to live with their sister who was recently widowed,' Marilyn explained. 'Come and have a look at the communal quarters, there's so much to do here.'

Sandra followed them down in the lift to a large lounge with various armchairs scattered about, sensible straight-back armchairs with wooden arms to hold on to, not the comfy armchairs she had at home that snuggled around her as she curled up and read a book. *You can have a comfy armchair in your flat, you can furnish it however you want*, she reminded herself.

There were a couple of residents dozing in the chairs. Each had a blanket over them and looked to be in their mid-eighties. It was clean and cosy but very quiet.

'It's used more in the evenings, and we also have some activity afternoons where we have a singer in, or a craftsperson, to entertain the residents,' Marilyn told them. 'It's very lively then. A lot of the residents are out and about all day, off out in their cars or visiting their families. Not everyone uses the communal hall.'

Sandra listened as Marilyn listed all the advantages of living there, the services she could opt in for, meals, cleaning, shopping. But whilst she could see the advantages for some people, she knew that it wasn't for her. How did she get Don to understand that though?

'When were you thinking of moving in?' Marilyn asked, as if it had already been decided.

'My house isn't on the market yet,' Sandra said quickly, taking charge of the conversation. She didn't want Don speaking for her. This was her life. Her decision.

'I see, well you can make an offer, if you're interested, but it will be subject to selling your own property, of course.'

'We'll get Mum's house up for sale right away and be in touch by the middle of next week with an offer for the apartment. Would you take it off the market for a couple of weeks then to give her chance to sell her house?' Don asked.

'We could, but only for three weeks,' Marilyn said. 'And if someone else comes along in a position to proceed, we'd have to go with them.'

They were discussing this as if she wasn't here, as if it was nothing to do with her. Sandra fought down the wave of anger that rose in her. Don was only looking out for her, she reminded herself, he was worried that she wouldn't cope when he moved away.

And how would they cope without her being on hand to childmind when needed, a small voice inside her head whispered. She'd always been happy to do that, she loved Rana and Kali but was that a strong enough reason for her to move away with them?

'I'll get in touch with our estate agent right away, Mum. I'm sure your house will sell quickly once we've tidied it up and decluttered a bit.'

They were outside now, where Laila and the children were waiting in the communal gardens for them. 'These gardens are pretty, Nanny. Mummy said we can play in them when we come to see you,' Kali, a mini version of Laila, said excitedly. As if it was all settled that she would move here.

'It looks very posh!' Rana gazed around approvingly, her big, brown eyes wide.

Yes, it did but it wasn't where she wanted to live.

'What did you think of the apartment, Sandra?' Laila was looking thoughtfully at her.

Sandra took a deep breath. 'It's very nice, and the place is clean and the staff are lovely. But I don't think it's for me, love. I prefer more space, a house with my own garden.'

'I doubt you could afford a house in Cambridge, Mum. And you really could do with somewhere without the stairs. What if you fall down them?'

'I live in a house now and I've never fallen down the stairs,' she pointed out.

'You're getting older now, Sandra. You have to think of the future,' Laila said.

She had a point. 'A bungalow then.'

Don's forehead creased. 'You'll still be living on your own, Mum. I'm worried about that. Anything could happen and there would be no one to help. This is the sensible option and I'm sure you'll love it once you get used to it.'

She could see why Don made such a good manager, he had the skill of commanding people without raising his voice, but that authoritative tone wasn't going to work with her. She had to think about this carefully, it was a big step and she wasn't sure she wanted to take it. Don was pushing her into making a decision, but this was too important to rush into.

5

'I need more time to think about it,' Sandra said firmly.

She knew why her son was worried about moving away from her. She understood it completely. But that didn't mean she should uproot herself and live somewhere she didn't want to live, and Don was speaking as if the apartment was her only option. He'd obviously decided that's where she was going to live and all he had to do was persuade her that it was the right decision.

'You are going to live near us, aren't you, Nanny?' Kali asked. 'Mummy and Daddy said you were.' She looked beseechingly at Sandra.

'We won't be able to see you much if you don't, and that will make us sad,' Rana added, her voice wobbling a little. 'We'll miss you.'

They both fixed their eyes on her, waiting for her to assure them she would move with them. She felt her heart melt. Of course, she wanted to see them and live near them. But she wasn't the one moving away, was she? This was Don and Laila's decision.

'I'll miss you both too, but I'm not sure about living in Cambridge. I like my house, I don't want to leave it,' she told them. 'Don't worry though, even if I don't move, I can still come and visit you.'

'If you refuse to come with us, then I'll have to turn down the promotion. I can't possibly move all that distance from you.' Don's tone was laced with annoyance.

'That's emotional blackmail,' she retorted, stung at his phrase 'refuse to move', as if *she* was being selfish, when he had sprung this on her and it was perfectly reasonable for her to want to consider, or even turn down, the idea.

Don kneaded the back of his neck with his right hand. 'That's a horrible thing to say when I'm only trying to look out for you. Like Dad would want me to. Like I've always done,' he added for extra effect.

'Please come and live near us, Nanny,' Kali begged, throwing her arms around Sandra and hugging her tight.

'We don't want to move if you don't come,' Rana sniffed, joining in the hug.

Sandra's mind was in turmoil at the downcast expression on her young grandchildren's faces. She loved them all so much and couldn't bear to live so far away from them.

What should she do?

'Please at least give it some serious thought, Sandra,' Laila said softly. 'I know it's daunting for you, but we'll all help you settle in and I'm sure within a couple of months you'll agree that it's the best thing you ever did.'

Bombarded with such persuasion, and because she knew that she would miss them terribly, Sandra agreed to seriously consider it.

They had a little tour around the local area, showing Sandra the leafy semi-detached house they were hoping to buy when they sold their present home. It had just come on the market, apparently, and they'd made an offer, which had been accepted subject to their house being sold.

'It's only a ten-minute walk from Orchard House so you can stroll over and visit us whenever you want.' Don told her. 'It's really convenient.'

'It's such a lovely area. You'd soon settle down here,' Laila added.

'Your house and the area does look nice,' she agreed. She had to say something. She couldn't let them talk her into this. 'I'll give some serious thought about moving here, Don, but I'm sorry, living in a retirement community wouldn't suit me at all.'

Don sighed and fidgeted with his collar. 'You'd be safe there and looked after...'

'And unhappy. Which I'm sure you don't want me to be.'

'How do you know that until you try it?'

'Because I know myself, and it's not for me.'

He frowned then his face brightened. 'Maybe, you could come and live with us, Mum?' he suggested. 'Perhaps you could put something towards us getting a bigger house, with an extra room for you. Or even an extension.'

Laila looked shocked. They clearly hadn't discussed this, Sandra thought as her daughter-in-law turned away to talk to Rana, who was tugging on her shirt to get her attention. She was obviously hoping that Sandra hadn't seen her reaction, but she had. However, Laila didn't need to worry, much as she loved Don, Laila and her grandchildren she most certainly didn't want to live with them.

'Thank you, dear, but I prefer my own space,' she replied, and Laila turned back, a smile of relief on her face.

'We need to respect your mother's wishes, Don,' she said quickly.

* * *

Later that evening, when she was back in her own home and Don and his family had finally gone, Sandra poured herself a glass of chilled white wine and thought over the day. This was all her fault, she'd allowed herself to wallow when Brian had died. She'd been so devastated, bewildered. Brian had dealt with all the finances, etc., and she had no idea how to cope so she'd leant on Don and now he thought she couldn't manage by herself. Well, she could. She'd learn to. Look at Patti, she lived alone and had overcome cancer.

Then a text pinged in. She glanced at her phone, expecting it to be from Don reinforcing all the reasons why she should move to the apartment, but it was from Patti.

PATTI

How did your day in Cambridge go?

SANDRA

Awful. Don had booked a viewing of an apartment in a retirement complex for me.

PATTI

Fancy a chat over a glass of wine? I can be there in five minutes.

She did. Company was just what she needed.

SANDRA

Yes please. I've got a bottle chilled and am already on my first glass!

PATTI

That bad? I'm on my way!

Patti arrived within ten minutes. 'I've brought cake. I had a couple of slices left.' She held out a plastic container when Sandra answered the door. 'It's chocolate fudge,' she added as Sandra stepped aside to let her in.

'Brilliant. Come through.'

Patti had only been to Sandra's house a couple of times when she lived in Worcester previously, Sandra remembered as her friend followed her into the lounge. They'd been work colleagues and both had been busy raising teenagers back then. She'd given Sandra a lift home once when her car had broken down, and had dropped a couple of things off for her when she'd been off ill. Patti had lived on the other side of the river then, not so convenient for popping in, and they'd been more work buddies than friends. But despite the years that had passed, it didn't seem awkward at all for Patti to be here.

'Grab a seat and I'll go and get the wine.' Sandra indicated the big, comfy beige sofa. 'Is Pinot, okay? I do have a Merlot if you prefer red.'

'Pinot is perfect.'

When Sandra returned with a tray bearing the opened bottle of wine in an ice bucket, another glass and two plates with a serviette on each and cake forks, Patti had taken off her coat and was sitting on the sofa looking very relaxed, her head resting against one of the rich chocolate brown furry cushions. 'This sofa is gorgeous, you just sink into it.'

'The grandkids love it, they often curl up on one of those cushions and fall asleep.' Sandra felt a wave of sadness that soon Kali and Rana would be living miles away and wouldn't be able to curl up on her sofa. You can take it with you if you decide to move, and if you don't they'll come to visit, and can still stay over in the holidays, she told herself.

'You didn't like the apartment then?' Patti asked as Sandra passed her a glass of chilled wine then sat down beside her.

Sandra shook her head vehemently. 'Definitely not. I mean it's clean and modern enough but there's no character. And I really don't want to live in a complex like that. I understand all Don's reasons, that I'll be warm and safe and have company, but it's not for me.'

'It wouldn't be for me either.' Patti opened the plastic container and put a slice of cake on each plate. 'What did you think of Cambridge itself? Is it somewhere you could see yourself living? If so, perhaps you could buy a house or bungalow there. Actually, some of these retirement complexes have bungalows with a bit of a garden, so that might be worth looking into. My aunt and uncle lived in a gorgeous one. Although the yearly fees can be quite hefty and they're usually leasehold.'

Sandra dipped her fork into the cake as she mulled over the question. 'I'm not sure. I mean, Cambridge seems very nice, but I like it *here*. I feel safe and settled.' She gazed around. 'I know my house isn't posh or modern, but it's full of memories and I'm happy.' She bit her lip. 'Actually, I did suggest that if I do decide to move, I might buy a house or bungalow, but Don doesn't like the idea. He's worried that I'm vulnerable living on my own. He's been like that since Brian died. Malvern is only a short drive away at the moment, so he's always popping in.'

'It's nice that he cares, but this is your life, your decision. Make sure you do what you think is best for you. Don't let him talk you into doing anything you don't want to.' Patti wiped a bit of chocolate cake from her mouth with the serviette. 'I hope that I'm not overstepping the mark but I'd hate you to move then regret it. It took me a long time to settle in Nottingham when Adrian was relocated, and I'm happy to be back in Worcester now.'

'It's only because they're worried about me.'

'I know, my family are the same. Amanda tried to talk me out of moving back here and is never off the phone. Kit is always checking in on me too. It's only natural that our families worry about us but we don't have to dance to their tune. We might be getting on a bit but we've still got a life to live, and we have to do it our way.'

Sandra picked up her wine and took a long sip. 'Don can be so persuasive that I find myself doing what he says before I realise it. It's as if the roles are reversed when you get older. I'm afraid I leaned on Don when Brian died and now he thinks I can't manage without him.'

'Well, that's only natural, we all need help at times. But now you have to show him that you've come through, you're stronger and you can cope. And if you can't, you'll ask him for help. It's best for them too, they have their lives to lead, and busy ones at that. Our families want to fit us into a box to make their lives easier but we don't have to climb into it. We live by our rules not theirs.' Patti finished her cake and reached for her wine glass.

Sandra nodded. 'You're right. I'll miss them all dreadfully though when they move. Don has said he won't take the job if I don't agree to put my house up for sale and move to Cambridge with them. He said he can't leave me here by myself.'

Patti rolled her eyes. 'Emotional blackmail. My lot try that sometimes too. Look, why not tell them to go ahead with their plans, your daughter-in-law and grandchildren will still be here for a while, so you won't be on your own yet and it will give you time to start making a life for yourself without them. Then, when their house is sold, you'll be in a stronger position to decide what you want to do.'

6

PATTI

'Yes I think I will.' Sandra's brow unpuckered a bit. 'Thanks for listening. It's good to have someone to talk to about this.'

'You're very welcome.' Patti smiled. 'Now let's forget about what your son wants and think about what *you* want. What would you like to do with the rest of your life?'

Sandra shook her head. 'I've no idea. Have you?' She reached for the bottle of wine and topped up both glasses.

'There's loads I want to do. I promised myself that if I survived cancer, I would make every moment count.' Patti pointed to her tattoo. 'I'm going to grab life by the horns.' She took a gulp of wine. 'We never ask ourselves what we actually want to do with our lives, do we? When I was married to Adrian we muddled along, worked, raised the kids, plodded on – as most people do. But when death stares you in the face, you wish you'd made more of your life.' Another gulp of wine. 'Surviving cancer has made me focus on what's important and what isn't. Of all the things I was scared to do, that held me back. Now I want to live, to experience life while I can. I've been given a second chance and I'm not going to waste it.' She leaned forward. 'Do you know I've never been on an aeroplane?'

'Really?' Sandra looked surprised. 'Are you scared of flying?'

Patti nodded. 'Terrified! But I'm determined to overcome that and visit my brother Keith and his wife Mary in Spain. They've been there a few years and keep asking me over. Keith had a heart attack a few months ago – he's okay now but he doesn't feel up to the trip over here and I'd really like to see him. I've applied for my passport so that's the first step.'

'You must go. It's not that scary once you've done your first flight. Brian and I were going to fly over to Australia to see our daughter Becky later this year.' She blinked her eyes as she fought back the tears. She'd obviously been looking forward to that trip.

'Will you go by yourself? Or are you nervous, as it's such a long trip?'

'I'm not nervous about flying. Actually, statistically you're more likely to have an accident driving,' Sandra told her. 'I've been wanting to go for years. Becky used to work as cabin crew for an Australian airline – that's how she met Hogan – and could get cheap flights so they've been over here a couple of times but we've never visited them. You know what it's like with work and everything. We said we'd go when we retired, we talked about it so much. We were going to spend a couple of months over there, have a bit of a tour around as well as visiting Becky and her family.' She bit her lip. 'I still want to but it's so difficult, the first time doing everything by myself. There's so many first times, Brian's birthday, Christmas, Easter... I've got through those three but there's still my birthday, our anniversary...'

Patti's heart went out to her. Her divorce had been painful but at least Adrian was still alive, and they both got on reasonably well, whereas Sandra's beloved husband had died. 'It's bound to be, love, but you're strong. You can do it.' She thought back to when they worked in the supermarket together. Sandra was on Customer Services, and she'd always dealt with everything so calmly.

'You know, I can! I will! And you must go and see your brother.' Sandra's eyes sparkled. 'We should each make a bucket list. I'd put go to Australia right at the top of mine.'

'Now that's a brilliant idea. Why don't we start writing it now? There might be things we both want to do,' Patti suggested. 'I've got a notebook and pen in my bag.'

'And I've got one in the kitchen drawer.' Sandra got up. 'I think this calls for another bottle of wine.'

Patti fished her notebook and a biro out of her handbag.

Sandra came in with a tray holding another bottle of wine, a small bowl and ice cube tongs plus a notebook and pen. She put it down on the coffee table. 'It's not chilled but I've brought ice cubes.'

'Perfect.' Patti popped a couple of ice cubes in each glass then Sandra filled them with wine.

'Now we're all ready to do our bucket lists.' Sandra opened her notebook and wrote 'Go to Australia to visit Becky' at the top.

Patti wrote 'Get over my fear of flying and go to Spain' at the top of hers.

'What a pair of wannabe jet-setters we are!' Sandra giggled.

'I'd like to get over my fear of heights,' Patti said. 'I can't even bear to go up a ladder.' She added that to her list and took a long sip of wine.

'If you're going to climb a ladder, then I'd like to learn to swim!' Sandra blurted out. 'It's not that I'm scared of water, but I have no coordination and have never managed it. And while we're at it, I've always wanted to go up in an air balloon.' She sounded excited.

Patti shuddered. 'Not me, I'd be petrified. Although I've always fancied jet skiing.'

'I don't fancy that at all! Mind, I would love to sail across the sea in a motor yacht. That would be amazing.'

'Me too. Let's add them to our lists!' They both wrote these on their list.

'I've always wanted to sit on a beach and watch the sun go down,' Sandra confessed. 'It sounds so decadent.'

'I'm up for that! Especially if cocktails or fizz are included!' Patti said eagerly.

'You know, I'd love to be able to make cocktails. I imagine inviting people around for supper and coming up with these amazing creations. I could create a new one, a Sandra Special.'

'You could add that to your list,' Patti suggested. 'I'll be your cocktail taster.'

'You're on!'

'I fancy trying different foods, something exotic like octopus,' Patti said.

'Yuk!' Sandra pulled a face. She tapped her mouth with her pen. 'I'd like to get my ears pierced. I've always wanted to wear a pair of long, dangly earring. I've got some clip-on ones but they pinch my ears,' she said. 'And I rather fancy wearing a hat. A beret maybe? I'm not sure it would suit me though.'

'Rubbish, you'd look fabulous in one! I'd love to stop biting my nails.

They're such a mess.' Patti held out her hands, revealing short, chipped nails. 'I'd love to grow them and decorate them with those pretty nail gems.'

They both chuckled, downing more wine as they added the things to their list.

'I've always wanted to go to London and see a musical on stage,' Sandra announced.

'I wouldn't mind doing that. Maybe we can go together!' Patti said.

They both added 'Going to a musical in London' to their lists. Then they compared lists.

Patti
Get over my fear of flying and go to Spain
Get a tattoo ✓
Get over my fear of heights
Go on a jet ski
Stop biting my nails
Grow my nails and wear nail gems
Eat some exotic food such as octopus

Sandra
Visit Becky in Australia
Learn to swim
Wear a hat
Have my ears pierced
Go up in a hot air balloon
Sail across the sea in a motor yacht
Create a new cocktail

Both
Sit on a beach watching the sun go down, drinking fizz
Go to London to see a musical on stage

'That's seven each and two joint ones, that's enough to start us off,' Patti said. 'We might be a pair of Old Gals but there's life in us yet!' She raised her glass. 'To the Old Gals' Bucket Lists!'

Sandra smiled and clinked her glass. 'The Old Gals' Bucket Lists,' she echoed.

7

SANDRA

Don phoned again the next morning to see if Sandra had thought any more about moving to Cambridge with them.

'I can't make up my mind that quickly, Don. I'm not rushing into this.' She put the phone on loudspeaker, propped it up against the bread bin then took a carton of orange juice out of the fridge and poured some into a glass, taking a sip.

'At least let the estate agent value your house, then you'll know what price you could expect. They could take photos so that when you're ready to sell, they can go ahead immediately.'

The thought of someone walking around her house, valuing it, made her shudder. She wasn't ready for that yet. Nor was she ready for the big tidy up operation it would entail. She wanted things to remain exactly how they were, Brian's coat hanging up in the hall, his shoes on the rack, his clothes in the wardrobe. A wave of grief flooded through her. She couldn't do this, not yet. She took a moment to compose herself then replied, her voice a little shaky even to her ears. 'There's no rush, dear. I know you have to leave next month, but Laila and the children will still be here for a while. I can put my house on the market when yours is sold. It will give me more time to sort things out.'

'Mum, our house might sell quickly, which means you could be there on your own for months. We'll be miles away. It will take me a couple of hours to reach you. It's not even as if you have close friends to turn to.' She could hear the exasperation in his voice.

'Actually, I do have a friend,' she said, irritated by his attitude. 'On Saturday, I bumped into someone I used to work with at the supermarket back when you were a teenager – Patti, you might remember her, she was a cashier. Though she moved away years ago. Anyway, she's moved back now and she's on her own too.'

'So, on the basis of meeting this one person you used to know decades ago again, you've decided not to move?'

'I never did decide to move. It was your idea,' Sandra replied calmly. 'I know you mean well, love, and I'm very grateful to you for looking out for me but I really think that it's best if I stay here until I decide what's right for me to do.' This house has been my home for years and is where all my memories are, she wanted to add, but she knew that Don would only tell her she had to let go of the past. 'Anyway, I must go now, Don, I'm in the middle of breakfast. I'll speak to you later.' She quickly ended the call before Don could say anything else, put the phone on the table, poured some muesli into a dish, added yogurt and sat down at the kitchen table to eat it.

To be honest she was dreading Don, Laila and the girls moving away, she would miss them terribly, but she had to get used to it. It was time she stood on her own two feet. What was that tattoo Patti had on her arm. 'Grab life by the horns.' That's what she had to do too. It's what Brian would want her to do. She loved him but he was gone, and she still had a life to live. It was a life without Brian, but she had to make the most of it.

Maybe she should have a tattoo done too, reminding her to live her life! Idly, she scrolled inspirational tattoos. She was amazed at the selection. One in particular caught her eye. It was a sideview of a small butterfly with half-open wings, written in a circle around it were the words 'Embrace change, love life.'

She studied it for a moment, something about it was calling to her. She imagined it just above her right wrist, reminding her to live her life. She clicked on the photo and saved it to her gallery then, on impulse, sent it to Patti with the message.

SANDRA

Just saw this. Tempted.

A reply shot back.

PATTI

Go for it, gal!

She wouldn't have done this if Brian was alive. Brian never took a chance, neither did she. They lived a safe life. But he'd confessed to her one day – when Martin had sent them a video of him bungee jumping – that he wished he could be brave enough to do something like that. 'I always take the safe route, worried that something might go wrong,' he'd told her. 'I wish I'd got Martin's sense of adventure to go off and explore the world like he's done.'

Tragically, Martin had died far too young in a paragliding accident. But he'd packed a lot in his short life, far more than they had done.

Brian had played safe, but he'd still died far too soon.

She messaged Patti back.

SANDRA

I'm going to do it. Can you give me the number of the tattoo studio we went to?

Within seconds Patti pinged the number back.

PATTI

Want me to come with you?

SANDRA

Yes please!

Sandra phoned the tattoo studio immediately and luckily they could fit her in that afternoon, so before she could change her mind, she booked the appointment, then messaged Patti. They agreed to meet at the bus stop, as they had the other day. Sandra was a bit nervous, she had to admit, but if Patti could do it so could she. And the tattoo was just the start. As Patti suggested, she was going to sit down and think about what she wanted to do with the rest of her life. She'd already started making her bucket list, which was rather exciting. Suddenly, life seemed full of opportunities rather than empty days.

* * *

Paul grinned when they both walked in. 'Hello again, ladies. Any more of your friends planning on having a tattoo?' he asked, a twinkle of amusement in his eye. 'I might offer Senior Rates.'

'You never know,' Patti replied with a wink. 'We might even be back for another one and we'll be wanting those Senior Rates if we do!'

Paul chuckled. 'It's a deal.'

Patti was right, having the tattoo done wasn't very painful, more of a scratching sensation. Although Sandra had to clench her teeth a couple of times, but Patti distracted her by chatting away just as she herself had done when Patti had her tattoo. She felt quite proud of herself when Paul had finished.

'Do you mind if I take a photo of you both showing your tattoos to put on Instagram?' Paul asked. 'I often do that with my clients.'

Sandra and Patti both looked at each other then nodded. 'Go for it!' Patti said.

'Can we pout?' Patti asked mischievously as Paul took his phone out of his pocket.

'Go ahead!' he said with a grin.

The two friends looked directly at the camera, pouting away. They giggled and tried a few different poses, making sure their tattoos were visible.

'That's fantastic. We'll take a look through the photos in a minute but first let me put a dressing on that tattoo.'

When the dressing was in place Paul gave Sandra a pot of tattoo healing cream. 'You know the rules.'

She nodded. 'I do.' She was feeling quite proud of herself for doing this.

Paul held out his phone and flicked through the photos until he found one they all liked. They were both laughing, half turned towards each other, Sandra holding out her arm to show her tattoo and Patti with her shoulder turned towards the screen so that her upper-arm tattoo was visible. They looked happy, vibrant, Sandra noticed in surprise.

'We look like a right trendy pair of "old gals",' Patti said with a grin.

'You certainly do. Are you on Insta, ladies? I could tag you in it.'

'No but my granddaughter is, so I'll get her to look you up. She'll be amazed to think we're Instagram models!'

They both went giggling out of the shop.

'Let's celebrate with a cocktail before we go home,' Patti suggested. 'A trendy cocktail bar has just opened around the corner.'

'Fabulous idea. And my treat this time.' Sandra hooked her arm in Patti's and they made their way to the bar.

'What are we like! It seems quite decadent to be drinking cocktails in the afternoon,' Sandra said as they sat down at an empty table.

'It's called living our life.' Patti picked up the drinks menu from the table. 'Why don't we go for something really wild?' Her eyes scanned the list then a smile formed on her face. 'How about a Porn Star Martini?'

Sandra hesitated for a second then nodded. 'Sounds good!'

Patti ordered the cocktails. 'I've been thinking, do you fancy taking up dancing? It would be fun to learn a new dance, and the exercise is good for us.'

'I'd love to do ballroom dancing, the dresses are gorgeous. I did mention it to Brian but he didn't fancy the idea.'

'I've always fancied a bit of jazz myself,' Patti replied. 'I'd love to keep it a secret from the family then at the next do take to the dance floor and surprise them. They're used to me having two left feet and jigging along completely out of step.'

Sandra tittered. 'I could just imagine Don's face if I started doing jazz! Why don't we see if there're any dance classes locally.' She paused as her phone rang and glanced at the screen. 'Sorry, it's Don. I'd better take it.'

'Go ahead.'

'Where are you, Mum? I called in to see you but you're not here.'

Drat. He always dropped in from work before going home and she'd forgotten the time.

'I'm in town having er... coffee with Patti,' she said, deciding it was best not to mention the tattoo yet. 'I'm fine, love. You carry on home, and I'll see you tomorrow.'

'Here you are ladies, two Porn Star Martinis,' the waitress said, bringing their drinks over.

'Mum!' Don practically screeched. Sandra held the phone a little way from her ear. 'Are you in a *bar*?'

Sandra was about to deny it but stopped herself. She was an adult. She could go for a cocktail if she wanted to. 'We've just stopped for a quick drink.'

'Marilyn phoned me about that apartment, Mum. Someone else is interested in it. If you don't put a deposit on it soon it will be gone and another one might not come available for ages. Please think about it. I really believe it would be ideal for you.'

Sandra was suddenly filled with resolve. 'I'm not going to move to that apartment, Don. I've told you, I want to wait and see how I feel when you've all moved before I uproot myself.'

'Mum, you're being ridiculous. I can't possibly move to Cambridge and leave you here alone.'

She bristled. Ridiculous for wanting to stay in her own home? 'That's your choice. Staying put is mine,' she said firmly. 'Now I must go, dear, I'll see you tomorrow.'

'Well done,' Patti told her when she ended the call.

Well done indeed, Sandra thought. The old Sandra was coming back. Brian's sudden death had shocked her, knocked her off kilter, now she was righting herself again.

And it was all thanks to Patti. She couldn't believe that her friend had moved nearby at the very time Don was trying to persuade her to sell up and move hundreds of miles away. It seemed like fate.

8

The persistent ringing of her phone jolted Sandra out of a deep sleep the next morning, the best she'd slept for a long while. For a few seconds she was startled, wondering why someone was phoning her in the middle of the night. Then she opened her eyes and was surprised to see that the bedroom was flooded with sunlight. Goodness, what time was it! She glanced at the clock. Nine fifteen! Every day since Brian had died, she'd tossed and turned half the night and finally got up at seven, knowing she wouldn't sleep any longer. Mind, the two cocktails they'd had yesterday probably helped. She and Patti had giggled in the back of the taxi all the way home.

The ringing continued. She groaned, she bet it was Don, he always checked in on her first thing. He'll be thinking she'd tripped over something and was lying injured on the floor. She sat up, rubbed her eyes and reached for the phone, her heart lifting when she saw that the incoming call was a WhatsApp video call from Becky. She did a quick calculation, it must be about eight thirty in the evening in Australia. Funny to think that in another few hours it would be Wednesday for Becky, a completely different day.

'Hello. You caught me having a lie-in,' she said as Becky's cheery face appeared on the phone.

'Good for you, Mum. Sorry I disturbed your sleep. I thought you'd be up.' Becky had been living in Australia so long her voice now had a distinctive Aussie twang to it.

'Normally I am, and please don't apologise. I'm always pleased to hear from you.'

'How are you doing? Don tells me you're all moving to Cambridge.'

Sandra brushed away the flash of irritation at Don's presumption that she would fall in line with his wishes, reminding herself that he was just trying to look out for her and that he and Laila had been there for her whilst she'd coped with the trauma of Brian's death. 'I haven't decided what I'm doing yet. Don, Laila and the children are definitely going but I might not be. I'm happy living here.'

A frown crossed Becky's forehead. 'You'll be a bit lonely there without them, Mum. You see a lot of them, don't you? And you know how much you love the kids.'

'I do, and I love living near them. But I love it here too. And what if Don is offered another promotion and has to move away again? I can't keep following them around, Becky. I've got to think about this carefully.' She edged herself up on her right elbow. 'I bet he's phoned you and told you that I'm being "awkward" and will you help him persuade me to see sense.'

Becky grinned. 'Spot on. I know what a fusspot Don is, but I can see his point. I worry about you, Mum. Truth be told, I hate to think of you on your own in that big old house since Dad died.' Her voice wobbled a bit. 'It's always reassured me that Don isn't too far away and can get to you quickly if you need help. And it is nice that they want you to move by them. A lot of parents complain that their grown-up kids don't bother with them.'

'I know. And I am grateful, really I am, but I have to do what's best for me. I can't allow myself to be railroaded into a decision I might regret. It's a big upheaval.'

'Of course not, but please think it over carefully.' Her eyes met Sandra's through the screen. 'I know it's a lot for you to leave that house, Mum, it holds so many memories for you. We had some happy times as kids and it's great to come back and visit you there. But it might do you good to start afresh in a smaller, more modern place.'

At least Becky understood how precious this house was to her and that she didn't want to erase all the memories. Although, even she seemed to think that Sandra should move on.

'Look, if you feel like you want to get away from it all, you can come over here. Stay as long as you want. We've got plenty of room. You've got an open invitation.'

Sandra knew that Becky and the family had been looking forward to seeing her and Brian this year. 'I will when I'm a bit stronger,' she said. 'I promise.'

'Good. Now what have you been up to?'

Sandra sat up straighter, grimaced at the image of herself in the bottom corner of the screen and ran her hand through her hair in an effort to tidy it.

'Mum! Is that a tattoo on your arm!' Becky squealed, her eyes sparkling with amusement.

'What?' Fourteen-year-old Honey ran over to join her mum on the video. 'Let me see, Nan!'

Sandra held her arm up straight so that they could see her tattoo, which was still red and raised.

'Cool! And it looks like you've only just had it done! What does it say? I love the butterfly, but I can't read the words,' Honey asked.

'It says "Embrace change, love life",' Sandra told them. 'Which is what I intend to do.' Then she remembered the Insta photo. 'Are you on Instagram?'

'Yes, we have a family account. Why?' Becky asked.

'My friend Patti had a tattoo as well, she had hers done on Saturday and Paul, the tattoo artist, took a photo of us both when I had mine yesterday. He said he was going to put it on his Instagram account.'

Honey's mouth dropped open and her eyes widened. 'You're on Insta? Nan, that's so cool. I've got to see that! What's the name of the tattoo studio?' She grabbed her phone.

Sandra told them. Honey tapped away then shouted, 'I've got it!'

'Let me see.' Becky peered over her shoulder. 'Oh, Mum, that's a smashing photo. You both look great.' She glanced up. 'Have you seen it?'

'I saw it in the tattoo shop but I don't have Instagram.'

'I'll screenshot it and send it to you after this phone call then you can see the caption as well.' Honey's face almost filled the small screen.

'Thank you, love.'

'Now who's Patti? I can't remember you mentioning her before.' Becky's face appeared on the screen now.

'She used to work at the supermarket with me years ago but then she moved away.'

'The cashier with the loud laugh?' Becky asked.

'That's the one. Well, she's moved back into the area. She's just recovered from cancer, and she's so upbeat, so determined to live her life. It got me thinking, your dad is gone but I'm still here. He would want me to pick myself up and carry on living.'

'He definitely would, Mum. You've got to live your life for both of you now.'

'That's what Patti said.' She told them about Patti having a tattoo to celebrate recovering from cancer. 'We've both come up with a bucket list of things we want to do and visiting you in Australia is top of mine.'

'Really! That's great, Mum. It will be so lovely to see you. It sounds like you're picking yourself up now.'

Sandra felt a surge of guilt as she saw the tears welling in Becky's eyes. It must have been hard for her to see Sandra so distraught in the early days after Brian's death, with her living so far away and not being able to help. She remembered how Becky had hugged her tight on the day of Brian's funeral and told her she wished she could be there for her more.

'Yes I am. I'm feeling much stronger now, and it's so lovely to have Patti living nearby.'

They chatted for a while, exchanging news, and Sandra felt a lot lighter when the call had ended. She always did after talking to Becky. She missed her daughter so much.

Then she remembered the screenshot Becky had sent her. She opened her message and looked at it, smiling again at the photo. Written across the top of it in white capital letters on a black background were the words 'You're never too old to ink.' She wondered if Patti had seen it yet. She sent it to her with the words:

SANDRA

We're Insta famous!

Patti messaged back a few minutes later.

PATTI

Kit spotted it on her Insta last night. She said it had over fifty likes. She said that we should open an Instagram account.

SANDRA

Isn't it just photos? What on earth would we put on it?

PATTI

Pop around for a cuppa in a bit and we can chat about it?

Sandra glanced at the clock. She needed breakfast and a shower, in that order. Her tummy was rumbling.

SANDRA

Eleven okay?

PATTI

Perfect. I'll have the kettle on.

She got out of bed, pulled on her fluffy dressing gown, and went downstairs, Becky's words about living her life for both her and Brian resounding in her mind. She and Brian had been so looking forward to going to visiting Becky, Hogan, Zac and Honey, in Australia this Christmas.

Was she brave enough to go by herself?

9

PATTI

Patti had the kettle boiling and a box with a selection of hats, scarves and other accessories on the kitchen table when Sandra arrived. 'I'm having a green tea, what do you fancy? I've got quite a selection of herbals plus normal tea and coffee.'

'I'll have coffee please. I don't really get on with herbals,' Sandra replied.

'I didn't at first, but they're healthier for me so I have a couple a day. Got to balance out the wine and cocktails.' She grinned and indicated the chairs around the table. 'Take a seat, I'll be with you in a minute.'

'Are you having a clear out?' Sandra eyes were fixed on a jaunty purple beret on the top of the box.

'No these are all for our Instapics. Kit often posts photos of herself wearing different hats, sunglasses, etc., so I thought we could do that too. It'll be fun.' She placed a mug of coffee on the table. 'I've had all these for years, let's have a sort through and see if there's anything we like.'

'I'm not too sure about this Instagram account,' Sandra said as she sat down. 'What would we post on it? I don't know about you but I don't think my life is interesting enough for people to want to see photos about it.'

'I thought that.' Patti put a plate of assorted biscuits in the middle of the table and sat down with her own mug. 'But Kit said that the photo of us both with our tattoos has got over a hundred likes now and we should open our own account. Kit often shows me her Insta, or some funny pics from other accounts. People post all sorts, what they had for tea, a new dress they bought, photos of their pets. You don't have to be living an exciting life for people to connect with you, you just have to be relatable. And how about we make it a joint account – two old gals having fun.'

Sandra nibbled away at a chocolate digestive. 'You really think people want to see photos of two older ladies messing around?'

'Why not? We can make it light-hearted and playful. It might inspire other older folk to try new things and have a bit of fun in their life.'

Sandra looked at her dubiously. 'How do we share the same account though?'

'Kit said that it's simple, if we both download Instagram and share the log in details then we can both access the account and post. She said we just need an email address, a username and a password.'

'I'm not sure it will be that easy. Sometimes it takes me ages to do something on my iPad that Rana and Kali do in no time. Still, we can try. Phone or iPad?' Sandra asked.

'Phone to set it up I think. We'll probably be using it mainly on our phones anyway as they're always with us. Kit said we can use it on our tablets and iPad too though.'

'Okay.'

They both picked up their phones, searched for the Instagram app and downloaded it. Then Patti set up a shared email account. 'Done.' She looked up from her screen. 'We'll need a name for the Insta account.' A smile twitched at the corner of her lips 'How about The Old Gals' Bucket List?'

'Good idea,' Sandra agreed. 'We can post photos of the various things we do as we tick them off our bucket list.'

'Right, that's our Insta account created. Now we have to write a short intro. How about something like, "You're never too old to make your dreams come true",' Patti suggested.

'Sounds good to me.' Sandra peered over her shoulder at the screen. 'And we need a profile photo of us both.'

'Hence the accessories.' Patti pointed to the box. 'Let's make the photo really fun.' She pointed to a mirror she'd propped up on the worktop behind them. 'I've brought this down for us to use.'

They both had a giggle as they tried on the various hats, sunglasses and scarves.

'What do you think of this?' Sandra finally settled for the purple beret, and a pink feather boa. She picked up a pen and held it like a cigarette holder. 'Do I look good, dahling?'

'I love it!' Patti chuckled. 'All you need now is a pair of big sunglasses to set it off. And I think I know the exact pair.' She searched through the box and found some pink heart-shaped sunglasses. 'Try these.'

Sandra slipped on sunglasses then got up to look in the mirror, studying her reflection this way and that. 'I don't think anyone will recognise me.' She sounded pleased.

'What do you reckon to this?' Patti asked. She'd donned a red bakers' cap, rainbow-rimmed sunglasses and a red chiffon scarf knotted at the neck.

'Fabulous, dahling!' Sandra told her.

'Thank you.' Patti blew her a kiss. 'Now let's see if I can take a decent selfie of us both. Kit said that the trick is to hold the phone up high.' She picked up her phone and went over to Sandra. 'Budge up and I'll take a couple of shots, we can choose the best one.'

They stood close together and Patti held up the phone, trying to get both their head and shoulders in the frame but it was hard to click the button with her thumb. 'Drat, this isn't as easy as it looks!'

She took a few shots but when they checked them out, one showed just the top of their hats, the other the wall behind them, and the third one was blurred.

They both turned as they heard the front door open and someone shout, 'Gran!'

'It's Kit,' Patti told Sandra. 'She has a key to the house, so that she can keep an eye on me, although it's more me who keeps an eye on her.' She winked. 'In the kitchen,' she called out. Great, now Kit could take a photo of them both.

She heard the front door shut then a few seconds later Kit bounced in, her hair – blue this month – tied up in a messy bun on the top of her head, her blue eyes sparkling. She was wearing her trademark baggy jeans slung low on her hips, rainbow-coloured trainers that she'd dyed herself and a purple top revealing a couple of inches of tanned (from a bottle) midriff.

A smile burst across her face as she looked at Sandra then back at Patti. 'You both look fab. I'm guessing you're Sandra. Nan has told me all about you.'

This remark was directed at Sandra who nodded and smiled. 'Hello, Kit. Delighted to meet you.'

'Back at you. Now, is all this for the Insta account?'

'Yes, I've been trying to take a selfie of us, but they haven't worked out.' Patti held out her phone so Kit could see the photos.

'It takes a little while to get used to it. And it's easier if you use a selfie stick. I've got one spare, so I'll bring it to you next time I drop by. Shall I take a photo of you both?' Kit offered.

'Please!'

Kit looked from one to the other thoughtfully. 'You could both do with some lipstick on – bright red would be good – and how about I paint your nails different colours and you can hold them up to your face like this.' She partly concealed her mouth with the palm of her hand, spreading out her fingers so her nails were showing. 'See what I mean?'

Patti screwed up her nose. 'I'd love that, but have you seen my nails?' She held out her hands. 'One of the things on my bucket list is to stop biting them.'

'No problem, I picked up a couple of packets of false nails today, you can have one. I'll do them for you.'

'Brilliant,' Patti said in delight.

Kit glanced at Sandra's nails. 'Shall I stick a pair on you too? Your nails are fine but it would be good to have long ones for the photo.'

Sandra nodded. 'Please. And you must let us pay you for them.'

'My treat – they're only cheap.' Kit rummaged in her bag, taking out two packets of false nails, a bottle of yellow nail varnish, and another bottle of blue. 'Do you have red nail varnish, Gran?'

'I do. I've got a few different colours upstairs. I'll go and get them.'

Patti returned with a bottle of red, a bottle of purple and one of pink. 'Will these do?' Kit had spread two sheets of newspaper on the table, Patti noticed in relief. Very thoughtful of her.

Kit nodded. 'Right, ladies, place your hands out on the newspaper and I'll get working on those nails. Shall I start with you, Gran?'

* * *

Kit looked at the finished sets of nails with pride. After fixing the false nails on, she'd painted each nail on Patti's right hand a different colour, then did the left hand to match. She'd done the same for Sandra but in a different order. 'Well, what do you think?'

Both women held out their hands and gazed admiringly at them.

'They are gorgeous. Thank you, darling. Now I'm even more determined to stop biting my nails,' Patti exclaimed. 'I'm going to grow them and stick some pretty gems on them!'

'They really are,' Sandra agreed. 'Thank you, Kit.'

Sandra's her eyes were sparkling. She's enjoying herself, Patti thought happily. She'd been worried how downcast her old friend had looked when they'd first met – even though it was natural in the circumstances – and felt so pleased she'd been able to cheer her up a little.

Kit took several photos of them together, calling out instructions, 'Pout – no not that much!' 'Turn towards each other' 'Look up' 'Pull your glasses down onto your nose and peer over them.' Finally, she finished and sat down to look at the photos she'd taken. Patti and Sandra peered over her shoulder.

'I reckon this one, what do you two think?' she asked.

Patti and Sandra crowded around the screen. The photo showed them both looking at the camera, hands with their fingers spread across their mouths, displaying their multi-coloured nails, glasses perched on the ends of their nose, hats jauntily poised on their head. They looked so alive. She loved it.

'It's brilliant,' she said.

'Perfect!' Sandra agreed.

'Right, let me filter it, then I'll upload it to your account.'

'No way. No filters here,' Patti said firmly. 'We're not bothering with any of that. What we post is going to be real. Right, Sandra?'

'Absolutely! If you can't be real at our age, when can you?'

Kit shrugged. 'If that's what you want.' She uploaded the photo to their Instagram account and handed Patti her phone back. 'Fantastic name. Old Gals' sounds sassy and fun.'

'That's the image we want.' Patti explained how they were going to upload photos of them attempting to fulfil their bucket list, and other fun things they did.

'That's so inspiring. And why don't you ask other people what they want to do for their bucket lists too? That would encourage interaction.'

Sandra turned to Patti, her eyes sparkling. 'Shall we?'

'Why not?' Excitement was buzzing through her. She was enjoying herself so much.

'Take a photo of your bucket list and tick off the things as you do them. That will get everyone's interest. You've already got your tattoos so that's one ticked off.'

'Good idea. Let me get my notebook.' Patti took it out of her handbag and opened it up to the written bucket list.

'I've got my list in my phone case.' Sandra opened the case and took out the piece of paper. 'Oh, I must add "get a tattoo". It wasn't on my original list.'

Patti ripped a piece of paper out of her notebook. 'Might be best to write it out again.'

'Thanks.' Sandra wrote out a new list and ticked off 'get a tattoo'. Then they both handed their lists to Kit who took a snap of them.

'Perfect! Now watch carefully.' Kit uploaded both the photo of the lists and the one showing their tattoos. Then she added a caption saying 'That's one ticked off both lists.' She grinned, 'You'll soon be influencers.'

Next, Kit showed them how to create a story and a reel then gave them a quick tutorial on how to find people to follow and how to accept followers. 'I've followed your account. Give your Instagram account name to your family, Sandra, then they can follow you and you can follow them back. Be careful though both of you, you get some weirdos messaging you. I'll turn off message requests from people you don't follow and disable message notifications, then you should be okay.'

'Thanks, love,' Patti told her. 'We'd better watch you, so we know how to do it.'

Kit showed them how to go into settings, and the options they could choose. 'There you are. I bet you soon have loads of followers.'

They both thanked her and Sandra picked up her list and put it back in her phone case which she slipped into her bag. 'It was lovely to meet you, Kit, but I'd better be going now.' Then she realised she was still wearing

Patti's beret, sunglasses and feather boa. 'Oh goodness, I almost went home with these on!' She took them off and went to put them back in the box.

'Take the beret, if you want. It looks great with your purple coat,' Patti told her. 'And you did say that you'd like to start wearing a hat.'

'Really? Thank you.' She put the beret back on. 'That's another one off the list!' She turned to Kit. 'Thank you, Kit. It's been a pleasure to meet you. See you tomorrow, Patti.'

10

Kit looked a bit relieved when Sandra left and Patti had an inkling that she had dropped by because she wanted to talk to her about something.

'Thanks for showing us what to do, darling. Do you fancy a cup of chai and a chocolate cookie? Freshly baked this afternoon,' Patti added. Chai tea was Kit's favourite and she'd never known her granddaughter to refuse a chocolate cookie. Or any cake for that matter. Kit was a high-wire of energy and dashed around so much that Patti was sure she could eat a dozen cakes a day and still be stick-thin. Amanda worried about her not eating enough and drinking too much, although Patti tried to reassure her that Kit was perfectly healthy and preferred chai tea to alcohol. In fact, from what she'd seen of Kit and her young student friends, they were a lot more sensible and clean living than Amanda and her friends had ever been. They were more aware nowadays of health, etc., and they couldn't let rip without it being all over social media. Goodness, the state Amanda had come home in sometimes, and the scrapes she'd got into. Actually, maybe that's why she worried so much!

'Please.' Kit rested her chin on her upturned hands. 'I still can't get over my gran being an influencer.' She reached for a cookie from the plate Patti had put down on the table, her sleeve riding up to reveal some musical notes on the inside of her wrist. Kit had a few other tattoos, an intricate dragon on her right upper arm, an orchid on her left shoulder, it was her birth flower, and some stars on her ankle.

'How is the tattoo by the way? Is it healing okay?'

'It's fine.' Patti rolled up her sleeve and showed her. 'It's a bit red and raised but that will go soon, won't it?'

'Yeah, keep putting the cream on it though.'

'I will.' She'd heeded this advice religiously. She frowned as she noticed that Kit's nails were bitten down to the quick. Something she always did when she was troubled. That must be why she had bought the packs of false nails. 'Now, how are things with you?'

Kit's dark-lined eyes met Patti's and she chewed her bottom lip. 'Seb wants me to move in with him.'

Patti sat back and studied her granddaughter's face. Kit had been going out with Seb for a few months now. He was a little older than her and seemed a nice enough lad, but she got the impression that he was a bit of a drifter. Not the sort to settle down. Not yet, anyway.

'And you don't want to?'

'I like living with Carly but Seb's flatmate, Noah, is leaving to live with his girlfriend and he can't afford the rent by himself.'

'That's not a good enough reason for you to move in with him, Kit. Let him get himself another lodger.'

'He said he doesn't want to. He wants to live with me.'

'Kit, darling, this is a big step. And if it's not really what you want to do you shouldn't do it. While you're living with Carly you can relax, have downtime, a night off from Seb now and again. If you're living together, you won't be able to do that.'

Kit's blue eyes met hers. 'Seb said if I loved him, I'd want us to live together.'

Patti felt a surge of anger flood through her but she kept her tone light. 'And if he loved you, he'd want you to be happy and do what's right for you.' She reached out and squeezed her granddaughter's hand. 'Why not take a bit of time to have fun before you shackle yourself to a lad?'

Kit nodded slowly. 'That's what I want to do but...'

'Seb's living arrangements aren't your responsibility. He can get himself another guy to share with.'

'The thing is,' Kit twisted a loose strand of her blue hair around her finger, 'he said he has to get someone quickly so it might be another girl.'

Now the fury sparked out of Patti. 'Then let him! How dare he try to emotionally blackmail you! You're worth more than that.'

'He's not blackmailing me, Gran, they'd only be flatmates. He can't afford the rent by himself, so he needs to let the first person who applies have the spare room. And that might be a girl.'

Patti was pretty certain that Seb *was* emotionally blackmailing her granddaughter. He was well aware that those good looks and lazy smile of his could charm the girls, that and the fact that he was the lead singer in an indie band. Kit had her head screwed on and would think this through, she told herself. Patti nagging her wouldn't change anything.

'Then let him. You do what's right for you,' she said firmly. Youngsters didn't like being lectured, so thinking it was best to change the subject now, she gave Kit a smile. 'Thanks again for helping us do our Instagram account.'

'I don't mind. It's a fab idea and Sandra's nice. I'm so pleased that you're thinking so positively, Gran.' Kit leaned over and gave her a big hug. 'I was worried at one time that we were going to lose you.' Her voice caught in her throat.

'Not me, I've got a lot of living to do,' Patti replied. 'Have *you* ever thought of doing a bucket list?'

'Not really. I mean, I'd like to travel, who doesn't? Maybe even work abroad for a bit. Me and Carly were talking about volunteering in an animal sanctuary abroad together once we've finished uni.'

'That sounds a wonderful idea,' Patti agreed.

'Seb doesn't want me to go...' Kit's voice trailed off.

'It's not up to Seb though, is it? It's your life, your decision,' Patti said firmly. 'Why don't you look into it?' She picked up her phone. 'Let's google it and see what we can find.'

Half an hour later, Kit had a list of places looking for volunteers that Patti had shared with her from her phone, and her eyes were sparkling with excitement. 'I can't wait to show this to Carly. Thanks so much, Gran.'

She hugged Patti and left, a spring in her step.

Well, hopefully that will put all thoughts of moving in with Seb out of her mind, Patti thought with satisfaction. She'd found that it always worked out better to show people another solution, or path, than to try and talk them out of something. All Kit had needed was a little nudge to think about what she wanted to do with her life, not what Seb wanted to do. A whole new horizon had been opened for her.

A video call came in.

It was Mary, her brother Keith's wife. Patti got on well with her and they often had a Facetime chat. She grabbed her iPad, preferring to use the bigger screen for video calls, and hit the accept button. 'Hi, what's it like over there in sunny Spain?'

'Sunny and not too hot. Why don't you come over for a week or so and see for yourself,' Mary said. 'We would love to see you, it would really cheer Keith up.' Mary and Keith had both asked Patti several times to go and stay with them. They'd moved to Spain five years ago when they both retired and Patti hadn't visited yet. She was too scared to fly, but had considered driving and taking the ferry over until cancer came along and upturned her life.

'I'd love to come. I'm just... trying to build myself up to it.'

'Please do. It would do you the world of good. And it would do Keith good to spend a bit of time with you.' Her voice broke a bit. 'I need you to come, Patti. I'm so worried about Keith. He's still not his normal self. I've tried to talk him into flying over to see you, but he's scared of taking the risk after his heart attack, even though the doctor said it's perfectly safe for him. He's really quiet and disappears into his shed for hours. I can't get him to go anywhere.' Her voice was laced with worry.

Patti was sad to hear that. Both Mary and Keith had thrown themselves into the social life when they'd first moved to Spain, they'd got a great bunch of friends and were always talking about the day trips they went on, nights out, or gatherings around each other's houses. Keith was usually a sociable person, it wasn't like him to shut himself away. She knew the heart attack had shaken him up but was surprised that he'd retreated into himself so much.

'I will come over very soon,' she promised.

She had to pluck up the courage and do it. Keith and Mary had flown over a few times to support her when she was going through cancer treatment. Now it was time for her to return the favour. And sooner rather than later. Something about Mary's tone had worried her.

11

SANDRA

'The estate agent is coming around to value our house on Thursday and said that she could fit you in too.' Don had dropped by after work later that day, whilst Sandra was weeding the back garden. 'I think you should do it, Mum, then you will know what you can afford to buy.'

Sandra stood up, rubbing her knees, then turned to look at her son's anxious face. He really had got the bit between his teeth over this.

'Surely you don't want to be rattling around in this house by yourself when we've gone?' Don continued. He looked around at the slightly overgrown garden. 'All this is too much for you. You shouldn't be on your knees weeding at your age.'

'I like gardening. And yes, I know I haven't kept on top of it, but I'm feeling a lot more positive now and the weather has brightened up, so I'll be spending more time out here.' She'd decided that today. She and Brian used to spend hours out here, potting plants, weeding, mowing the lawn, deadheading flowers but she'd let it go a bit. Meeting Patti again had given her a new lease of life and made her determined to get on with things. Tidying the garden was a start.

'I know it's a big step, Mum, but that apartment really would be ideal for you. You should grab the chance before it's gone.'

For goodness' sake, she had told him repeatedly that she didn't want that perishing apartment! 'Don, I am not moving into an apartment! I know you mean well but I'm not being pushed into this so will you please stop going on about it!' she snapped.

Don recoiled as if he'd been slapped across the face. 'Pushed! That's a horrible thing to say!' He thrust his hands in his pockets and jutted his chin out. 'Christ, Mum. I'm just trying to look after you! That's all I've ever tried to do. There's only me to look after you since Dad died. Becky's too far away to do anything useful.'

He looked so upset that Sandra felt awful. She hadn't meant to react like that, but she had to be firm with him. She reached out her hand and touched his arm. 'I know that, love, you and Laila have been wonderful.'

Suddenly Don's eyes widened as he stared down at Sandra's lower arm. 'What's that on your arm?'

Sandra went to pull her sleeve down and stopped herself. She had nothing to be ashamed of. She pulled it up further instead and turned her wrist so that Don could see the tattoo clearly. 'It's a tattoo. I had it done yesterday. It's to remind me to embrace change and make the most of my life.'

Don looked aghast. 'So that's where you were yesterday! I can't believe this. You're seventy-one, for Christ's sake!'

'What difference does it make what age I am? Patti is only a few years younger than me and she's had a tattoo.'

'First drinking cocktails in the afternoon and now this tattoo. I think this Patti is a bad influence on you, Mum.'

'Don't be silly. Patti is a good friend. I'm enjoying her company.' Then impishly she added, 'and the tattoo came before the cocktails!'

His eyes widened in horror. 'I don't know what's got into you just lately! You're acting totally out of character.'

'You should be pleased that I'm picking myself back up again,' she said firmly. 'I know that I was devastated when your dad died, and that I relied on you a lot. I'm very grateful how kind you all were to me, how you supported me. But I'm ready to live again and you need to step back and let me do that. You can't tell me how to live my life, Don.'

Don looked wounded. 'That's a cruel thing to say, Mum. I thought that you'd want to be with us. My mistake. I think I'd better go.' He turned on his heel and strode away without as much as a backward glance.

Sandra took a deep breath and sat down on the wooden bench underneath the window. She hadn't meant to hurt him but he had to back off and let her figure things out for herself. Maybe she'd give him an hour or so to cool down then send him a text and try to explain.

She continued with her weeding but her mind was in turmoil. Had she been too hard on Don? Was she being foolish not jumping at the chance to move to Cambridge with them rather than staying here by herself in this big, run-down house?

The house she loved.

How complicated everything had suddenly become. She was pleased that Don had been given a promotion with a much-needed increase in income but she wished it wasn't so far away. She didn't want all this pressure, she wanted things to remain as they were. Which was selfish of her, wasn't it? She put the trowel down and went into the kitchen to make a coffee, black and strong. As she sipped it slowly, a message pinged in. It was from Laila.

LAILA

Don't worry about Don, he'll come round. You know how he frets. He would love you to move by us but of course you must do what is best for you. xx

Sandra bit her lip as she read the message. She couldn't shake the feeling that Laila was a bit relieved Sandra wasn't moving with them. Which was understandable. She was her mother-in-law, not her mother. It must have been hard for Laila to have Sandra so dependent on them all when Brian had died, even if she did help look after the children. Laila's parents lived and worked in London so weren't near enough to help on a regular basis, although Laila and Don often travelled down to spend a weekend with them. Actually, they hadn't done that since Brian died, she remembered. Is that because Don didn't want to leave Sandra alone? They'd invited her over every weekend, sometimes she'd stayed over on a Saturday night, or they'd come to her for Sunday lunch. Laila had never complained, but Sandra had seen the looks she'd shot at Don when he had suggested she accompany them somewhere, or stay over another night, when she thought that Sandra wasn't looking. Especially on Sunday, when

Don had suddenly suggested that Sandra move in with them. She had to set them free.

She went over to the sideboard where she kept a photo of Brian, by the pot containing his ashes, a vase of flowers and a candle. Brian hadn't wanted to be buried so in the absence of a grave to visit she'd made this little memorial corner for him. She refreshed the flowers every week and sometimes lit the candle as she sat and thought – make that, cried – about her beloved husband. The grief had been all-consuming in those early, dark days and this little ritual had comforted her so much.

She picked up the silver-framed photo of Brian and traced his face with her finger. It was such a lovely face. He was almost bald, and wore glasses, the kindness in his eyes shining out through the lens. He could be stubborn, and pig-headed, and they'd had some massive arguments, especially in the early years. But he was considerate, like Don, and he had always tried to look out for her, even if it felt at times that he was smothering her. Again, like Don. Her youngest son had a lot of his father's traits.

'I'm going to be okay, Brian,' she said softly. 'I'll always miss you and carry you in my heart forever but I'm going to be okay.' She kissed the frame and put it back on the sideboard again.

12

Thursday morning Laila asked Sandra if she would pick up the children from school, as the estate agent was coming around about three and she needed to tidy up. Don would collect them from Sandra's on the way home, she'd said. Sandra had readily agreed, she enjoyed spending time with her grandchildren.

Kali and Rana came running over when they saw her waiting at the school gates.

'Nanny!' They both flung their arms around her.

'Steady, you'll knock me over!' she told them playfully.

'I like your hat, Nanny,' Kali said, looking admiringly at the purple beret Sandra was wearing.

'Thank you, darling.' Sandra was so pleased that Patti had given it to her, wearing it made her feel chirpier somehow.

'Can we go to the park?' Kali asked.

'And have a Maccies.' This was from Rana.

'Of course you can.' Laila and Don didn't really like them having fast-food but were okay with Sandra taking them once a week.

The children walked beside her, clasping onto a hand each, over to the car. She loved moments like this, and now that Don and Laila would be moving away, they were even more precious.

They both scrambled onto their booster seats in the back of the car and fastened their seat belts. Sandra checked to make sure they were secure then got in herself and set off, the children's favourite songs blasting. They all joined in and as she glanced in the mirror and saw their happy faces she felt a lump in her throat. She would miss Kali and Rana so much.

She pulled up in the parking area by the play park and they all got out. The children immediately ran off to play, Kali jumping onto the swings, Rana hurtling down the slide. There had been a time when she'd had to coax them, hold their hands, help them onto the swings, stand at the bottom of the slide to catch them. Those days were gone.

They're growing up fast, and soon they won't need you to pick them up from school, she reminded herself. They won't want you to take them to the park, or to have sleepovers. They'll be off with their friends, and too busy to see you. Don and Laila will be busy too, you'll be lucky if you see them all for an hour a week. You'll be on your own in a home and city with no memories.

* * *

Don was late, and in a hurry to get home when he picked up the children. She'd known he'd be in a rush, so had made sure Kali and Rana were both ready.

'Can't stop, Mum. I'll call you later. Thanks for having the kids.' He gave her a peck on the cheek, as usual, as if the other afternoon had never happened. 'Oh, by the way, our house is going on the market on Monday and the estate agent said this is a good time to sell. They're actively looking for properties. And there's some lovely bungalows for sale in Cambridge,' he added.

She could obviously decipher the barely hidden message, and Don was looking at her, waiting for a response. 'I'm still thinking about it.'

He pursed his lip. 'Don't take too long, Mum. The clock's ticking.' He ushered the children out, calling over his shoulder, 'See you over the weekend.'

When they'd gone Sandra sunk down onto the sofa, her head in her hands. What should she do? She felt like her whole life was being turned upside down. And she was terrified of making the wrong decision.

Her phone pinged. It was Patti.

PATTI

Do you have time to chat?

Sandra phoned her immediately. 'Hi, what's up?'

'You know you said that you've always wanted to swim? Well, I was passing by the local swimming pool earlier and saw they were advertising swimming lessons for seniors twice weekly. Mondays and Thursdays. Fancy joining? I'll come with you.'

'You can swim already,' Sandra pointed out. 'And I'm not sure. I think I'm a bit old and wrinkly to be parading around in a swimming costume.'

'It's for seniors, everyone will be old, wrinkled and have droopy boobs. Anyway, I'm a bit self-conscious too, you know. My boobs are lopsided since the cancer and I haven't swum for years. Might not have the energy now. I'm not going to let it stop me from trying though.'

Of course Patti would be a bit anxious about how her body had changed but if she wasn't going to let it deter her, neither was Sandra.

'Let's do it,' she agreed. 'Then when I go to visit Becky in Australia I'll be able to swim in their pool instead of sitting out on the side or wearing a float.'

'Good for you! There's life in us "Old Gals" yet! I'll book us both in for Monday, shall I? Now how about we go swimming cossie shopping?'

'I have a couple of costumes somewhere...'

'Yes, but we need new ones, brightly coloured, for our Insta.'

'You want us to put photos of us in our swimming costumes on our Instagram account? Goodness, I'll look a right sight!'

'Rubbish, we'll look like a pair of older women having fun. And we might even inspire others who can't swim to learn too.' Patti always put a positive slant on things. 'Now what are you doing tomorrow? We could go shopping then, if you fancy it. Followed by coffee and cake, of course. Or another couple of cocktails.'

Sandra spirits lifted. A shopping trip with Patti sounded just what she needed. Once again, Patti had brightened up her day.

'Perfect. Shall we meet at the bus stop?'

They agreed a time and chatted for a bit longer. When the call ended, Sandra went upstairs to sort out her swimming costumes. It would be good to have a new one for Monday, but if they were going twice a week she wanted a variety to wear.

Patti phoned again to say she'd booked the lessons. 'They start at eleven,' she said.

'Brilliant. I've been sorting out my swimming costumes. I know we're going to buy some new ones tomorrow, but I don't want to wear the same ones in every photo.' She chuckled. 'Goodness, listen to me! Anyone would think we're one of those... what did they call them? ...influencers.'

'We are,' Patti told her. 'We're going to shake up "the oldies" and get them to enjoy their lives.'

Well, this was one 'oldie' who was starting to enjoy her life again, Sandra thought as she looked at the two swimming costumes on her bed, one black and one navy Both very boring. I definitely need a few coloured ones, she thought, ones that would look bright and fun.

A text pinged in from Patti. She opened it up and chuckled when she saw the photo of two old ladies in Victorian swimming costumes with frilly swim caps on their heads.

PATTI

How about we turn up in these?

She replied with a laughing emoji.

SANDRA

Maybe not the first week

13

It was a busy weekend. Don and Laila asked Sandra if she could have Rana and Kali over on Saturday night so they could go out for a meal together, then they'd spend Sunday packing and getting the house ready for any viewers, it would be on the market from Monday. Sandra was more than happy to oblige, wanting to spend as much time as she could with her precious grandchildren before they moved away. She and the two children had a splendid time and when she told them about their swimming lessons, they were delighted. 'You can do it, Nanny, just keep your legs up,' Kali said.

'And don't swallow the water,' Rana added.

'That's the trouble. I just can't keep my legs up, no matter how I try – and I always end up swallowing the water,' she told them.

'You need to kick your feet really quick,' Rana told her. 'That's what I do.'

'And really stretch out your arms, it helps you move faster,' Kali added.

'I'll try. Thank you both.'

Kali gave her a big hug, 'You can do it, Nan. Just keep trying.'

'I will. Now, I bought some new swimming costumes on Friday and I can't decide which one to wear tomorrow. Can you help me choose?'

They both nodded eagerly and she went up to fetch the swimming costumes. She'd ended up buying three, a blue one with pink flowers on it that held in her tummy and had a little skirt that made it seem not so revealing, one with a lilac top and black bottom and a red polka dot one.

Kali studied them thoughtfully. 'I think the blue one with the pretty flowers.'

Rana nodded. 'Me too.'

'That's the one I thought,' Sandra agreed. She leant forward and said conspiratorially, 'My friend is wearing a leopard print one.'

'You should have got a zebra print one, Nanny, then you could have both pretended to be animals in the water,' Rana said. 'That's what me and Kali do when we're swimming.'

Sandra smiled at the thought of her and Patti pretending to be a leopard and zebra. That would certainly liven up the swimming lesson!

* * *

'I'm not sure about this,' Sandra said when Patti called for her on Monday morning. She'd almost chickened out when she'd packed her bag this morning with the new blue and pink swimming costume and a towel. She'd suddenly thought, what the hell was she doing? Apart from the occasional dip up to her knees in the pool when they'd been on holiday, she hadn't worn a swimming costume for years. It had been decades since she'd gone to the swimming baths, and then she'd only sat on the side while Brian went into the water with the kids. Butterflies were whirling around in her stomach as she thought of getting in the pool with all those strangers, memories of her swimming teacher at school shouting, 'Legs up, Sandra. Legs up!' But try as she might she could never get her legs to stay afloat and always ended up with her head under water. Gradually all the other kids in her class had learnt to swim, jumping off the side into the water with abandon, then streaking across to the other side. She could never pluck up the courage to dive in. She'd held gingerly onto the bar along the side of the pool all through the lesson, to the despair of her teacher. 'Let go of the bar, Sandra. You'll never learn while you're clutching the bar.' She was so relieved when she moved on to secondary school and didn't have to do swimming lessons.

What if she made a fool of herself? She'd always been hopeless at swimming, why should she be any better now? She'd probably be splashing around, sinking under the water, not able to keep her legs up, just as she used to, while the others would soon pick it up and be swimming across the pool like fish.

'It'll be fun. Everyone else will be around our age and in the same boat,' Patti told her. 'Think how proud you'll be when you can swim. You can surprise your grandkids by joining them in the pool.'

Yes, she would like to do that. Don and Laila were good swimmers and so were the children. Sandra had often envied them as they'd raced across the pool while she remained in the shallow end. It suddenly occurred to her that 'she'd been holding on to the bar' all her life. Maybe it was time she let go.

'You're right.' She grabbed the tote bag that held her swimming costume and towel, then picked up the purple beret and perched it jauntily on her head. 'Let's do this.'

* * *

'Are you ready?' Patti called from outside Sandra's changing cubicle.

'Coming!' She stepped out to see her friend wearing her leopard print swimsuit and holding her tote bag. 'We need to pose for a selfie for our Insta account.'

'Can I put my towel around my waist?' She didn't fancy a photo in her swimming costume. Despite Patti's pep talk she was feeling anxious and self-conscious about being so undressed in front of a whole bunch of strangers.

Who would be in swimming costumes too and were also no longer in their prime, she thought. *Patti had body issues too but wasn't letting that stop her.*

'No need, I've brought some props.' Patti took some swimming goggles, a snorkel and some colourful arm floats out of her bag. 'Blow these up and put them on and I'll try to take a selfie. I wish I'd remembered to bring the selfie stick Kit gave me at the weekend.'

'Okay,' Sandra agreed. At least she wouldn't be recognisable with her swimming goggles and snorkel. Besides it was only a bit of fun.

'I'll do it, dear, if you want.' A woman of about their age, dressed in a lilac costume, her silver hair pinned up in a bun, offered. Another woman, in a plain black costume, was with her. 'Are you both here for the "learn to swim" class?'

'We are. Thanks so much.' Patti passed her phone over. 'Just give us a sec to get ready.'

Sandra couldn't help but giggle as they pulled on their goggles and now-inflated floats. The woman was smiling too. 'Are you going in the water with those?'

'No it's just to make the photo look fun for our Insta account,' Patti explained. 'We're documenting our attempts to do everything on our bucket list. Learning to swim is one of them.'

'Actually, Patti can already swim, it's me that can't,' Sandra added.

'I can't either. I'm going on holiday with my son and his family this year and I want to surprise my grandchildren by diving into the pool and swimming to the other side. I'm tired of sitting and watching them all have fun. I'm Beryl, by the way. And this is Madge.'

'I'm Sandra, and this is Patti. That's why I want to be able to swim too. I want to visit my daughter in Australia and be able to swim in their pool.'

A few others had come out of the changing cubicles and had heard what Sandra said so all started sharing their reasons for wanting to learn to swim. They introduced themselves and were delighted when Patti asked if they were happy to be in the photo too. As they all posed together, Sandra felt her anxiety fade away. They seemed a friendly bunch and were all around the same age as her and Patti. This might be fun.

They made their way to the pool, chatting together, where some more wannabe swimmers were waiting. There were ten other seniors in the class, two of them men, and three of them over eighty, most of them a bit anxious but all of them determined. Tess, the friendly instructor, who looked like she was just out of school – didn't everyone now? – asked them all to introduce themselves and checked that they had all filled in the medical form. Then she got them started with some stretching exercises to warm up before they went into the pool. Madge was so nervous that she didn't even want to get into the water at first. Sandra's trepidation eased when she saw that the others were just as nervous as she was. Tess was a patient and inspiring instructor. By the end of the lesson, Sandra had actually managed to keep her legs up whilst she swam holding on to a float. Patti, meanwhile, had soon found her sea legs again and swam swiftly across the pool.

'Take your time, Patti, don't push yourself,' Tess called.

But Patti carried on swimming.

Sandra watched her enviously. 'I wish I could swim like that,' she said when Patti completed a width and pulled herself up onto the side to sit down and catch her breath.

'It was hard work,' Patti puffed.

'Are you all right?' Sandra asked, concerned for her friend.

'I will be... once I've caught my breath.'

Tess came over to check on her. 'Well done, Patti but I think you need to take it a bit slower,' she said.

Patti nodded. 'I will. I haven't got the stamina I used to have.'

'That was hard work, but fun,' Sandra said when the lesson was over and they all climbed out of the pool.

'We're going for a coffee. Anyone want to join us?' Beryl asked.

Patti shot Sandra a questioning glance and she nodded. So they all agreed to meet in the café once they were dry and dressed.

They spent an enjoyable hour chatting to everyone, and by the time they left the café Sandra felt invigorated. Why had she never taken swimming lessons before? Brian had suggested it a couple of times when the children were young because she always stopped in the shallow end of the pool whilst he and the kids swam off when they were on holiday, but she had been too embarrassed. It had seemed ridiculous that she couldn't swim, now she knew that lots of people couldn't and it was nothing to be ashamed of.

'You did great today, I bet you'll be streaking across the pool in a couple of weeks,' Patti told her.

'I think it's going to take longer than that,' Sandra said. She had to admit though, she felt a lot more confident than she had when they set out this morning.

They went back to Patti's house and Patti mixed them a mojito while they selected a photo to put onto their Instagram page, breaking into hysterics as they looked at them all. Finally, they chose the funniest one, where Patti's goggles had slipped down and Sandra was posing, orange floats on her arms, hands on her hips. They posted it onto Insta and captioned it:

Another one off the Bucket List. Learning to swim. Wish us luck.

'We should put one of you wearing that beret, you look great in it! And it's another thing off your bucket list,' Patti said. She grabbed her phone and took a quick snap, then uploaded it.

'Hey, there's already loads of comments about the swimming photo. And we're getting a bit of a following now,' Sandra said. 'Look, lots of people are saying that they're going to learn to swim too. They thought they were too old until they saw our posts.'

'You're never too old to do anything!' Patti said firmly. 'Remember,' she pointed to the tattoo at the top of her arm. 'Grab life by the horns!'

14

Don dropped by after work that afternoon and Sandra could see that he was unhappy about something but before she could even offer him a drink he blurted out, 'Laila said you have an Instagram account with that friend of yours and that you've posted photos of your tattoos.' He paused, his lips tightening, 'And of you both in swimming costumes.' Disapproval was written all over his face.

She took two mugs off the holder. 'Yes, we started swimming lessons today. You know how I've always wanted to swim. It was fun.' She looked over her shoulder at him. 'Coffee?'

He nodded then asked sternly, 'Do you really think it's appropriate to post photos of yourself in your bathing costume for all and sundry to see?'

She made the coffee and handed him a mug before replying. 'It's a very decent swimming costume. I don't see why I shouldn't.'

He shook his head, as if she was a naughty child. 'Mum, you need to be careful what you post on Instagram. There are lots of scammers out there, people who pretend to be someone they aren't. You're making yourself vulnerable. There are people who pretend to be men... who admire you... and send you messages in your inbox.'

'Oh, so you think I'm much too old for a man to actually admire?' she teased.

Don reddened. 'No but,' he floundered. 'I'm serious, Mum, you could be inviting the wrong kind of attention.'

'Look, don't worry, I know all the risks. Patti's granddaughter Kit has told us all about that, and she's fixed our settings so that no one can contact us if we don't follow them. Besides, we're not stupid enough to reply to someone dodgy.' She seated herself in the nearest chair. She might as well be comfortable if Don was going to lecture her.

Don put his mug on the worktop and leaned back against it. 'It's not easy to spot scammers, Mum. Lots of people have been taken in by them. They contact you and pretend to be all sorts, then before you know it they've emptied your bank account.'

'I promise you I won't be giving money to anyone.'

'Make sure you don't. If someone contacts you, let me know. I'll sort them out for you.'

'I will. There's no need to worry. Like I said, Kit has explained everything to us.'

'Well, it doesn't look like she has. If you post that you're going swimming – or anywhere else – then everyone will know you're out and someone might break in.'

'How would they know where we live? We haven't put our full names and address on our account! Stop fretting, Don, it's only a bit of a lark. And if it encourages other older people to learn to swim, surely that's a good thing?' She took a sip of her coffee.

He folded his arms across his chest. 'I really don't think this is a good idea. I don't know what's got into you just lately. You're acting completely out of character! I mean, what do you actually know about this Patti? She could be a scammer, she might have befriended you to get some money out of you.'

Sandra almost choked on her drink. 'You do have a vivid imagination! She's an old friend and is recovering from cancer. We're both just having a bit of fun, that's all. Like I used to do before your dad died and my world fell apart,' she reminded him. 'Lots of people have Instagram accounts.' She put her cup down, 'I do wish you'd stop stressing. It really isn't a big deal.'

Don sucked in his breath. 'I can't help worrying. I won't be near enough to help you out if you get into trouble when I live in Cambridge. That's why I want you to move too.'

'I am not going to get into any trouble. Now please sit down and drink your coffee and let's talk about something else. How are the girls?'

Thankfully he sat down and started talking about Kali and Rana's latest exploits. Don was a good father and adored his daughters. There was no mention of Sandra moving again but later that evening she received a message from him with a link. 'Here's a couple of bungalows for sale in Cambridge in your price range. They look ideal for you and aren't far from where we'll be living.'

Curiously, she clicked onto the first link and up came the details of a detached two bedroomed bungalow with a paved front drive. She scrolled the images, a small kitchen, small lounge, equally small bedrooms – one just a box room – and a pocket-sized garden. Reading the details she could see that it was also on a retirement complex, with a resident warden. There were community fees of a couple of thousand a year. The other link showed a similar property.

She got up and walked over to the window, looking out at the garden. She knew that Don was only trying to look after her. She could see that it probably would be the sensible thing to move into a bungalow like that. But she didn't think she could do it. Not yet. Maybe not ever. There were no memories between those bland walls, none of Brian's clothes hanging in the wardrobes, no marks on the bedroom doorposts to mark the children's height, no memories of the children playing in the garden, of Martin's motorbike leant against the garage wall, of Brian sitting in the armchair sipping his nightly tot of brandy with hot water. How could she leave all that behind?

But if she didn't move, she was losing the only family who lived nearby.

She put on a film hoping to distract her thoughts, but she couldn't settle. Finally she gave up and went to bed, but slept restlessly, tossing and turning. When she did drift off she had mixed up dreams of Don and Martin. The next morning she woke up with a headache, feeling decidedly out of sorts.

She pulled on her dressing gown and went downstairs to make herself a hot drink which she took out into the garden, hoping the fresh air would make her feel better.

Then a text pinged in. She glanced at the screen, fearing it might be from Don asking her what she'd thought of the links he'd sent over. Her spirits lifted when she saw that it was from Honey.

HONEY
Wow, Nan, your Insta account is fab. And you have hundreds of followers already.

She clicked open her Instagram. Three hundred and ten followers. And lots of comments from people saying what a splendid idea their bucket list was and telling them the things they would like to do. Who would have thought it?

HONEY
Wanna chat?

It was another text from Honey.

SANDRA
Of course.

A chat with her granddaughter was just what she needed.

'Hello, Nan. You're getting famous!'

Sandra chuckled. 'I don't think so, pet. But it is nice that so many people are liking our page. Now, tell me what you've been up to.'

They chatted for ages, with Honey's brother Zac coming in and waving to her before he dashed back out again, and by the time the call ended, Sandra felt a lot more cheerful. She was meeting Patti later today, and Mabel and Beryl from the swimming group, for lunch. She'd better get herself ready.

After showering she went into the bedroom to get dressed, wondering what to wear. She wasn't used to having such a social life! She glanced over at the photo of Brian and wondered what he would have thought of it. She could imagine him. 'Go for it, Sandra,' he'd have said. 'Live your life. But be careful.'

15

PATTI

It was a fun lunch, with them all agreeing to meet up again. When they'd said goodbye to Mabel and Beryl, Patti and Sandra went to do a bit of shopping.

'I need a light bulb, the one in the hall went out on me last night. I had to take the torch with me to see up the stairs when I went to bed,' Patti said.

'Goodness, that's dangerous,' Sandra said. 'Are you okay to change it? Is it the downstairs hall or the upstairs one?'

'Downstairs, thank goodness, but I'm going to need a ladder.'

Sandra remembered that Patti was scared of heights. 'Do you want me to do it for you? I've got a stepladder if you haven't got one.'

'I have, and I'll be brave and change it myself. It's my first step to getting over my fear of heights. But I'd love you to come and hold the ladder and give me some moral support, if you don't mind,' Patti said.

'I'd be delighted to.'

Patti bought a couple of light bulbs, saying it was best to have a spare in, and some STOP to help her stop biting her nails – 'Kit said it was very good'. Then Sandra bought a couple of big plastic storage boxes. She hadn't decided if she was moving yet, but it was probably time she decluttered a bit anyway.

Back at Patti's house, they had a cup of coffee then Patti fetched the ladder from the cupboard under the stairs whilst Sandra held the light bulb, intending to pass it to Patti when she got to the top.

'Bring your phone too. If I'm going to do this, I want a record of it,' Patti said. 'We can put it on Insta.'

'Okay.' Sandra went back for her phone, placing it on the little table in the hall, beside the light bulb. Then Patti opened the stepladder and positioned it under the light hanging from the ceiling before stepping back and studying the ladder nervously. 'I know it's only four steps but...'

Sandra wanted to offer again to change the bulb for her but knew that it was best for Patti to overcome her fear. 'I'll be right here, holding the ladder,' she promised.

Patti nodded and took a deep breath. 'You can do this, Patti,' she said firmly to herself.

'You definitely can,' Sandra assured her, holding on to the ladder.

Patti went up slowly, pausing after each step. When she reached the top, she stretched up and took out the old light bulb.

'Well done!' Sandra told her. She handed Patti the new bulb and took the old one from her.

'Can you take a photo of me as I put this new one in? But be quick! I'm not sure how brave I can be if you're not holding the ladder.'

Sandra put the old bulb down on the table, picked up her phone and quickly took a couple of shots of Patti screwing in the new bulb.

'Well, actually that wasn't as bad as I dreaded,' Patti said in relief when she was safely down the stepladder again. 'I'm not sure I could have done more than four steps though.'

'You did well. And here's the proof!' Sandra showed her the photos.

Patti's face broke into a huge grin. 'I think this calls for a wine to celebrate.' She winked. 'And there just happens to be a bottle chilling in my fridge.'

When the wine was opened and two glasses poured, Patti took a photo of the two glasses, then uploaded that, and the photo of her standing on the stepladder to change the light bulb, onto Instagram.

The first step to overcoming my fear of heights

'You should put a photo of that "STOP" nail stuff too, let everyone know that you've taken the first step to stop biting your nails. It might encourage someone else to stop.'

'And you should take a photo of the storage boxes you bought and add "start decluttering" to your list.'

'The way we keep adding things to our lists, we'll never do it all.' Sandra chuckled as she did as Patti suggested.

16

SANDRA

Sandra was surprised at how much she enjoyed the swimming lessons. It helped that Tess was patient and inspiring and that the other members of the swimming class were all friendly and up for a laugh. Every week they happily posed for photos for Sandra and Patti's Old Gals' Bucket List Instagram page, coming to the lessons in colourful costumes with over-the-top accessories such as swimming hats with big plastic daisies on them and fun swimming goggles. Madge even wore a bright pink flamingo rubber ring and Beryl donned a Victorian swimming costume which she'd bought from eBay. Then the two men, Bill and Sid, got in on the act and turned up in one piece bathing suits and snorkels. Tess took it all in good spirits and allowed Sandra and Patti to take photos before the swimming lesson started. It made for some good material for their Insta feed, which now had quite a following, with people sharing that they had started swimming lessons too, and or were intending too, and thanking the two women for inspiring them.

Kali was having swimming lessons at school, so was eager to ask Sandra how she was getting on. It was a topic of conversation every time they had Sunday lunch together and even Don had started showing an interest. Over in Australia, Becky and her family were following the page in amusement and Honey often sent Sandra photos of unusual swimming costumes or floats that she could wear for her next lesson. Sandra enjoyed these fun exchanges with her.

Many other members of the swimming class had started a bucket list themselves. Sid a keen cyclist, wanted to cycle around the coast of England and was already training for the trip, Bill had decided to learn to play the guitar, Madge had started a class for flower arranging – something she'd wanted to do for ages – and Beryl had taken up yoga and proudly showed them all in the canteen after their lesson how she could now balance on one leg. Everyone applauded even though she lost her balance and ended up clutching onto Madge for support, almost pulling her over in the process. Because everyone had bonded so well, they all encouraged each other along and two of the group had already learnt to swim a few strokes. Tess had told them that the breaststroke was the easiest to learn – as the least tiring stroke and one that keeps your head out of the water – so that's what they all started with.

Sandra found her confidence growing and finally, after a few weeks of lessons, she let go of the bar and swam her first strokes.

'You've done it! Well done!' Patti clapped enthusiastically as Sandra lowered her legs to the floor and took a few deep breaths, elation flooding through her. She had done it. She'd finally done it! She'd let go of the bar as her swimming instructor had told her, both literally and metaphorically.

'Well done, Sandra,' Tess shouted and Sandra's face flushed with pride as they all cheered.

'That's another one off the bucket list,' Patti told her. 'Now you have to do it again so I can video you for our Instagram page. I'll go and get my phone.'

'I'll do it, I've got my phone with me.' Tess took her phone out of her pocket and held it up. 'Ready, Sandra?'

Sandra swam again – she managed a couple more strokes this time – and Tess filmed it, then sent the video to Patti's phone.

A little later in the café, Patti took a photo of the group, all raising their cups and grinning, and posted that on Instagram along with the video that Tess had taken and the caption:

Celebrating! Sandra swam today! What will be ticked off the bucket list next?

* * *

Sandra felt proud as she watched the video. Who would have thought that she'd finally learnt to swim at seventy-one!

'You should do something to celebrate,' Tess said.

Sandra nodded. 'I will. I'm going to have my ears pierced.' She'd noticed that a local beauty store had a walk-in ear-piercing service.

'That's a great way to mark the occasion,' Tess told her.

'And then we'll celebrate with a cocktail!' Patti said.

Which is exactly what they did.

17

'It's this weekend your son is moving to Cambridge, isn't it?' Patti asked as they caught the bus to go home.

'Yes, he's got a flat over there. Laila and the children are going to spend the weekend with him.' Don had told her this when he'd dropped by yesterday and invited her over tonight for dinner.

To say goodbye.

Laila and the girls would still be here and Don would be coming home weekends, she reminded herself.

This would be the first weekend that she hadn't spent with them since Brian died. She'd be alone. She'd buried her head in the sand a bit about Don's transfer, caught up with learning to swim and spending time with Patti and their new swimming club friends. Now it was staring her in the face.

'Fancy a day out on Sunday to celebrate you learning to swim and getting your ears pierced?' Patti asked as if sensing her thoughts. 'I was thinking of getting the train into Birmingham, taking a look around the shops and having lunch somewhere nice.'

'I'd love to,' Sandra replied. She hadn't had a wander around Birmingham City Centre for ages. Since before Brian died.

* * *

She was hanging her swimming costume and towel on the line when Don came to pick her up.

'You're early,' she said in surprise. She wasn't expecting him until five thirty, his normal time.

'I finished at lunchtime, Mum. It's my last day. I've got tomorrow off so that I can pack and move into the Cambridge flat.' He glanced at the swimming costume on the line. 'You've been swimming again?'

'Yes, and I actually swam a few strokes today. I can't believe it!' She turned to him. 'Your dad would have been so proud.' Brian had always wanted her to learn to swim. He'd have been there, cheering her on today. And they'd have celebrated tonight with a nice bottle of Merlot, Brian's favourite wine.

Don put his arm around her shoulder and gave her a hug. 'He would. Well done, Mum.'

'Thank you. Now, how are things with you? How was your last day at the office. I expect you had mixed feelings about that,' she said sympathetically. And his last week with his family. He'd only be seeing them at the weekend now until the house was sold.

'Yes, a bit, but I'm excited about this new job. Even though it will be hard being away from Laila and the children. And you.'

'I know it will, dear, but you'll be home weekends,' she told him, although she had to admit that she was going to miss him dreadfully.

* * *

Kali and Rana were waiting eagerly for Sandra. 'We saw you, Nan! We saw you swimming on your Insta,' Kali said.

'Did you?' she asked, surprised.

Laila laughed. 'They insist that we check your account every day to see what you've been up to. Congratulations, Sandra. It's quite an achievement.'

'It was. And I've had my ears pierced too.' Sandra proudly showed them her new earrings.

'You're like us now, Nanny. Remember to keep them clean,' Rana said. Both girls had their ears pierced a couple of years ago.

It was a lively but rather poignant meal, with everyone being extra cheerful. Don was leaving tomorrow, when the girls had finished school.

Laila and the children were going with him for the weekend, then coming back on the train. It was sad to think that the little family would be split up for a while.

Life goes on and it's a great opportunity for Don, she reminded herself.

They'd just finished dessert when Don's phone rang. 'It's the estate agent,' he said.

He left the table to take the call, coming back a few minutes later looking a bit shocked.

'We've got someone interested in our house. They're coming around tomorrow morning for another look.'

'The couple from earlier?' Laila asked.

'Yes. Their house has sold too, so if they go ahead, it will be a quick sale. Unfortunately the house we liked in Cambridge has sold now but we'll soon find another one.'

Kali and Rana jumped up and down in excitement. 'We're moving! Hooray we're moving! We're going to have a bedroom each and a trampoline in the garden.'

'We promised them that so they would look forward to moving. You know how anxious kids are about leaving their friends,' Laila whispered.

Sandra nodded, her mind whirring. If these people made an offer, her precious family would be gone in a couple of months. Quicker than she'd thought. She'd be here alone. It really was happening. No Don, Laila and family nearby.

'Look why don't you come to Cambridge with us this weekend, Mum?' Don suggested. 'We can make room in the flat. There's two single beds in the spare room. The kids can bunk up together and you can have the other bed.'

Sandra saw that look cross Laila's face again, before she scooped up some dirty plates and took them into the kitchen. Clearly Laila wanted to spend the weekend just with Don and the children, as a family. Which was only natural. Besides, she had plans herself, didn't she? She was going out with Patti.

She chose her words carefully, knowing that Don was fully expecting her to fall into his plan. 'That's a lovely idea and normally I would love to, but not this weekend, dear. I've made plans to go out.'

His eyebrows raised and his jaw slackened. 'Surely you can cancel them?'

'I can but I'm not going to. I think you need to spend some time looking around as a family this weekend. I'll come another time, I promise.'

He looked disappointed. 'You really should come, Mum. Once you get familiar with the place you'll want to move there. Cambridge is beautiful. And there's lots to do, shops, entertainment, some lovely walks.'

'I'm sure it is, but I don't think this weekend is the right time. Don, you're moving away. You'll only see your wife and children every weekend from now on, until your house sells. You need to spend this weekend with just them. Stop worrying about me and concentrate on your family.'

'You're my family too, Mum. And I want you to live by us. You've got time to get an estate agent around before we go. They could value the house and get it on the market in a couple of days. You can move when we do, rent a little flat or stay with us for a while until your house sells. If you leave your keys with the estate agent, they'll show people around.'

Goodness, he just wouldn't listen to her.

'I told you I've made plans for this weekend. And I need a bit longer to think about the move, love. Now stop worrying about me and concentrate on you, Laila and the children.'

Back at home, she walked around the house, going from room to room, savouring the memories. Becky's former bedroom was the first room. This was the one Kali slept in when she and Rana stayed over. She and Brian had redecorated it when Kali was born, using a pale grey and pink scheme, so that it would still be suitable when Kali was older. There were pictures of animals all over the walls; Kali was mad about animals. The same colour scheme was used for the bed, the desk that doubled as a dressing table, the bookshelves and the wardrobes. Kali loved it. The next room was Don's old room. This was similarly decorated but in grey and blue, with stars and planet pictures over the walls because Rana was fascinated by the night sky. If she moved to a bungalow in Cambridge, she would probably only have two bedrooms so the children wouldn't be able to have one each.

They're getting older, they probably won't even want to stay over in a few years' time, she realised.

The next room was now a study but this had once been Martin's room. Dear Martin. She walked over to the tall cupboard in the corner and opened it. Shelf upon shelf of Martin's things. His school books, his first roller skates, his skateboard. He had been such a daredevil, never showed any fear. She glanced over at the framed quote on the wall over the desk, white words on a background of grey cobbled stones.

> The inner fire is the most important thing mankind possesses.
>
> — EDITH SŐDERGRAN

Martin's favourite quote. He had that inner fire, that urge to do, explore, test his boundaries, right from an early age. He lived – and died – by it. What would he tell her to do? He'd probably tell her it was time she boxed up his things, she thought ruefully, remembering the big storage boxes she'd bought to do just that. Not yet though, she needed a little longer.

She walked all around the house, the memories comforting her. The king-size bed in her bedroom that, until that awful day last year, she and Brian had slept in side by side. The wardrobe that still contained his clothes. Then down into the kitchen where they had sat opposite each other, eating breakfast, her chatting away and Brian head deep in the daily newspaper, nodding and grunting occasionally. Sometimes that had irritated her, but now she would give anything to have him sitting there, reading the paper. Then the lounge where they sat watching TV. Brian loved documentaries, she loved dramas and watching the soaps, so they took it in turns to choose what programme to watch, the other one reading. It didn't matter, they had still been together.

She walked out into the garden, the neatly mowed lawn – Don had arranged for a gardener to come in and do that now, although Sandra still tended to the flower beds, she found it relaxing – the shed where Brian kept all his gardening tools. Some men had a 'man shed' where they retreated for some peace and quiet but not Brian, he used the study for that.

Could she walk away from all this?

She sat down on the bench, her thoughts whirring around in her head.

It seemed like she had to choose between having her memories around her or having her family nearby.

18

PATTI

On Sunday morning, Patti scrolled through the Old Gals Insta page to see if their followers had increased and was pleased to see that they had. The video of Sandra finally learning to swim had gained a lot of likes and comments. She smiled as she played the video again. She was so pleased that she'd suggested they go to swimming lessons. That was another thing ticked off Sandra's bucket list. Two things actually, she corrected herself, remembering that Sandra had also had her ears pierced. She had to get herself together and tick off another one from her list now.

A WhatsApp message pinged in from Kit.

KIT

Your Insta page is looking fab, Gran. I'll have to show you how to do reels again, that'll get you more attention.

Patti remembered her mentioning the reels when they'd first installed the app. 'I might be able to manage it myself. I'll have a try,' she replied. 'How are things with you?'

'OK. I've decided not to move in with Seb. I think I should see a bit of the world and have a few adventures of my own before settling down.'

'Good for you.' Patti wrote back.

They messaged back and forth for a while then Kit said she had to go and would see Patti later in the week.

Patti made herself some toast and poured a glass of juice. She'd just finished them when Mary and Keith Facetimed. They were both sitting in the garden, drinking iced tea against a background of blue skies and fluffy white clouds. Patti couldn't help feeling a bit envious. It was overcast and drizzly here in the UK.

They had a chat for a while, catching up on each other's news, then Keith went to watch a programme on the TV, leaving Mary and Patti to talk.

'What are you up to today?' Mary asked.

'I'm meeting my friend Sandra later. Remember I told you she couldn't swim so we were having swimming lessons. Well, she learned to swim on Thursday so we're off to Birmingham for a shopping trip and a meal to celebrate. The weather's not good here though, not like over there, but luckily we'll be under cover most of the time.'

'That's brilliant, well done her,' Mary said. 'Now how about you tick something off your bucket list too? Come over here and see us, warm up your bones with a bit of sunshine.' She leant closer to the screen and lowered her voice. 'It will cheer Keith up no end. I'm so worried about him.'

Patti could see why. Keith hadn't been anywhere near as chatty as he usually was. They used to talk for ages, but ever since his heart op he'd been quieter, more distant. It was like the spark had gone out of him. She could go. Her passport had arrived in the week so she could actually book a flight now, if she could pluck up the courage that is. 'I do want to, really I do. It's just a bit daunting, especially flying for the first time by myself.'

'Then why don't you ask your friend Sandra to come with you, she sounds fun,' Mary suggested. 'You can stay in the casita, it's got two bedrooms, a lounge/kitchen and bathroom, so you'll have plenty of room. Or you can share the spare bedroom in the house, if you prefer.'

It would be much more pleasant to travel with a friend. And although they'd only quite recently reconnected, she got on so well with Sandra. 'You know, that's a great idea. I'll ask her when I meet up with her today.'

* * *

Sandra seemed a little pensive when they met up. Patti wondered if it was an anniversary of some sort. She remembered Sandra saying the first times of doing something without Brian were the worst. As soon as they sat down on the train she asked, 'Is everything all right, Sandra?'

Sandra raised troubled eyes to hers. 'Don's got someone interested in his house. They had a second viewing on Friday and he thinks they might make an offer.'

So that's what was bothering her. 'That's quick! It's only been on the market a few weeks, hasn't it?'

'Yes, but the estate agent said that spring and early summer are prime time for selling. Of course, Don is now putting even more pressure on me to put my house on the market too.'

Patti could imagine. Although it was laudable that they wanted Sandra to move with them, she wondered if they actually realised what a big step that was. 'And how do you feel about it?'

Sandra sighed, reached in her handbag for a bag of boiled sweets, and offered one to Patti.

'Thanks.' Patti took a strawberry flavoured one, and waited for her answer.

'I don't know. It's sort of brought it home that they really are moving away. I'm going to have to give it some serious thought, as to whether I go with them or not.' Sandra popped a lemon sweet into her mouth, put the packet back and closed her bag.

'Well... I do have a bit of a suggestion that might give you the chance to think things over without feeling under so much pressure. My sister-in-law Mary and my brother Keith phoned me this morning, asking me to come and stay with them for a couple of weeks in their villa in Spain. She said that the weather is lovely now, warm enough to sunbathe in the afternoon but not too hot to make sightseeing uncomfortable...'

'Oh, Patti, that's marvellous. Do you think you'll go?'

Patti tugged at her earlobe. 'I'd like to. I did think about driving over there, I could go on the ferry to Santander, but it's a bit of a trek as they live down in Málaga. And I'm nervous about driving on the wrong side of the road. Besides, it would be good to knock something off my bucket list. I'd really like to go on a plane if I could pluck up the courage.'

'You must go, really, you'll be fine. Maybe take a few drops of Rescue

Remedy before you get on the plane. And take a book to read. The time will soon go. It's only about a two-and-a-half-hour flight.' She paused. 'Hang on, how does this give me more time to think things over? You're not that much of a distraction to me!'

'Well, Mary suggested…' Patti paused. Just ask…

Sandra was looking at her questioningly. 'What is it? Did you want me to drop you off at the airport? I don't mind.'

Patti shook her head. 'Mary said they have plenty of room and suggested I ask you to come with me. She knows we're good friends. And I'd feel much happier if I was travelling with someone. Don't feel pressurised though,' she added. 'I know that you have a lot on your plate. But maybe a change of scenery would be good for you?'

Sandra looked surprised. 'Me? Do they have enough room for both of us?'

'Yes, they have a spare bedroom and a little casita – it's like a little cabin – in their grounds. We could both stay in that. Or I can stay in the house, and you can have the casita if you'd prefer your own space?'

'Go to Spain with you?' Sandra repeated as if she couldn't believe Patti had asked her.

Maybe she shouldn't have asked. Sandra might feel awkward staying with strangers. 'It's okay, I know it's a lot to ask of you. It's just we get on so well and it would be lovely to travel with someone.' She patted Sandra's hand. 'It was only a thought, don't worry. I can manage by myself, I'm determined to. I'm not going to let fear rule my life.'

To her surprise, Sandra nodded. 'I'd love to come. If you're sure your brother and sister-in-law don't mind. It would be lovely to get away for a bit and have some sun!'

'You would? Oh that's brilliant! Of course they won't mind, it was their suggestion.' The words were rushing out of her mouth, she was so pleased. 'We're going to have a wonderful time. I know we are.'

'When are you planning on going?' Sandra asked.

'They said we could come anytime. And we're pensioners! Footloose and fancy free! When do you fancy? Have you any plans for the next few weeks?'

'None at all.'

'Well when we've finished our shopping why don't we take a look at flights over lunch?'

'Great idea,' Sandra agreed.

Patti was pleased to see that her friend looked much brighter already.

'Well now we're both off to Spain, how about we treat ourselves to some new holiday clothes?' Patti suggested as they got off the train. 'We're definitely going to need sun hats. Mary and Keith were sitting outside in T-shirts! And they've got a fabulous swimming pool.'

'It's a good job I've learnt to swim,' Sandra said with a grin.

They had a great time around the shops, both of them buying a summer hat, a couple of new summer dresses, shorts and T-shirts, and another new swimming costume.

'We can take some fun holiday pics to post on our Insta account when we're out there too!' Patti said, as they walked into a restaurant for a late lunch. 'Now, how about a bottle of wine to celebrate?'

Over lunch they used their phones to search flights to Spain. 'I can't believe how much the price differs from hour to hour, never mind day to day,' Patti said. 'We don't want to go at silly o'clock just to save a few bob though, do we? Especially as Keith will be coming to pick us up over there. We can't drag him out of bed in the middle of the night.'

'Definitely not,' Sandra agreed. 'Ah here's one, it's only just over £100 return. We have to add luggage and seats onto that, of course, but it's very cheap for this time of year. Ooh, it's next Wednesday. I didn't realise it was that soon.'

'Is it?' Patti asked. 'That sounds perfect to me, it won't give me much time to fret.'

'What about your brother and sister-in-law? It's only a few days away.'

'They said they always keep the casita ready for guests. Why don't you drop into mine when we get home and we can call them?'

19

SANDRA

Back at Patti's house, Patti sent a WhatsApp to Mary to let her know that Sandra had agreed to come to Spain with her and to see if she was free to chat, then opened the fridge. 'Fancy a glass of chilled rosé to celebrate our new adventure?'

'Why not?' Sandra said. Life was one long adventure and celebration with Patti.

Patti had just poured them a glass of wine each, when her phone rang. 'It's Mary,' she said, pressing the button to accept the vid call, then sitting down at the table and motioning Sandra to do the same.

A friendly looking woman with a tanned face and grey curly shoulder length hair appeared on the screen. 'Hi Patti, that's fabulous news. I can't believe that you're coming over! And how kind of Sandra to come with you. Keith will be delighted, he's inside watching the TV. Do you want to talk to him?'

Mary was standing beside a sparkling blue swimming pool. The sky looked cloudless and sunny, and was that an orange tree behind her head? Sandra wondered excitedly.

'No, I'll leave you to tell him! I'd better introduce you to Sandra.' She held out the phone so that Sandra was visible on the screen too.

Mary waved cheerily. 'Hi there. Thanks so much for accompanying this one, we've been trying to get her to come and visit for years!'

'It's a pleasure. Thanks for asking me. It's so good of you,' Sandra replied. Mary looked genuinely pleased that Sandra was accompanying Patti.

'Nonsense, it's lovely to have company. Now, when were you both thinking of coming?'

Sandra looked worriedly at Patti, was it too soon to go next week?

'We haven't booked yet but there's some flights next Wednesday, great times and a good price. Is that too soon?'

'Not at all. That's perfect. The weather's sunny and warm but not too hot. July and August can be scorching. And if I'm not wrong, that means you'll be travelling just before the school half term holiday too, so the flights will be cheaper.'

Goodness, she'd forgotten it was soon going to be half term. She usually had the grandchildren for a couple of days, to share the load. Laila hadn't mentioned it though, and they always worked out a schedule together well beforehand. Maybe she was having the time off to do a bit of packing, or they were all going to Cambridge to spend time with Don, seeing as Kali and Rana were off school. Should she check?

'Look, I forgot it was half term coming up. Can I just message my daughter-in-law and check that she doesn't need me to have my grandchildren any of the days? We'll be away over half term and I often look after them in the school holidays.'

'Of course, go ahead. Mary and I can carry on chatting here.'

Sandra sent Laila a quick WhatsApp to say her friend had invited her to go away with her to Spain so she wanted to check that Laila didn't need her for childcare.

Laila replied.

LAILA

That's fantastic. You go and enjoy yourself, you deserve it. We'll be fine. I've booked some time off so will be here for the kids

'All good, Laila's booked time off work,' Sandra said as she joined Patti again.

'Brilliant. Now why don't you come for a couple of weeks? The casita is ready. A couple of women to natter to is just what I need. Keith either potters about the garden or sits in front of the TV all day. I can't get a word out of him half the time.'

'We'll soon jog him out of that. We've got a list of things we want to do,' Patti replied. 'You both don't mind running us around, do you? Or we can get taxis, or the train.'

'You will not! I'd be delighted to run you around.'

'That's great then. We'll book now and I'll call you later for a catch-up, tell Keith.'

'I will. And no need for you both to lug heavy suitcases around with you. There's a washing machine in the casita so you can wash as you go.'

'That's great as we can bring a 10kg case free,' Patti said. 'I can't believe I'm actually flying over to see you!'

'Keith won't believe it either. It's just what he needs to cheer himself up.'

'That's good. I'm really looking forward to seeing you both. Anyway, we'll book now, and I'll call you back later,' Patti told her.

'Send us the flight times too, so we know when to get to the airport,' Mary told her. She waved. 'Pleased to meet you, Sandra. See you both on Wednesday.'

They said their goodbyes and Patti closed the chat. 'I told you she wouldn't mind. Now let's get those flights booked.'

Patti topped up their wine while Sandra booked the flights. 'If you get your passport I'll check you in now, and check myself in when I'm back at home,' she said.

A little while later the flights were all booked and Patti checked in.

'Oh my God, we're actually doing this!' Sandra said. 'Spain here we come!' She held out her glass and they both chinked glasses, squealing with excitement.

'Thank you for coming with me,' Patti told her. 'I feel a lot better now that I have someone flying with me. I actually can't believe that we're going.'

Sandra smiled at her. 'It's me who should be thanking you. Two whole weeks in Spain! It's just what I need.'

'I'm just glad you know your way around the airport. All of this is new to me.' Patti said, taking a long gulp of her wine.

They'd both just finished their drinks when Sandra's phone rang. She glanced at the screen. 'Goodness, I didn't notice the time. It's Don. He was popping in to see me after he dropped Laila and the children off, they've stayed with him at Cambridge this weekend and he dropped them back home, so he could collect more of his things. I must go.' She pressed answer and grabbed her bag. 'See you tomorrow,' she said to Patti as she hurried off home.

'What do you mean? Aren't you coming home tonight?' Don sounded worried.

'Sorry, love, I was talking to Patti. I'm on my way now. Put the kettle on for a cup of tea, will you? I'll only be five minutes.'

When she hurried in a few minutes later, Don was pouring hot water over teabags in mugs.

'You seem to be spending every minute you can with this Patti,' Don said scathingly. 'No wonder you don't want to move to Cambridge.'

'I thought that you would be pleased that I have a friend,' she told him. 'And actually I'm going to Spain with her next week to visit her brother and sister-in-law. That's why I'm late, we were booking our flights.'

'Laila told me. It's very short notice, Mum.'

'I know. Isn't it exciting? I can't believe that we're flying out on Wednesday for two whole weeks.' She stepped past him and swiftly took the teabags out of the mugs before it was too strong, then added milk. She put one of the mugs in front of Don and carried hers over to the table, sitting down in the nearest chair. Don leant back against the worktop.

'Do you think this is wise, Mum? These people are all strangers to you. You've only reconnected with this Patti a month or so ago.'

'Almost two months actually and will you stop calling her "this Patti"! She's a very good friend. And stop overreacting. What on earth do you think's going to happen? They're not going to kidnap me and sell me to traffickers.'

'There's no need to be so flippant.' Hurt flickered in Don's eyes. 'I'm worried about you, Mum. I think the grief has got too much for you. You're so impulsive just lately. It's not like you.'

'I'm making a life for myself, Don. Partly so that you don't have to worry about me being lonely when you move.'

Don looked a bit guilty. 'I guess you are, and it is good that you're getting out and about now, Mum. But please be careful.'

'Of course I will. I'll be fine I promise. I'll be enjoying two weeks in the sun with a good friend.'

At least she hoped she would. As Don had pointed out, she didn't know Patti's brother and his wife. It will be okay, I can always take myself off for a bit if things are awkward. She looked at her tattoo. 'Embrace change, love life.'

That's exactly what she intended to do. Now she was going to get her passport and check herself in. She couldn't wait to go to Spain.

20

MARY

Spain

'Patti's coming over on Wednesday and she's bringing a friend with her,' Mary said as she walked into the lounge where Keith was glued to the TV.

'That's good,' he replied without glancing away from the screen.

Mary suppressed the annoyance that flooded through her. Patti was his sister and was making a big effort to come and see them. He could at least show an interest.

'Keith!' she said in exasperation.

Irritation flickered in his eyes as he dragged his attention away from the film. 'What?'

'We need to plan where we're going to take them both. I was thinking Fuengirola, Mijas Pueblo and maybe Málaga for shopping. And we could have a couple of meals out. What do you think?'

'They'll probably be happy to sunbathe by the pool most of the time and have a bit of a chat. Me and Patti have a lot to catch up on.'

'They're coming for two weeks, Keith. They'll want to do more than sit around the pool. They'll want to see a bit of the place.'

Keith's eyes flicked back to the TV. 'That's okay, you girls go off out for some day trips. I don't mind.'

Mary plonked herself on the sofa next to him. 'You should come too.

Patti's your sister. She's travelling all this way, for the first time too, and you know how scared she is of flying. You should make an effort and spend some time with her and show her and her friend a bit of Spain.'

'There will be plenty of chance for us to have a natter and catch up, but I don't want to cramp your style and hang around with you all. I'm sure you'd much prefer to have a couple of hours out shopping by yourselves.'

Make that, he didn't want to go. He didn't want to do *anything* since the heart attack – which had been months ago. But he also didn't like her going out and leaving him alone for long either, in case anything happened. He was obviously prepared to make an exception for her to go out with Patti and Sandra, but wasn't going to make the effort himself.

She sighed. Keith's attention was now back on the TV programme. He couldn't carry on shutting himself away like this. It wasn't good for him. She knew that the heart attack had frightened him. It had happened late at night, and Mary had only just returned from a night out for a friend's birthday. Apparently, Keith had been having what he thought was indigestion for the past hour and was going to bed to sleep it off, but Mary knew it was a heart attack right away, gave him an aspirin and took him to the hospital. The aspirin and Mary's prompt action had saved his life, the surgeon told them. They were marvellous at the hospital and treated Keith immediately, he'd had a stent fitted the next day. It had been a harrowing experience for both of them, she couldn't stop thinking of what might have happened if she hadn't come home when she did, if she hadn't given Keith that aspirin, and like Keith, she lived in fear for a while afterwards that it might happen again. She couldn't bear to lose him. And she certainly didn't want to be here in Spain all by herself.

Gradually she learnt not to worry so much. Keith had a couple of follow-on check-ups and the nice Spanish doctor, who spoke very good English, informed them that Keith was fit and well, and to get on with his life. 'Everything in moderation,' he'd said. 'A bit of wine, the occasional piece of cake – those are fine. Just make sure you take regular exercise and eat lots of fruit, veg, white meat and fish too.'

Keith's regular exercise consisted of walking around the garden and doing a bit of weeding. His anxiety hadn't lessened with time though. He still lived in fear of having another heart attack and not being so lucky, so didn't want to exert himself or go far from home. She really hoped that Patti and her friend, Sandra, coming over would encourage him to get out a bit. Surely he wouldn't want to stay home alone while they all went sightseeing?

'We need to do a shop for when they come. And we'd better give the casita a bit of clean, ready for them,' she said.

'We've got plenty of time. There's a couple of days yet before they arrive,' he said. 'Don't stress.'

'Don't stress' was his new favourite expression. The doctor had told him not to stress after his heart attack, so it was a mantra he kept repeating, both to himself and to her. The trouble was, his attitude caused her a *lot* of stress, because it meant everything was left to her.

'I'll make a start now, no good leaving everything to the last minute.' She got up and walked out, fighting down the urge to shake him.

Patti's visit couldn't come soon enough.

The casita was past the pool, down a short path tucked in behind a couple of fir trees. It hadn't been used for a while. The last visitors were Mary's sister and partner last year before Keith's heart attack, but she always kept it clean and tidy. A quick vacuum and wipe around was all it needed. There was a decent sized lounge and kitchen area, with a cooker, microwave, wooden table and four chairs, and a range of cupboards along the wall containing cutlery, pots and pans, etc., then two bedrooms, each with a double bed and a wardrobe, a bathroom with a shower and the inevitable bidet. Out front was a small, fenced patio area with a table and chairs, so that their visitors could sit and enjoy the sunshine while enjoying a cup of tea in private, if they wanted. She suspected Patti would want to go over to the big house and chat to Keith, but she was sure that Sandra might want a bit of time to herself. Patti said that she and Sandra had worked at the supermarket together years ago, and she'd recently lost her husband. It was kind of her to travel with Patti, she didn't think her sister-in-law would have plucked up the courage to travel alone. She'd always been terrified of flying.

This was a big step for Patti. She'd come through a lot too. Mary remembered how shocked she and Keith were when Patti had told them, fighting back the tears, that she had cancer. Patti had tried to smile, talk positive, tell them she was going to fight it, but even through the computer screen, they could hear the sadness in her voice and see the fear in her eyes. She'd done it though. Keith had been worried when she'd taken the step to move back to Worcester a couple of months ago. 'Why put herself through all the stress of moving when she's just come through cancer?' he'd said. 'She should be taking it easy.' And now she was getting on an aeroplane for the very first time. Patti had clearly decided to grasp this second chance of life. Mary just hoped she could convince her older brother to do the same. Patti was only a few years younger than him but she was embracing life whereas Keith seemed to be giving up on it.

21

SANDRA

'It's lovely to see you getting out and doing things again, and now planning on going to Spain with your friend. We've been so worried about you since Brian died,' Laila said when she popped around to see Sandra the next morning after dropping Kali and Rana off at school. It was her day off. 'Don's fretting about you, of course, that's his nature. He'll get over it. The new job and the move to Cambridge will keep him busy. And it will do you good to get away.'

'Thank you.' Sandra had always got on well with Laila, she was calm and level-headed, good for Don who was always too anxious. Laila stood for no-nonsense, and you knew where you were with her. Brian had thought she was too outspoken sometimes, but Sandra preferred people to be straight, things got complicated if people didn't say how they really felt.

'It's nice that Don wants to look after me, but I think that it's best if I don't make a rush decision to move to Cambridge with you. I'd like to give you all time to settle down and see how you like living there. You're young and can move again if you're not happy, but I don't want to be uprooting myself again and again. I have to make sure it's the right decision for me.'

'Of course you do. We will all miss you, especially Kali and Rana, you've been great with them. And I'm really grateful for the free childcare and babysitting you've given us, but now it's time for you to live your life.'

'Thank you, I've been more than happy to do it. Are you sure that I haven't left you in the lurch with childminding over the half term?'

'Not at all. I have some time off work, so we're going to spend the weekend with Don and then my parents have been asking me to visit for ages, so I'm taking the girls down to London to spend a few days with them.'

Sandra was pleased that she was going away because it was setting Laila free to do what she wanted and take the children to see their other grandparents, Sandra realised.

'I'm delighted to hear that and I hope you haven't put off visiting your parents because you didn't like to leave me alone. You and Don have been such a support to me, but I'm stronger now. I don't want you to put your life on hold for me, worrying about me, and thinking you have to protect me. I've been very grateful for you both but I can cope now. I don't want to be a burden to you.'

'Of course you aren't a burden.' Laila's voice was soft, kind. 'Please don't think that. I didn't mind at all. You were our priority while you were working through your grief.' Her tone was warm. 'We're always happy to help you, Sandra. You mean a lot to us all. And my parents understand the situation. It will be good to spend a few days with them though, and to know that you are enjoying yourself too.' Laila's parents owned, and ran, an Indian restaurant in Camden. It was very much a family business. Laila's brother worked there too, and his uncle and aunt. The family were a little disappointed when Laila took a business studies course and got herself a job in Birmingham as a project manager for a manufacturing company, which is where she met Don. Don and Laila then moved to Worcester a few years later and Laila now worked for a healthcare company whilst Don was still in manufacturing. Her parents kept hoping that Laila, Don and the children would move down to London and eventually all work in one of the restaurants – they now owned three – but there seemed no likelihood of that happening.

They might do sometime in the future though. This was one of the things that worried Sandra about uprooting herself to Cambridge, in a few years she could end up being there alone or moving again. She couldn't keep following Don and Laila about. And she wouldn't do it if Brian was still alive, would she? He wouldn't have wanted to uproot himself to follow Don and his family. They'd just make regular trips to see them and have the children to stay in the school holidays now and again. Surely that's what she should do?

'Well if I can help in any way when I come back… I can have the children overnight a few times, so you and Don can go out together when he comes home for the weekend perhaps?'

'I would really appreciate that. Thank you,' Laila told her.

'It will be a pleasure.' It would too, she wanted to spend as much time with her grandchildren as she could before they moved away.

'Now tell me all about this holiday you've got planned. Whereabouts in Spain are you going?'

'It's somewhere in Málaga, on the Costa del Sol,' she told her. 'Patti's brother and wife have lived there a few years now but she's never been to visit. She's terrified of flying. So she asked me to go with her.'

'You two really have got friendly, haven't you?' Laila asked. 'I'm so pleased that you've reconnected again. It's good to have a friend to share things with. I will miss my friends Suzy and Clare, but they're going to come up for a weekend when we're settled.'

'That's great that you're not going to lose touch.' Sandra put her empty cup down in her saucer. 'And I'm sure you'll soon make new friends too.'

They sat chatting for a while then Laila had to go. Sandra cleared away the cups then renewed her lipstick, grabbed her tote bag with her swimming gear and set off. She was meeting Patti at the bus stop.

* * *

'Well done, Sandra,' Tess shouted as Sandra completed her second width.

'I'm going to try and swim a length now,' Sandra said, looking across to the other side of the swimming pool. 'I'm a bit worried about going in the deep end though.'

'I'll swim alongside you,' Patti offered. She didn't add 'in case you get into difficulties', but Sandra knew that was the reason. And she really appreciated it. She was nervous, but she could do it. She was sure she could.

'Can I make a suggestion?'

Sandra turned to Tess.

'Start off at the deep end, then if you tire – and you might – you're in shallow water and can stand on the bottom. It will be less daunting for you.'

That was a good idea. Although stepping down into the deep water was nerve-wracking. It would be easier if she could jump or dive in, but she hadn't managed that yet.

'You'll find it easier if you go down the steps until you're waist deep then reach out for the bar and hold on to it, put your feet against the wall, press hard and launch yourself off,' Tess said.

'I'll do the same. We'll launch off together,' Patti said.

They both padded along the side of the pool to the deeper end. Sandra hesitated as she looked at the mass of water below. It was so deep there was no way she could stand on the bottom if she got tired. What if she panicked? Maybe she should have brought a float to hang on to.

'I'll be right beside you and I'll grab you if you start to go under.' Patti's voice was firm and reassuring. 'I'm sure you won't though. You've got this.'

Sandra looked at the water and at the steps in front of her. *You can swim. Don't think about how deep it is. Just swim, like you do in the shallower end.*

'Want me to go first?' Patti asked.

Sandra nodded.

Patti turned around to descend the steps and Sandra followed her. As soon as she was level with the bar she reached out and grabbed it, then turned around so her feet were against the side. Patti was doing the same.

'Ready?'

'Ready.' Sandra pushed her feet against the wall, let go of the bar, shot forward and she was swimming. A couple of splashes and Patti was beside her. Grateful for her friend's reassuring presence, Sandra swam steadily through the water. Patti kept her pace beside her.

Her arms were aching by the time she reached the other end but she felt elated as she touched the bar and lowered her feet so that she could stand on the bottom of the pool.

'Well done, Sandra.' Tess looked delighted.

The others clapped and cheered.

'If you can do that, I can swim without my float,' Madge said determinedly. It had been an effort for her to get into the water at first but now she swam happily, holding on to the white float.

'Start small, Madge,' Tess told her. 'Remember "achievable aims". Wait until you're a little away from the bar, then let go of your float and swim the rest of the way.'

It took Madge three attempts but finally she did it. The look of sheer delight on her face as, with a final lunge, she grabbed the bar, had them all applauding. To think this was the woman who had been too scared to even go down the steps only a few weeks ago.

'You did great,' Patti told her. 'So did you Sandra. A whole length! I think we all need to celebrate with coffee and cake.'

Everyone laughed. They were all used to Patti's coffee and cake celebrations now. She celebrated every win. Sid jumping in, Bill doing a few strokes, Beryl letting go of the bar. Every week there had been some reason to celebrate.

'What will you celebrate when we've all finally learnt to swim?' Sid asked.

'Life,' Patti said simply.

22

Laila invited Sandra around for dinner the following evening, so that she could see the children before she went on holiday, Don was away in Cambridge so it was just the four of them. Kali and Rana were full of questions about Spain and what Sandra would be doing there. She showed them the photo of Keith and Mary's house, that Patti had sent her. The children were wide eyed with wonder as they gazed at the photo on her phone screen.

'There's a swimming pool!' Rana exclaimed.

'And oranges growing on trees!' Kali pointed to the oranges hanging from the branches.

'Yes, and lots of other fruit too. I'll send Mummy some photos when I'm there, so you can see what I'm doing and where we go. I'll bring you both a present back,' she promised, hugging them both. 'And I want to hear all about your trip to London, and see lots of photos. You are going to have a fabulous time with your Nani and Nana.' She used the Indian names for maternal grandmother and grandfather, that she had heard Laila use. 'I'm sure you'll both have lots of fun.'

'We will, I hope you do too. It will do you good to get away, give you time to think things over,' Laila told her. 'That couple made a formal offer for the house today. I'm talking it over with Don later tonight but am pretty sure we'll accept it. The house we liked has come back on the market and these are cash buyers, so we should be able to move in a couple of months. You can come and stay with us whenever you want and if you eventually decide that you want to move, we can find you a little bungalow nearby, with a small garden.'

Sandra nodded. 'I will miss you all but...'

'But it's a big move and you're not sure that you're ready to make it?' Laila said softly.

'I've lived here so long. It will be such an upheaval... I'm still giving it serious thought, but I don't know if I can do it.' She had to think long and hard about this. Maybe Laila was right, going on holiday to Spain, taking her away from the situation, would give her the perspective that she needed. Patti had suggested the same, she remembered.

Later, when she was back at home, suitcase packed, passport in her handbag, she felt a surge of excitement. Tomorrow, she was going on an adventure.

Don phoned to wish her a safe journey. 'Keep in touch, Mum. Make sure you message me every day. I'm worried about you travelling by yourself like this.'

'I'm not by myself, I'm with Patti, and we're staying with her brother and his wife,' she said for the umpteenth time.

'I know but you're thousands of miles away from home.'

After reassuring him that yes she would be careful, and keep in touch, and yes she would think about putting her house on the market when she came back, Don ended the call, saying he had to prepare for an important meeting in the morning. She could almost see the frown in the middle of his forehead, worrying because she was going away with someone he didn't know and was thinking of remaining in Worcester when they'd moved to Cambridge. Don didn't like change, it was a wonder he'd accepted this job, he liked things to stay the same and to have all his ducks in a row. She knew that he was fretting about her and she felt a little guilty about that. 'You're not doing anything wrong, you can't live your life how Don wants you to,' she reminded herself.

A text pinged.

PATTI

All packed?

SANDRA

Yep. Can't wait! Have you got your passport?

PATTI

In my bag.

SANDRA

Good. How are you feeling?

She knew that Patti was anxious about the flight.

PATTI

My stomach is in knots but I'm going to do it. You know what they say, Feel the fear but do it anyway!

She admired Patti for her sheer grit. They were both taking the train to the airport tomorrow, not wanting to leave either of their cars in parking for two weeks. It was a straightforward journey, changing over at Birmingham New Street station to the airport, which was perfectly manageable with only a 10kg case and hand luggage. Hopefully it would give them both chance to relax rather than have to deal with the heavy traffic on the motorway. Despite reassuring Don that she was perfectly fine she was a little apprehensive about the holiday, after all she had only reconnected with Patti a few weeks ago and didn't know her brother and sister-in-law at all. It will be all right, Sandra told herself. You can do this. What's the worst thing that could happen?

That they didn't get on, and she lost her friendship with Patti too.

You're good with people, you can be diplomatic, you had years of experience working in customer services, just take yourself out of any difficult situation, she told herself. Anyway, think positive. You'll probably all get on and have an absolutely fabulous time.

She felt lighter, happier than she had done for a long while and even though grief for Brian still frequently hit her, bringing on a fresh wave of anguish, she was coping much better. She walked over to the sideboard and picked up the photo of Brian in the frame.

'I'll always love and miss you, Brian, and I know you'd want me to live my life. To make it count for both of us.'

She could imagine him now, a twinkle in his eyes. 'You go for it, Sandra. Good for you,' he'd say.

He'd always wanted her to be happy. She blinked the tears from her eyes. When Brian had died it had seemed impossible to be happy without him, but now she was ready to try.

23

PATTI

Patti had hardly slept all night worrying about the flight today. She felt jittery with anxiety. She'd tried not to think about it as she and Sandra chatted away on the train, but once they entered into the airport the fear stepped in big time. She was glad that she was travelling with Sandra, she didn't think she'd have coped alone – she'd have turned back and gone home. The airport was much bigger than she'd expected and so busy she felt that she couldn't breathe. It was all so confusing, with signs, screens and queues everywhere but thankfully Sandra was very composed and knew exactly what to do and where to go.

'I usually go straight through security to get it over with, then have a drink and maybe a snack,' she'd told Patti.

Patti nodded in agreement and followed her friend. Her hand shook so much as she placed her printed boarding pass on the scanning machine, but the scanner couldn't read it and Sandra had to turn back to help.

Patti couldn't believe that all the people milling around them weren't nervous too. They were all getting in a metal contraption and then flying through the sky! The thought of it made her feel nauseous, shaky and want to run out of the airport. Why had she agreed to do this? Why hadn't she booked on a coach, travelled over on a ferry? It might have taken a bit longer – days longer actually – but at least she'd have arrived safely.

It's statistically safer on an aeroplane than on the road, she reminded herself. *And you're doing it because you want to get over your fear of flying. It'll be a big thing to cross off your bucket list. And you can do it. Stop panicking. Everything is going to be all right. You are going to get on that plane and fly over to see Keith and Mary.*

She looked around at all the people in the airport. There were old people, middle aged people, harassed parents travelling with their children.

If they could get on that plane, so could she.

Couldn't she?

Sweat was breaking out on her brow and her hands were shaking as she started piling her things into the plastic trays on the security belt. Sandra had suggested that they both travel in comfortable trousers, slip on shoes and a light cardigan over a tee shirt. 'We don't want to faff about with laces and belts when we're going through security,' she'd said. 'And it'll be warm in Spain.' It was good advice, Patti realised as she slipped off her shoes and put them in the tray, while others struggled with laces and buckles.

Sandra was behind her, doing the same. Patti wondered if Sandra had told her to go first so she could make sure that Patti didn't turn and run. If so, it was a good move as that's exactly what she felt like doing.

'You need to go through the scanner now. And don't panic if it bleeps and they want to do a body check.'

Patti has seen a few airport scenes on the TV, so knew that this was only a pat down over clothes and that the customs staff often did random checks on passengers as a matter of course. She hoped she wasn't stopped though, she was sure that she would look so guilty they might decide she must be carrying drugs and insist on a full body search!

Sandra nudged her. 'You're being called through.'

Patti turned to see an officer beckoning her towards the big body scanner. She cautiously walked through slowly, sighing with relief when it didn't bleep. Thank goodness for that. And there was her luggage waiting on the security belt for her to collect, it had all gone through the scanner fine too. She'd been dreading being pulled aside, being told that she'd packed something she shouldn't have done and couldn't go on the plane.

Even though, right now, she didn't want to go on the plane.

'All done. Now let's have a wander through duty free then have a cuppa and chill for a bit,' Sandra suggested. 'Are you hungry?'

Patti shook her head. 'I don't think I could keep anything down. I'm a bag of nerves.' She lifted her hands to chew her nails, as she always did when she was stressed, and pulled a face. Yuk! She'd forgotten she'd put some of that STOP stuff on this morning. It was working well actually, but the trouble was now she picked her nails instead of chewing them.

Sandra gave her a sympathetic look. 'It's only natural for you to be nervous as this is your first time, and not many people, even seasoned travellers, like the actual travelling, it's tiring. I always find that it helps to think about the place you're going to rather than the journey. Maybe focus on seeing your brother, finding out where he lives, catching up on his news. When you get there you'll be so glad that you did this.'

Sandra was right, she would be pleased with herself. It would be so good to see Keith and Mary again.

'I know. I wish I could just teleport myself there though.'

Sandra grinned. 'Me too. It would make life much easier, wouldn't it? Mind, can you imagine your brother's face if you appeared out of thin air right in front of him?'

Patti chuckled. 'Yeah, you'd have to get the logistics right – and maybe check with them that they were decent!'

The light-hearted exchange lifted her spirits. *Look on it as an adventure, you're ticking off one of the things on your bucket list*, Patti told herself.

'Remember how scared I was about going swimming? I'd never have been able to do that first lesson without your support – and wearing all those daft goggles and snorkels you brought along! Come on, let's have a giggle looking at all the madly expensive stuff in duty free. We can take a few pics of us trying on the accessories and put them on our Insta page,' Sandra suggested.

Patti grinned. 'That's a great idea!'

They headed for an accessory shop and Sandra picked up a red felt fedora. 'What do you think of this?' she asked, popping it onto her head.

'You need some shades!' Patti picked up some designer sunglasses and handed them over. Sandra put them on and pouted as Patti took a photo.

The assistant came over. 'Can I help you?' she asked.

'We're taking some photos for our Instagram page,' Patti showed her the page. 'Is that okay?'

The assistant smiled. 'Certainly. If you tag us in we'll share them. It's good publicity for us.'

'No problem!' Luckily Kit had shown her how to tag people in.

'Let me take a photo of you both,' the assistant offered.

So Patti and Sandra both tried on several hats, scarves and shades. It was such fun and the assistant snapped away. Quite a crowd had gathered around and were watching them.

'Are they influencers?' Patti heard a woman whisper, and she grinned. She guessed that they were!

'Remember to tag us in and we'll follow your page and share the photos,' the assistant said as they put the accessories back. 'Enjoy your holiday.'

'We're going to see my brother and his wife in Spain,' Patti told her proudly. 'It's my first flight.'

'Is it? Congratulations. I'm sure you'll have a great time.'

Patti felt a lot more relaxed as they made their way over to a restaurant. 'You know, I think I could eat a little snack. A cookie perhaps.'

'Great – you grab a table and I'll get the refreshments. Tea?' Sandra asked.

'Please.'

Patti flicked through the photos whilst she was waiting for Sandra to come back, there was quite a queue at the restaurant. She chuckled, they looked like they were having great fun. When Sandra returned, they chose a couple of photos to upload with the caption:

At the airport to tick another one of the bucket list! #getoverfearofflying.

Then Patti tagged in the accessory shop.

'This is more fun than I expected,' Patti said as they sipped their tea and bit into the crisp chocolate chip cookies that Sandra bought them both. She looked around and took in their surroundings. There were lots of cafés and restaurants and a selection of shops. 'I didn't realise there were all these shops, as well as the Duty-Free section in the airport. That must be handy if you've forgotten to pack something.'

'Yes, and if you want to take back a present for someone. Actually, I should buy something for Mary and Keith for putting me up,' Sandra said. 'I'll get something when we've finished here.'

Snack finished, they had a look around the shops for a gift. Sandra picked up some shortbread biscuits in a souvenir England tin. 'Would Mary and Keith like these, do you think?'

'Definitely, and the tin is a wonderful keepsake. I'll take them a big box of chocolates to share. And we could treat them to a meal as a thank you,' Patti said.

'Good idea.' Sandra looked at her watch. 'Our gate will be up soon. We'll take a look at the screens when I've paid for this.'

'I'm glad you're with me, I'd have had no idea what to do!' Patti said.

'You soon pick it up,' Sandra told her. 'And you can always ask the staff, or other travellers, if you need help.'

Gifts paid for, they made their way over to the screens. 'There's our flight and the gate number is up,' Sandra said. 'Come on, let's make our way there. No rush, we've got plenty of time.'

They strolled over to the correct area and took a seat. Then Patti's nerves took over again.

'I'm not sure I can do this.' She clutched the side of the chair in the airport lounge with shaking hands.

'Take some deep breaths,' Sandra said softly. 'Breathe in through your nose and as you count to five in your head, hold it, then let the breath out slowly through your mouth. I'll do it with you.'

Patti nodded and turned to face her friend. Together they inhaled, held their breath, then slowly exhaled. They did this a few times and Patti was relieved that she felt a little more relaxed.

'If you do that whenever you feel panicky, it will help you destress,' Sandra told her.

'I'll try.' Patti clasped and unclasped her hands. 'I really want to do this, but I'm petrified.'

'It will all be okay, I promise,' Sandra told her. 'Did you load your iPad with a couple of favourite films you can watch, as I suggested? That will keep you occupied. I've bought a couple of puzzle books with me too. The trick is to keep your mind busy then the time will pass quicker.'

'I think the trick might be to have a few gins and knock myself out!' Patti said. She smiled wanly. 'No, seriously, I'll be fine. I really want to do this. Feel the fear and do it anyway, eh?' She gazed around. 'Besides, look at all the little kids here. If they can do it, so can I!'

'That's the spirit. Did you bring some Rescue Remedy?'

'I already put a few drops on my tongue before I left home. I don't know how much I can use.'

'That was a couple of hours ago. You could take a few more drops now. Or would you prefer to wait until you get on the plane?'

Patti considered it, she was incredibly nervous, but would she be even more so when the plane was about to take off. She'd heard that was a trigger point for people. There again she felt like her legs were so wobbly, they wouldn't actually let her get on the plane.

'I'll take a few drops now,' she said. She took the small bottle out of the plastic bag where she'd put all her liquids, opened it, and squeezed four drops onto her tongue. She placed it back in her bag and took out the black travel bands Sandra had given her this morning, in case she felt nauseous on the plane. She didn't usually suffer from travel sickness, but then she had never flown before, had she? She leaned back in the plastic chair and closed her eyes, taking deep breaths.

'The gate should be open now. The plane must be late.'

Patti snapped her eyes open. 'Why's the plane late?'

'It's nothing to worry about, it could be a number of things, traffic congestion, crew shortages. It happens sometimes.'

'I'd better let Keith know,' Patti said, taking her phone out of her bag. She looked up at Sandra. 'How late exactly are we?'

'Fifteen minutes, but we might make up the time on the journey. Ah, the gate's open, time to go.'

Sandra stood up. 'Ready?'

Patti could see several people were now queuing up by the checkout desk.

'Ready.' She slowly got to her feet.

Sandra led the way. Shoulders back determinedly, Patti walked over to the waiting cabin crew, showing them her passport and boarding pass, then they made their way together to the aeroplane. Patti paused at the bottom of the steps, looking up at the plane. 'I can't believe that I'm actually doing this.'

'I'm proud of you. Now up the steps, find our seats and we'll be off in no time,' Sandra told her. 'Do you want to go first?'

'No, you lead the way.' Patti picked up her suitcase and purposely followed Sandra up the steps. They'd booked a middle and aisle seat so

Patti wouldn't feel penned in, and as Sandra had pointed out, looking out of the window during the flight could be triggering for Patti, seeing how high up they were. Plus it was easier to get out of their seats and walk up and down – another good distraction technique. Patti had been happy to go along with Sandra's suggestion, she'd read up about aerophobia and knew that some sufferers could really panic during take-off. She was determined not to, even if she had to grit her teeth and dig her stubby nails into her hands!

'We need to take a photo of you on the plane to show that you've struck off another thing on your bucket list.' Sandra fished her phone out of her pocket and selected the camera app. 'Smile!'

Patti gave her a big smile. She was doing it! She was actually flying for the very first time.

She kept calm as the plane taxied across the runway but when the cabin crew gave their talk about safety and what to do in an emergency, she felt her heart race. She could do without them reminding her that the plane could topple out of the sky! She gulped, gripping the arms of the seat as the plane took off. Heck! She was actually doing this! She was in an aeroplane, flying through the air. She took a deep breath, allowing that fact to sink in.

'Have a boiled sweet to suck, sometimes the pressure as we go higher up – and when we descend – can hurt your ears a bit.' Sandra held out a bag of barley sugars and Patti took one. As she sucked the sweet, she felt herself start to relax.

'Fancy doing a wordsearch?' Sandra whipped a puzzle book out of her bag. 'We can do one together or one each, which do you prefer?'

'One together,' Patti replied.

They chatted away, solving the puzzle, then another one, and gradually her nerves subsided. The cabin crew came around selling duty-free goods, hot drinks and snacks and they had a cup of coffee each, then they watched a film on Patti's iPad and the time went remarkably quickly.

'Only half an hour to go,' Patti said, looking at her watch. 'That's gone fast!'

'It does if you keep yourself occupied.' Sandra smiled at her. 'I bet Mary and Keith can't believe that you're actually coming to visit them.'

'I can't believe it either. I wish I'd done it before. Never mind! I intend to make up for lost time.'

She tried not to think about the landing, and chatted to Sandra about Keith and Mary, and what she knew about where they lived, sucking away at another barley sugar, and before they knew it, the captain was announcing they were preparing to land and – with a little bump – they were in Spain.

Patti's face broke out into a triumphant grin. She'd done it. She'd actually done it. 'Well that's another one off my bucket list!'

Sandra took a photo of Patti as she came down the steps of the plane and posted it on their Insta account with the caption:

Well done, Patti. This was top of her bucket list!

Then she added a tick to 'Get over my fear of flying and go to Spain' on Patti's bucket list and uploaded that.

'We're acing this bucket list,' Patti said with a grin.

24

MARY

Mary had spent the last few days tidying the house, and sorting out fresh linen and towels for the casita. She hadn't seen Patti for a few years and she didn't know her friend, Sandra, at all. She wanted both women to be comfortable while they were here. She'd got a shop in, stocking up the cupboards and fridge in the casita with basics, though she was planning on taking them shopping when they'd had chance to settle in so they could choose some things for themselves. The gardener had mowed the lawn – something Keith had always done until his heart attack – and Keith had done a bit of weeding and tidying up.

Wednesday morning, she and Keith were both up bright and early, ready for their guests. Mary opened up the blinds and sunshine blazed into the bedroom. 'Well, that's a good start,' she said, taking a few moments to gaze at the view of the mountains in the not-too-far distance. She loved this view.

'I checked the app yesterday, it looks like they're going to have good weather all the time they're here. That makes things easier, we can have barbecues, and sunbathe around the pool.'

'They'll want to do a bit of sightseeing too, Keith, but maybe we can alternate days out and then relax around the pool on the other days.' She turned from the window to face Keith, who was sitting on the bed taking his blood pressure. He took it religiously every morning and every night. She knew from the expression on his face if it had gone up a little. To her relief it was okay today. 'I'll go and start breakfast.'

She had just popped four slices of wholemeal bread into the double toaster when Keith came in, wearing patterned shorts and an olive-green T-shirt. 'I'll spread my own,' he said as he did every morning. She had butter, Keith had sunflower oil margarine, and he didn't trust her not to get them mixed up and spread his toast with butter. Or to spread it thinly enough.

'Shall we eat on the terrace?' she suggested as Keith took a jug of fresh orange juice out of the fridge, then two glasses out of the cupboard.

'Okay.' He placed the jug and glasses on a tray and took them outside.

The toast popped back up, golden brown, just as they both liked it. Mary placed it in a toast rack, put it on a tray with butter, margarine, two plates and two knives and stepped out onto the back terrace where Keith was sitting at the wooden table. 'It will be good to have Patti here at last,' she remarked, putting the tray down.

'Yes it will. What time are you leaving to pick them up?' Keith took a slice of toast out of the rack.

'I was hoping you'd come too.' Mary smeared butter onto her knife.

'It doesn't take two of us and I've got some things I want to finish here.' Keith concentrated on spreading margarine thinly on his toast, refusing to meet her eye.

Mary sighed. Here we go again. She put down her knife. 'Keith,' she said firmly. He looked up sheepishly. 'You need to come with me and be there to greet your sister when she steps through Arrivals. This is a big thing she's done, overcoming her fear of flying to come and visit you. You need to make an effort.'

'Patti won't mind.'

'*I* mind. I'll drive if you want, but you have to come along too. She's your sister.' She batted down her annoyance and kept her tone soft. 'Patti's expecting you to be there. She wants you to be there. I really think she'll be disappointed if you aren't.'

She bit into her toast and watched the myriad of expressions on Keith's face. He was battling with the decision, she could see that. He and Patti were close, they messaged each other every week. He'd been so upset and worried when she had cancer, and over the moon when she came through. Patti had been very brave to overcome her fear and fly over to see them and the least Keith could do was show up to greet her. She chewed her toast as she considered how much to push him.

He nodded slowly. 'I guess I'd better come then. I'll drive. I've got to watch my blood pressure.'

Bloody cheek, insinuating that her driving would push his blood pressure up! Still, he'd agreed to come, that was a first. It was usually 'you go, but don't be long'. Before the heart attack they'd gone almost everywhere together, now she was always racing around alone to get the shopping in and chores done. She even walked Rags, their little terrier, by herself now. They used to have such a busy, fulfilling life. She missed it.

'What time do they arrive again?' Keith picked up his glass of fresh orange juice and took a sip.

'Elevenish,' she replied.

He frowned, a V forming between his eyebrows. 'You don't know the actual time? Didn't Patti send you the flight details?'

'She sent them to you.'

He picked up his phone. 'Oh, there's a message from Patti to say they're running fifteen minutes later. We'd better leave about ten thirty then.'

'It takes us twenty-five minutes max to get to the airport,' she reminded him. 'We'll be waiting around for ages. And the cost of parking is extortionate.'

'We can go to Plaza Mayor and park up and wait until Patti texts and says they've landed, it's only a few minutes from the airport.'

She sighed. 'If you want.' She wasn't going to argue, at least she'd managed to persuade him to leave the house and drive to the airport to pick up his sister. That was a miracle in itself. Hopefully they could build on that and, once Keith had reconnected with Patti, he'd be accompanying them all on day trips. She longed for life to go back to how it was.

They got ready straight after breakfast but then Rags escaped through a hole in the fence and she had to get him back, locking him in the large, fenced area where he had a kennel – although he was house trained, she didn't like to leave him inside when they went out. It was gone half past before they finally left and then they got caught in a traffic jam.

'Damn. We're going to be late at this rate,' Keith muttered. 'I knew we should have left earlier.'

'Relax, we've got plenty of time. I've just checked and the flight is still ten minutes away, then they still have to disembark and get through passport control,' Mary told him. She almost wished she hadn't persuaded him to come with her now. He'd been on edge ever since he got in the car, grimly holding on to the steering wheel, his gaze fixed on the road ahead and insisting on total silence. He hated driving since his heart attack, but he hated being a passenger with Mary driving even more. How she longed for the days when they used to chat and sing along to music in the car.

Finally, the jam ended and the traffic picked up speed. They arrived at the airport just as a text pinged in from Patti to say they'd landed.

Parking was a nightmare, it seemed that quite a few people had taken advantage of the cheaper midweek flights, as Patti and Sandra had done.

'Hurry up, they'll be waiting.'

'They probably won't even be through yet. Stop panicking,' she told him as they strode over the road and up to the Arrivals entrance.

They stood by the canteen near Arrivals watching the passengers pour through. Then Mary spotted Patti's bright red hair. 'There she is!' She waved cheerily, her heart lifting.

She couldn't wait to have a bit of company, someone to chat to and get out and about with. And hopefully, Patti would be able to get through to Keith, bring him out of the doldrums. She desperately wanted the old Keith back.

25

SANDRA

'There's Mary and Keith,' Patti said, waving to Mary, dressed in a loose, brightly coloured top over three-quarter white leggings, who was leaning over the barrier, waving to them. Beside her was a tall, slim, almost-bald man with a smile just like Patti's wearing a T-shirt and colourful shorts. They were both smiling and waving frantically.

'So lovely to see you.' Mary pulled Patti into a big hug. 'And you look really well. Doesn't she look well, Keith?' She kissed Patti on both cheeks.

'She does.' It was Keith's turn to hug and kiss Patti now and they both clung tightly to each other as Mary turned to Sandra.

'Hello again, Sandra. Welcome, love.' She gave her a hug then kissed her on both cheeks. Keith did the same.

'That's the Spanish way,' Mary said, noticing Sandra's surprise.

'It's so kind of you both to put me up,' Sandra told them.

'Nonsense, it's no trouble at all. And we're the ones who are grateful because this one would never have travelled by herself and we've been trying to get her over here for years,' Mary replied. 'A holiday will do her good, give her chance to relax and have a bit of fun.'

'How was the flight? Better than you were dreading?' Keith asked, linking his arm with Patti's, leaving Mary to follow with Sandra. Patti and her brother were obviously very close, Sandra thought. She was pleased that she'd accompanied Patti to Spain.

'Actually, I even rather enjoyed it once we'd taken off and I'd calmed myself down. Sandra taught me some breathing exercises, and we took plenty with us to keep us occupied. Now I've done it once, you might not get rid of me,' Patti said, glancing over her shoulder at Mary.

'You're welcome anytime. Both of you,' Mary replied. 'Now let's get to the car, I'll make us a spot of lunch at home, then perhaps you might like to relax for the rest of the day and we can do some sightseeing tomorrow?'

'That sounds perfect.' Patti turned to Sandra for confirmation and she nodded. 'It certainly does.' They'd had an early start and she was hungry. It would be nice to settle in and relax for the rest of the day.

'Where exactly do you live?' Sandra asked.

'Just outside Cártama,' Mary replied as they made their way over to the car park. 'It's only twenty-five minutes or so.'

They got into Keith's sturdy estate car, Mary in the front with Keith, Patti and Sandra in the back, then set off. Keith pointed out various landmarks as they whizzed past the commercial area, then past mountains with white houses dotted here and there, some of them ridiculously high up.

They all chatted away and soon Keith was turning up a dirt track, and after a few minutes, they pulled up outside some white gates. A sign on the wall to the right of the gates said *Casa de Árboles*.

'What does that mean?' Sandra asked as Mary got out to open the gate.

Keith looked over his shoulder. 'House of Trees. And you'll see why in a minute.'

Mary opened the gates to reveal a long drive lined with palm trees. At the end of the drive was a pretty white house with a roof terrace and white balustrading all around it.

'Hey this is incredible!' Patti exclaimed. 'What a gorgeous place to live.'

'It really is beautiful,' Sandra agreed, gazing around in wonder.

'Isn't it? We fell in love with it immediately.' Keith drove through the gates and into the huge garden, past the palm trees and onto a large, paved area to the left of the drive, just before the house. Mary locked the gates and walked up the drive towards them.

As they got out of the car, the heat and a heady mix of jasmine and citrus hit them.

'Gosh, it's hot!' Sandra exclaimed. She and Patti put on their sunglasses and gazed around at the mountains in the distance, and the large garden with orange, lemon and olive trees dotted amongst huge succulents and cacti.

'Oh wow!' Patti gasped. 'Your photos don't do it justice, Keith.'

'Wait until you see the pool area, that's where we spend most of our time.' Mary led the way along the path to the back of the house where there was a large, tiled terrace with a big wooden table and six chairs, plus a comfy sofa. A little brown and white terrier dog was standing in a fenced area with a kennel to the right, barking and wagging his tail.

'That's Rags. Let me introduce you to him, then he'll settle down.' Mary opened the gate and the dog bounded out, tail wagging. Both Patti and Sandra stroked him, then he settled down by the sofa, leaving them to explore the rest of the grounds.

A few steps led down to a large pool. The water was shimmering blue, and several sunbeds were placed invitingly on the paved area around it.

'The water is lovely and warm if you fancy a dip later,' Mary told them. 'It's not that deep, you will be able to stand on the bottom and keep your head above water, so don't worry if you can't swim.'

'Oh we can both swim,' Patti told her, smiling at Sandra.

'I've only recently learned how,' Sandra added.

'Really? Well done you, things don't come easy as we get older, but it means you'll be able to enjoy the pool. Now how about I show you the casita and you can unpack, freshen up, then we can have lunch on the terrace.'

Mary led Patti and Sandra past the pool and down a small pathway between two fir trees to another white building. There was a small fenced front garden with a mosaic table and two matching chairs, several colourful plant pots and a white stone Buddha statue.

'This is the casita,' Mary said as she opened the gate.

It looked pretty, Sandra thought, and private although it wasn't too far from the house. It looked quite big too. She'd expected something smaller, with basically just room to sleep, but when Mary opened the door she was amazed to step into what looked like a small apartment with a lounge/kitchen area, two small bedrooms and a bathroom.

'This is gorgeous,' Patti said.

'It certainly is,' Sandra agreed. She couldn't believe they had this all to themselves.

'I hope you'll be comfortable here.' Mary opened the blinds to let some light in. 'We tend to keep the blinds closed all day in the summer, it keeps the heat out. Decide between yourselves what bedroom you're each having. There's a washing machine you can use and a cooker if you want to rustle up a snack, but you're very welcome to have your meals over in the big house with us.' She glanced at the watch on her wrist. 'Shall we say half an hour for you to unpack and freshen up? Is that long enough?'

Patti looked questioningly at Sandra and she nodded her agreement.

'I'll leave you to it then.' Mary went out.

'This is amazing. What a wonderful home your brother and his wife have,' Sandra said. 'And how kind of them to put us both up.'

'I think we're going to have a fantastic two weeks here. Thanks so much for coming with me,' Patti said. 'It's so lovely to see Keith and Mary again.'

'No, thank you for asking me.' Sandra was so pleased that she'd agreed to accompany Patti, a couple of weeks away in the sun was just what she needed to get her head straight, and sort out her life.

'Now shall we draw straws for who picks their room first then get unpacked?' Patti suggested.

'I'm happy with any room, so you choose, it's your brother we're staying with, so that's only fair.'

'In that case, I'll take the one on the front so I can look out on the little garden.'

Sandra was quite happy with that. The second bedroom looked out the back, to the mountains. It would be a glorious view to wake up to every morning. She took a photo of the view and sent it to Don.

SANDRA

Arrived safely and this is the view from my bedroom.

A text came straight back.

DON

What a relief. I was worrying that I hadn't heard from you. That's a fantastic view. Oh, and we've accepted that couple's offer so the wheels are in motion.

Sandra read the message thoughtfully. It was definitely happening. Don, Laila and the children were leaving.

26

PATTI

Patti couldn't believe that Keith and Mary lived in such a beautiful place. It was like one of the houses that were featured on *Homes in the Sun*. She was so pleased that she'd finally plucked up the courage to come and see them, thanks to Sandra. She was really looking forward to spending a couple of weeks here.

After they had unpacked, she and Sandra joined Mary and Keith on the terrace, where their gifts of biscuits and chocolate were accepted with delight and thanks. Then they sipped home-made sangria and tucked into a gorgeous Caesar salad with garlic bread. Now that Rags had been introduced to them, he was quite happy to lie on the sofa or have a wander around the garden.

'So how long have you two known each other?' Mary asked.

Patti filled her in on how she and Sandra had worked together at the supermarket years ago. 'We bumped into each other again on the bus – gosh, really only a few weeks ago – when I was on the way to have my tattoo done. One of the things on my bucket list.' She smiled at Sandra. 'Sandra came with me for moral support. And then ended up having one herself a few days later.'

'A tattoo, where?' Mary asked.

Patti slipped of her light cardigan and showed her the tattoo on her upper arm.

'Grab life by the horns,' Mary read out. 'It's an admirable sentiment.' She shot a glance at Keith who was focusing intently on eating his salad. Then she turned to Sandra. 'And where's your tattoo?'

Sandra pulled up her thin sleeve so that Mary could see the tattoo just above her wrist. 'Embrace change, love life,' Mary read out. 'Have you had cancer too?'

'No, thank goodness. But...' Sandra took a breath to compose herself. 'I lost my husband nine months ago. It was so sudden. An aneurism. We'd been together a long time and it hit me hard. For a while life seemed a bit pointless. My tattoo is to remind myself that I still have a life to live.'

'Oh, love.' Mary's voice was full of sympathy.

Suddenly there was a crash and they all looked in alarm at Keith who had thrown his fork down, pushed his plate aside and sprung to his feet. 'See, her husband died instantly. I was lucky, I survived. Yet you still want me to take risks!' He stormed into the house.

There was a stunned silence.

'Wow, what was that all about?' Patti asked.

Mary's bottom lip quivered. 'Ever since Keith had the heart attack he's been scared to do anything. We used to go out for day trips, meals, socialise with friends, but now he just shuts himself away. You know how he loved to spend hours in the garden? All he will do now is a bit of weeding, we have had to get a gardener in to do the mowing and anything remotely strenuous – even though the doctor said that it was important Keith did physical exercise.' She leaned back in her chair a little. 'Keith's convinced that if he exerts himself, he's going to collapse and die. He wouldn't even go back to the UK for a visit. And he hates me going out for long in case anything happens to him while I'm gone.' She glanced from Patti to Sandra then back to Patti. 'I can understand his concern. I know it was a scary time for him, for both of us. He could have died. But... he survived, thank goodness, and this fear is taking over his life – and to be honest, it's ruining mine.'

Goodness she hadn't realised that's how Keith had felt. He'd never mentioned it to her in one of their Facetime chats. 'I'm so sorry, I had no idea.'

'He doesn't want to worry you, so he pretends he's fine, but he isn't. He's become a hermit and I can't get him to go anywhere. He tells me to go by myself but not to be long and is constantly on the phone to me when I am out.'

This sounded serious. And it was obviously putting a strain on their marriage, Patti realised worriedly.

'I'm so glad that you've both come to stay for a while. You have such a positive attitude, Patti, and you too, Sandra. Hopefully it will rub off on Keith. And he'll come out and about with us, you and Keith were always so close.'

Not as close as she thought seeing as Keith hadn't confided his fears to her. Patti felt a pang of regret that she hadn't known how much her brother was suffering mentally. But then as Mary said he didn't want her to know, probably because she had her own health issues. She remembered how scared she had been that the treatment wouldn't work, and even when she got the all clear she was terrified that the cancer would come back. Still was, if truth be told. She had pulled herself together though, told herself there were no guarantees with anything and she had to make the most of her life however long – or short – it was going to be. Maybe, she could talk to Keith and convince him to do the same.

'I'll have a chat to him, see if I can get him to open up,' she promised. 'And we'll definitely encourage him to come out with us.'

'Thank you.' Mary reached out and squeezed her hand. 'It's so lovely to see you, Patti. I'm so glad that you managed to pluck up the courage to fly out here. And thank you for accompanying her, Sandra.' She smiled at both of them, then said, 'Now tell me about this bucket list you've both made. What sorts of things are on it?'

Sandra swallowed down the last piece of garlic bread before replying. 'We have some things we both want to do, and some things separately. I wanted to learn to swim so I had some swimming lessons and now I can swim a little.'

'That's great. What else is on it? Let's see what we can cross off it while you're over here,' Mary said. 'Maybe we can even get Keith to start one. It could be the push he needs.'

'We're still thinking of ideas,' Patti told her, opening up the files folder on her phone and showed the list to Mary.

Patti	Sandra
☑ Get over my fear of flying and go to Spain	☐ Visit Becky in Australia
☑ Get a tattoo	☑ Get a tattoo
☐ Get over my fear of heights	☑ Learn to swim
☑ Stop biting my nails	☑ Have my ears pierced
☐ Grow my nails and wear nail gems	☑ Wear a hat
☐ Eat some exotic food	☐ Start decluttering
☐ Learn a new dance	☐ Create a new cocktail
☐ Go on a jet ski	☐ Sail across the sea in a motor yacht
☐ Sit on the beach drinking fizz as I watch the sun go down	☐ Go up in a hot air balloon
☐ See a musical on stage in London	☐ Sit on the beach drinking fizz as I watch the sun go down
	☐ See a musical on stage in London

Mary read the list out. 'So, Patti, you've finally managed to stop biting your nails?'

Patti held out her hands. 'I'm still trying to grow them though so I can paint them and wear gems.'

'Good for you. And you still have to get over your fear of heights...'

'I'm working on that, I've been up a stepladder,' Patti interrupted.

'Well done!' Mary continued reading the list. 'And you still need to go on a jet ski ...'

'And eat octopus, but I said exotic food in case I couldn't bring myself to do it,' Patti added.

Mary wrinkled her nose. 'Can't say I fancy that!'

'Nor me!' Sandra agreed.

Mary glanced back at the list. 'Learn a new dance? Do you have a particular dance in mind?'

Patti shrugged. 'Something different. I was thinking maybe jazz or the jive.'

'I suggested ballroom dancing, I love the fabulous dresses,' Sandra added. '*Strictly Come Dancing* is one of my favourite programmes. Me and Brian used to watch it regularly.' Her eyes misted over for a minute and she glanced down at her drink.

'I'll have to take you to see some flamenco dancers while you're here. I think you'll enjoy that.' Mary said. 'Now let's take a look at your list, Sandra. Go to Australia – is Becky your daughter?'

Sandra nodded. 'Becky, her husband and their two teenage children live over there. Brian and I were planning on going this year but...' Her voice trembled a little and Mary squeezed her arm reassuringly.

'Hard, isn't it, love?'

Sandra nodded. 'It never really leaves you, but I'm learning to live again.'

'So it seems, judging by this list!' Mary continued reading. 'Go in an air balloon, sail across the sea in a motor yacht, create a cocktail, have your ears pierced.'

'Done.' Sandra pushed her hair behind her ears to reveal tiny gold studs. 'Another couple of weeks and I'll be able to change these to dangly ones.'

'Gosh, you two have been busy.' Mary scanned the list again. 'And you both want to go to London to see a musical on stage and sit on the beach drinking fizz while you watch the sun go down.' She handed Patti her phone back. 'You know, this is a really good idea. Maybe I should make a bucket list. One thing I've always wanted to do is go on the Caminito del Rey, in fact we both planned on doing it. But now Keith won't come with me and I don't want to go alone. Would you two be up for joining me?'

'What is it?' Patti asked.

Mary jabbed at her phone a few times then held up a picture of a wooden pathway running along the side of a sheer cliff top. 'This is it! It's perfectly safe now, and there are barriers to stop you falling – children over eight can even go on it. I'd love to do it. The views are spectacular.' She glanced at Patti. 'And you did say that you wanted to get over your fear of heights.'

Patti looked at the photo again. This was a *lot* more daunting than climbing a stepladder to change a lightbulb. The pathway seemed very narrow and scarily high up above the gorge.

Could she do it? She wanted to get over her fear of heights but was this too much?

Sandra peered over her shoulder. 'I'm up for it, if you are?'

'Please say that you'll both come! I would love the company and Keith won't even hear of it now.'

'No pressure then.' Patti nodded slowly. 'Okay, but I might need someone to hold my hand.'

'Really! Oh, thank you both. And don't worry, Patti, we'll both hold your hand. You can walk in the middle of us,' Mary promised.

Patti didn't think the platform looked wide enough for the three of them to walk in a row but she didn't say anything. This was something Mary really wanted to do. Besides, hadn't she promised herself when she recovered from cancer that she wasn't going to let fear stop her from doing anything?

Mary's face broke into a huge smile. 'I'm *so* glad you two have come over for a visit. I've got the feeling we're going to have a fabulous time. Keith seems to think that we're past having fun now, but we can show him that we're not. And you never know, he might join in with us.'

They clinked their sangria glasses then Mary picked up her iPad. 'Let's book us in for the Caminito del Rey now, otherwise we might not get in. Sometimes it's booked up for weeks.' After a few minutes she looked up. 'It's fully booked all next week but there's a few free slots the week after. Shall I book us for then? Is Tuesday morning okay? It's closed on Monday and will be too hot in the afternoon. The next slot is Wednesday and that's the day you go back.'

'That's fine by me,' Sandra said.

'Me too,' Patti agreed. She could do this.

'Right. That's all done, and it's my treat. Now what shall we do tomorrow? Do you fancy going on a boat trip? We could go to Málaga and get a boat at the port. I've always wanted to do that, but Keith doesn't fancy it.'

She looked at Sandra. 'It could be another one to tick off your list – although it isn't exactly a motor yacht.'

'Definitely! That sounds amazing!' Patti said, turning to Sandra. 'Are you up for it?'

'I certainly am,' Sandra agreed.

Patti glanced towards the house. 'Should we go and check on Keith?' she asked.

'He'll be sitting watching the TV, but you go in if you like,' Mary told her. 'It's no use me saying anything, it just causes an argument.'

Patti wasn't sure what to do, she felt she ought to talk to Keith, but she didn't want to make things worse. Fortunately, while she was still dithering about it he came out again to ask if anyone wanted another drink. No one mentioned his outburst and they all sat chatting pleasantly for the rest of the afternoon.

* * *

'Your brother and his wife are such a lovely couple,' Sandra said when they were sitting in the casita later. 'They've made me feel so welcome.'

'They are, aren't they? We used to see quite a bit of each other when they lived in the UK, so I'm glad I've finally managed to visit them. And it's all thanks to you agreeing to come with me. I don't think I would have been able to do it on my own.'

'I'm glad to help – and to have the chance to get away for a while and sort my mind out,' Sandra told her. 'I had a text from Don earlier. The buyers have put in an offer for the house, which means that Laila and the children will be gone in a couple of months too.' She looked wistful. 'I'll miss them so much.'

'Have you decided if you want to go with them yet?' Patti asked.

Sandra shook her head. 'It seems such a big move and I thought I couldn't do it. But look at your brother and Mary, they've moved all the way over to Spain and made a happy, new life for themselves. Maybe I'm being a bit of a stick in the mud.'

'It's a massive decision and there's nothing wrong with taking your time over it,' Patti told her. 'Whatever you decide, just make sure it's what you want.' She didn't add that she wasn't sure if Keith and Mary were actually that happy. Mary had seemed so pleased to see them, so eager for company, and Keith was obviously struggling to cope. She needed to find time to speak to him alone, but she knew her brother, he was stubborn and when his mind was made up, it was hard to change it.

27

SANDRA

They all tried to persuade Keith to join them on their trip to Málaga the next morning but he shrugged them off. 'You girls go and have fun, I'll stay and keep Rags company.' So Sandra, Patti and Mary drove down to Málaga, parking in an underground car park near the port.

'We can spend the whole day here, if you both want,' Mary said. 'We can go shopping, take a walk over to the beach, and go on a boat trip later. How does that sound?'

Sandra thought it all sounded splendid. She and Brian had been to Barcelona but never to this part of Spain. Brian hadn't wanted to go to either Benidorm or the Costa del Sol saying that both regions attracted the wrong kind of Brits. Maybe he was right in some coastal areas, but certainly not here. Málaga was a thriving, cosmopolitan city, with rows of shops and restaurants opposite the seafront. It was a warm, sunny day, and the sunlight was shimmering on the ocean, where three large ships were moored. 'It's beautiful,' she said.

'I love it here. We used to visit a lot when we first moved to Spain,' Mary told them. She didn't add but now Keith won't go anywhere, but the undertone was there. 'Now how about we have a cool drink at one of the cafés before hitting the shops?'

They sat down at one of the tables outside a café facing the port and ordered a soft drink each from the waitress who spoke very good English.

'Is English widely spoken over here?' Patti asked.

'It is in the big cities where lots of tourists go but not so much in the smaller towns,' Mary replied.

'Can you speak Spanish?' Sandra asked.

'A little. Enough to get by for everyday things such as ordering a coffee or buying stuff from the shops but it can be difficult in more formal situations or when we go to the doctors. Thankfully, when Keith was in hospital, most of the doctors spoke English.'

'I seem to remember that you went to Spanish lessons when you first came over to live,' Patti said.

'We did, then Covid came along and everything was cancelled. We just couldn't get back into it. We have a couple of apps and keep trying but it's harder to remember things as you get older.'

'Tell me about it. I can't remember where I've put my house keys most of the time and spend ages looking for them only to find that I'd stuffed them in a coat pocket,' Patti replied.

'I was looking for my glasses the other day and they were on my head,' Sandra said.

'We're all as bad. Keith was on the phone to someone yesterday and shouted, "where's my mobile?" at me!'

They all laughed. It was good to share things, Sandra thought. It made you realise that you weren't the only one who was forgetful, lonely or scared sometimes. When you were younger, working and bringing up a family, there wasn't really time to think about things, you just ploughed through. But when you were on your own everything seemed bigger, scarier, worse. Well, it did to her anyway. She'd even started worrying that she might be getting dementia because she was so forgetful, but listening to Mary and Patti, it was perfectly normal at their age to forget a few things or get a little mixed up.

The waitress returned with their drinks, placing them on the table in front of them. They all thanked her.

'Would you like anything to eat?' she asked.

They all shook their heads and she went off to serve someone else.

'This is gorgeous,' Sandra said, gazing across at the sparkling ocean.

'It is, isn't it? Málaga Port is one of my favourite places.' Mary picked up her glass and took a sip of the cool fruit juice.

'I wouldn't mind going on that yacht.' Patti pointed to a huge white luxury yacht. 'I wonder where it's going.'

'That's probably belongs to a Greek or American billionaire. We'll go take a closer look at it when we've finished our drinks, if you want,' Mary suggested.

'A billionaire! It's like something out of a novel. Maybe we should have glammed ourselves up a bit more,' Patti said with a grin. 'Do you think he might invite us on board for a few cocktails?'

'If only! Perhaps if we were forty or so years younger.' Mary gave a mock sigh and they all chuckled.

'I don't think I'd want to be young again, would you?' Patti sipped her drink thoughtfully. 'All that angst and drama. I wouldn't want to go through it all again.'

'I don't know,' Mary cocked her head onto one side. 'I was so positive back then, so full of life and hope. Now I feel a bit jaded and life's so mundane.'

Patti shot her a questioning look. It seemed a strange thing to say when she lived in such a beautiful place, Sandra thought. Mind you, going on holiday was one thing, but living in another country was completely different.

Mary had her eyes still focused on the big yacht. 'When you're young, you think anything is possible. But when you're older your best years are behind you.'

'Maybe your *youth* is behind you, but your best years could still be ahead of you. There's so many money worries and problems when you're raising a family, don't you think? And so easy to make the wrong decisions.' Patti looked thoughtful. 'You don't realise when you're young how much one decision could alter your life.'

'I can see what you both mean. When Brian died, I thought that was it, my life was finished. Lately though, I've come to realise that it isn't finished, it's just different. It's a life without Brian, and that seems empty and strange, but it's still a life and it's up to me what I make of it,' Sandra said thoughtfully.

Patti nodded. 'I was so grateful to come through cancer, and to feel almost normal again, that I promised myself I would make the most of every day.'

Mary seemed to give herself a little shake, then she downed her drink. 'Which is exactly what we all should do.'

'Let's go and check out that billionaire's yacht, we can take a few photos for our Instagram page,' Patti suggested. 'And maybe we could book ourselves on a boat trip for later. That would be another thing off your bucket list, Sandra.'

'That would be fantastic,' Sandra replied. This was only the first proper day of their holiday but already they had done so much.

'If I had a bucket list going, a sail on that billionaire's yacht would be on it!' Mary quipped.

'Why don't you make a bucket list?' Sandra suggested. 'It's fun. You could do an Instagram page like us! I think a lot of people would be interested in your life out here. You'd have some fabulous photo opportunities.'

Mary's eyes clouded. 'To be honest, if I made a bucket list now, it would only have one thing on it. To get Keith to go back to how he used to be. We used to have such fun. We were always out and about—' Her voice broke and Sandra felt sure that behind the sunglasses there were tears in her eyes.

Patti reached over and gave her sister-in-law a hug. 'I'm so sorry love.'

They paid their bill then crossed the road to look at the yacht. It really was magnificent.

'Look, there's even a helipad,' Patti said. 'Whoever owns this has serious money.'

'Sorry, ladies, but I'm afraid we'll have to settle for a smaller boat to have a ride in,' Mary said. 'Let's check them out and see what times the sailings are then we can plan our afternoon.'

There were a few catamarans offering tours at various times of the afternoon and evening, they decided on a sunset trip which was an hour long. 'That will give us time to do a bit of shopping and see the beach. It's only a small one but worth a visit,' Mary said.

'We won't get home until late though. Won't Keith mind?' Patti asked. 'You did say he didn't like to be left for long.'

'I'll message and let him know, he'll be fine. It was his choice to stay at home. To be honest I'm hoping he will get bored being on his own and decide to come with us next time,' Mary said. 'Now, how about we check out the beach, before we go to the shops.'

She paid for the boat ride tickets, insisting that it was her treat – the man spoke English well enough for them to understand – and headed for the small beach.

'The sand is a bit gritty so you might want to keep your sandals on until you get to the sea,' she said.

'But we'll get sand in them,' Patti protested.

'Don't say you weren't warned!' Mary said as Patti slipped off her sandals, and held them in her hands, dangling them from her fingers. Sandra followed suit. Then they both tiptoed over the sand, with gasps of 'Ouch!' 'Ow!'

They were now paddling in the clear blue ocean, sandals still dangling from their fingers, big smiles on their faces. When she reached the water's edge, Mary took off her sandals and joined them.

'It's beautiful,' Sandra said. 'And so warm.' She felt herself relaxing as the sea gently lapped over her feet. It was so wonderful to be here. 'This is the life!' she said, standing with her legs wide open, arms outstretched, head back and eyes closed. She felt invigorated and free, her worries seeming completely insignificant in this beautiful place.

Suddenly a shower of water splashed over her and she jolted her eyes open to find Patti grinning. 'Wake up, daydreamer!'

Mary kicked up a spray of water over Patti from behind. 'You should always watch your back!' She laughed.

The three women larked about for a while, paddling in the sea, basking in the warm sun. Then they dried their feet with a tissue, luckily they all carried a packet, slipped on their sandals and walked back along the front, where there were quite a few shops and some pop-up stores selling a selection of clothes and gifts.

'This is so pretty,' Sandra said.

'It's even prettier at Christmas with all the lights and the stalls selling festive things,' Mary told her. 'You'll have to come over again and see for yourself.'

'Sandra might be in Australia for Christmas,' Patti said.

Mary shot Sandra a glance. 'Really? That would be amazing. I'm sure your daughter will be delighted.'

After checking out the shops along the front they walked through the park into the town, where there were bigger, more well-known stores, stopping again for a drink and snack.

Much later, laden with a couple of shopping bags, they went back to the port, put their shopping in the boot of the car then stopped for a meal before heading out on their boat trip.

They sat at the front of the catamaran watching dusk fall and the sky glow with shades of red, yellow and orange, clicking away with their phones. It was stunning.

'I could sit here forever,' Patti said.

'Me too, it's so beautiful,' Sandra agreed.

Then the captain let them have a go at steering the boat; again the phones came out to record the moment.

'I can't wait to show the grandchildren these photos,' Sandra said in delight. 'They won't believe it. That's another thing ticked off my bucket list, and with the extra bonus of being at the helm too,' Sandra continued happily.

'Jet skis next on the list!' Patti told her excitedly. 'Imagine racing each other across the sea on one of those.'

She'd rather not, Sandra thought, the idea of it filled her with dread. Maybe she could persuade Patti and Mary to go without her.

'I'm so glad you two came over. We're going to have a fabulous fortnight,' Mary told them.

'You bet we will,' Patti agreed. 'What shall we do tomorrow? We don't have to go out,' she added hastily, 'we can have a day in and laze around the pool.'

'I was thinking that we should only go out on alternate days,' Mary suggested. 'We don't want to tire you out. I know you've come through cancer but I've heard that you still tire easily for ages after finishing the treatment. I'm sure you still get days when you feel exhausted.'

Patti nodded. 'I do. So a day by the pool tomorrow then. I can have a natter and a catch up with Keith.'

Sandra felt a surge of excitement as the boat turned back for the return trip to the port. It had been a really enjoyable day.

When they arrived back home, Keith was watching TV, a zero beer in his hand. 'Have you had a good day?' he asked. 'You've been ages.'

'It's been wonderful. Why don't you come with us next time?' Mary suggested. 'It must be boring being here by yourself.'

'I'm fine here. You women enjoy yourselves, don't mind me.'

Sandra saw Mary purse her lips with annoyance and glance at Patti. Would Brian have been like this if he'd survived his aneurysm, she wondered. He was always cautious, never one to take risks, would the aneurysm have made him even more cautious. She guessed that you could go two ways when you survived a major health crisis, wanting to make the most of your life like Patti, or scared to live it like Keith. It was the same after a bereavement. You could hide yourself away, as she had done, or step back into the world and live life for both of you, as she was doing now. Perhaps she and Patti could help Keith take that step. She hoped so, because a life of fear wasn't living, it was existing.

28

PATTI

The next day, as planned, they spent sunbathing and relaxing by the pool. Keith had joined them and was lying on a sun lounger reading the local paper. Patti decided to see if she could get him to open up about his health anxiety. It troubled her that he was too scared of having another heart attack to live his life to the full.

'Can you read Spanish?' Patti asked, taking the seat next to him.

'A little, but this is the English language version.' He turned to the front page where the heading said Sur in English. He glanced at Patti. 'Are you okay in the sun?'

'As long as I'm covered.' She was wearing a sun hat and a thin cotton shirt over her swimsuit. 'I'll have a swim in the pool before the sun gets too strong.' She eased her legs up on the sunbed. 'Are you going in?'

'In a bit. Swimming is good exercise for the heart. As long as you don't overdo it, of course.'

'It gave you a big scare, didn't it? Your heart attack?'

'You bet it did! I thought I was a goner. And I could have been if Mary hadn't got me to hospital so quickly.' He put the newspaper down. 'You were scared too, when you had cancer, weren't you?'

She nodded, remembering the conversations she'd had with him over the phone when she couldn't even bear him to see her on Facetime because she looked so gaunt. 'I was. I was terrified I was going to die. But I didn't. I'm in the clear and I feel like I've been given a new lease of life. And you have too. You should make the most of it.'

His mouth set into a thin line and his brow wrinkled in annoyance. 'Has Mary put you up to this?'

'Not at all. I'm just worried about you. It's not like you to shut yourself away. You and Mary have always gone places, done things.'

'It changes you when you look death in the face, Patti. You should know that.'

'I get that you don't want to put yourself at risk, of course I do. But a day out sightseeing, a boat trip like we did yesterday, a day at the beach – what harm could it do?'

Keith fixed her a long look. 'Do you know the full circumstances of my heart attack?' he asked.

Patti shook her head. 'Not really. Mary phoned me from the hospital to say that you'd had a stent fitted because you'd had a heart attack. But you've not really talked to me about it since. So that's all I know.' That call was embedded in her mind. It had been six thirty in the morning when Mary had phoned her, which would have been seven thirty in Spain. Apparently, Keith had taken ill late the previous night so Mary had taken him to hospital, they'd run a few tests and realised he'd had a heart attack. He'd been fitted with a stent a few hours later.

'I had a few pains in my chest when we were getting ready for bed. They weren't really painful, a bit like indigestion. I took a Rennie and was going to sleep it off, but Mary insisted I take an aspirin and took me to hospital.' His eyes met hers. 'I could have died if I'd got into bed and gone to sleep, Patti. I might never have woken up again.' He choked. 'I can't risk that happening. And Mary had only just returned from a night out. I keep thinking, what if Mary hadn't come home when she did? I don't want to die.'

She reached out and squeezed his hand. 'I understand your fear, and you're right to be cautious, but the way I see it, you had a problem with your heart and it was dealt with. There is no reason why it should happen again.'

'I can't take that for granted. What if I don't get a warning next time? Like Sandra's husband. And don't tell me it won't happen because it does.'

'Of course it does. People die unexpectedly – especially as you get older, like us. There's no guarantees with life, but that doesn't mean you shouldn't enjoy it.'

A peal of laughter rung through the air as Mary and Sandra jumped into the pool.

'You know, Sandra couldn't even swim until a few weeks ago. We both wrote a bucket list of things we wanted to do while we were still fit enough to do them, and swimming was top of hers, so I encouraged her to take lessons and look at her now.'

'What was top of your list?' Keith asked.

'After my tattoo, to get over my fear of flying and come here to visit you,' she told him.

She saw him digest this information.

'What about you? Have you got a bucket list of things you'd like to do while you still can?' she asked softly.

He shook his head. 'There's only one thing I want to do.'

She cocked her head onto one side. 'What's that?'

Keith picked up his glass and finished his drink. 'Stay alive.'

Patti watched worriedly as her brother got up and walked into the kitchen. Keith really did have a serious anxiety problem. How was she going to help him through it?

After lunch, they all went to have a siesta. Patti and Sandra went to the casita, wanting to give Mary and Keith time alone. Patti told Sandra about her conversation with Keith. 'He really is scared of having another heart attack, and I feel guilty about us all going out for the day and leaving him here but it's not healthy for either of them to be like this, and poor Mary is desperate for some company.'

'Is there somewhere we could go tomorrow that Keith will come?' Sandra asked.

'I don't know. I mean the boat trip wasn't that energetic, was it? It seems like he doesn't want to do anything.'

They both went to their rooms for some quiet time.

When they joined Mary and Keith for the evening meal, Mary asked them to remind her again what was on their bucket list. Patti got the list up on her phone and showed it to her.

'Look, they've already ticked a few things off,' Mary said, holding out the phone to Keith.

Patti	Sandra
☑ Get over my fear of flying and go to Spain	☐ Visit Becky in Australia
☑ Get a tattoo	☑ Get a tattoo
☐ Get over my fear of heights	☑ Learn to swim
☑ Stop biting my nails	☑ Have my ears pierced
☐ Grow my nails and wear nail gems	☑ Wear a hat
☐ Eat some exotic food	☐ Start decluttering
☐ Learn a new dance	☐ Create a new cocktail
☐ Go on a jet ski	☑ Sail across the sea in a motor yacht
☐ Sit on the beach drinking fizz as I watch the sun go down	☐ Go up in a hot air balloon
☐ See a musical on stage in London	☐ Sit on the beach drinking fizz as I watch the sun go down
	☐ See a musical on stage in London

His eyes scanned the list. 'Going on a jet ski and up in an air balloon is a bit risky!'

'I'm sure it's quite safe. And there's other more sedate stuff we want to do too. Such as sitting on the beach drinking fizz and watching the sunset,' Patti said. 'So we'll definitely do that one of the days we're here. Why don't you and Mary join us? We can get a taxi there and back.'

'Count me in! That would be fantastic!' Mary said. 'We could even do that tomorrow. There's a beach at Fuengirola and it's not far to drive. I'll only have a small glass of fizz so I can drive us.' She turned to Keith. 'Please say you'll come.'

He gave a mock shudder. 'No thanks. I can watch the sunset here without getting sand in my shoes.' He picked up his phone and slid it open, tapping the screen. 'It says here that the sun sets about ten to nine, so bear in mind it will be quite chilly by then.'

'That's okay, we can take a throw for our shoulders.' Mary turned to Patti and Sandra. 'What do you say we go out for about four, take a walk around the shops, have a bite to eat then wrap up a bit warmer to sit on the beach.'

'That sounds fantastic.' Patti couldn't believe that one by one she was ticking off the things on her list, with the help of her friend and sister-in-law.

If only Keith would join them. Still, it was his choice and she wasn't going to let him stop her from enjoying this holiday, and neither was Mary, thank goodness. It couldn't be easy for her, first she'd had the worry of Keith's heart attack and now she'd got the stress of how he was coping with it. Hopefully me and Sandra being here would ease the strain a bit for Mary and give her chance to enjoy herself, she thought.

29

MARY

When they got up the next morning it was such a bright, sunny day that Mary suggested they go out earlier than planned. 'We can sit on the beach for a while, then go around the shops, although they will probably be busy as it's a Saturday. Then we can have an early supper at a restaurant and go back to watch the sunset. What do you think?'

'It's a great idea,' Patti said, and Sandra agreed.

'What, you'll be gone for the day and most of the evening too?' Keith asked, sulkily.

Here we go. He didn't want to go out with them, but he didn't want them to go out without him either. This was going to be a difficult two weeks if Keith carried on like this. She sympathised with him, she really did. But she wanted to give Patti and Sandra a good holiday. And she wanted to get out and about herself. She was sick of being stuck at home. 'Yes, we will. You're welcome to come along if you want.'

'Yes, do come along, Keith. It won't be very strenuous and it will do you good to get out a bit,' Patti suggested. 'Besides, I came over here to spend some time with my brother.'

'I prefer to stay here. The doctor said I had to be careful and not put any strain on myself.'

'That was months ago, when you were recovering from your heart attack, Keith. And he also said that gentle exercise was good for you,' Mary reminded him.

Keith set his lips in a firm line. 'I'm not taking any risks.'

'I don't want you to take any risks either, Keith, but you have to live your life,' Mary told him.

He shot her a dark look and continued eating his breakfast in silence.

Oh dear, this was awkward, Mary thought. She glanced at Patti and Sandra hoping that they didn't feel uncomfortable but Sandra kept her eyes firmly fixed on her plate.

Patti was looking at Keith sympathetically. 'Why don't you come along later then and join us to watch the sunset,' she suggested softly. 'You'll only be out a couple of hours then.'

Keith shook his head. 'Like I said, I'd prefer to stay here. You ladies go off and enjoy yourselves, don't worry about me.'

* * *

'Honestly, I love your brother but he drives me mad,' Mary said as she drove them down to Fuengirola a few hours later. Patti was sitting in the front beside her as she suffered from travel sickness in the back.

'He does seem to have got trapped into a spiral of worry,' Sandra said. 'My son Don is a bit like that. He's convinced something bad is going to happen to me. He's been promoted and moved to Cambridge, so he's selling the family home. His wife and children are joining him there. They want me to go too.'

Mary's eyes met Patti's in the mirror. 'And are you going to?'

'I don't know. But Don is stressed out about moving away and leaving me on my own. He's messaged and called me a few times already since I've been here. His older brother, Martin, died some years ago, and now his dad. So he's petrified that something is going to happen to me. I guess that's a bit how Keith is feeling.'

'I understand but it's so frustrating. It's not much of a life, if you're with someone who is living in fear.' Mary turned off onto the seafront.

Fuengirola was a typical seaside resort, vibrant and bustling, the beach running along one side of the seafront whilst bars, cafés and shops selling clothes and souvenirs ran along the other side. There were a few families with young children on the beach already and several people paddling in the clear blue ocean, the sun's rays making little sparkles on the surface.

'I guess a lot of families travelled last night or early this morning, as it's half term now,' Patti said. 'It's a good job we booked our flights for midweek, I bet the airport was packed this morning.' She glanced out of the window. 'There doesn't look anywhere to park. Is there a public car park nearby?'

'There's one at the port, I usually park there,' Mary told her as she continued driving along the seafront. She turned off into the big port car park and saw that there were a couple of vacant places. Thank goodness. She wound down the window, took the ticket from the machine, and headed towards a parking space.

'Do you want to stop for a drink and snack or head for the beach first to have a paddle?' she asked as they got out of the car. 'The water will be quite warm now, with the afternoon sun on it.'

Patti and Sandra both looked at each other. 'Beach?' Patti asked and Sandra nodded eagerly. 'I can't wait to feel the sea ebbing over my feet again.'

Luckily, as Mary had suggested, they'd all dressed in shorts, T-shirt and sandals, but had put longer trousers and a warm throw in the boot of the car for when it got cooler. 'We'll come back to change into the warmer clothes later,' she told them as they headed off towards the beach.

They paddled for a while then spread out the towels they'd packed into their beach bags, along with a bottle of water, and sat down on the sand. Taking out the water, they had a much-needed drink as they watched the holidaymakers frolicking in the sea.

'Look, there's some jet skis! Maybe we can hire one each from here,' Patti said.

Mary looked up and saw two people on a jet ski speeding over the water, leaving a foamy trail in its wake. 'I'd love to go on one too. It looks so exciting. I'm sure we can arrange it.'

Sandra shuddered. 'Really?' she asked. 'Aren't you scared of falling off?'

'You wear life jackets, and don't have to go that far out,' Mary told her. 'Me and Keith used to talk about having a go but...' Her voice tailed off.

'Keith wanted to go jet skiing?' Patti repeated in surprise.

Mary nodded. 'He used to be more adventurous, even just a few years back.'

'Then we must definitely do it,' Patti said. 'What do you say, Sandra?'

Sandra hesitated then nodded. 'Okay,' Sandra agreed. 'Things don't seem so scary if we do them together.'

'We're like the three musketeers,' Patti said. She held her hands out, crooking the two little fingers. Mary linked her little finger into the right one and Sandra linked her little finger into the left one then they formed a circle. 'All for one and one for all!'

Mary felt a glow flood through her. It was so good to have these women as friends and to spend this precious time with them. She'd been so lonely the past few months. 'Thank you so much, both of you. Let's leave jet-skiing for another day though. Going around the shops and watching the sunset is enough for today.' She fastened her water bottle and put it back in her bag. 'Are you both ready to hit the shops?'

'You bet,' Patti said, and Sandra nodded in agreement.

They had a wonderful afternoon shopping, Mary enjoyed their company so much. They were warm, friendly and fun. Sandra bought some souvenirs for Kali and Rana, and Patti bought a gorgeous top for Kit. They each bought a fun beach hat, and a colourful sarong for around the pool. And a selfie stick. Which they tried out straight away, taking several photos of the three of them for their Insta account. Then Patti noticed a huge inflatable giant unicorn hanging up in one of the shops they passed. 'Oh, I must get that for the pool!' she exclaimed. 'Do you mind, Mary?'

'Go for it! It will be fun,' Mary replied with a grin. 'Why don't we all get an inflatable pool toy each and we can have a pool day tomorrow?'

Sandra was already checking out a giant pink donut ring. 'I fancy this!'

Mary went for a white and gold Pegasus. She felt a surge of excitement as they all paid for their purchases, luckily the shop sold deflated ones in sealed packets so they didn't have to struggle carrying blown up ones. She hadn't enjoyed herself so much for a long time.

'I'd better check how Keith is,' Mary said. She had already messaged him a couple of times and received one brusque 'I'm fine, enjoy yourselves x' message back.

This time, there was no reply.

'I think he's sulking at being left on his own for so long,' she said. 'But I'll be blowed if I'm staying in when you two are here. That's rude. Besides, I want to enjoy myself too.'

The shops were open late so they stopped for a bite to eat then had another wander around until about eight o'clock then went back to the car and put their shopping in the boot. They changed into trousers and long-sleeved tops in the toilets, then took the cool box with the bottle of fizz in it out of the boot, wrapped their throws around their shoulders and set off for the beach to watch the sunset.

Mary poured them all some fizz, only half filling her glass, and they took several selfies as they sat there sipping the sparkling drink watching the sun set over the ocean, the sky melting into shades of red, orange and yellow, reflecting on the still ocean and transforming it purple and pink mixed with the blue. They all took a photo of the spectacular scene. Then watched as the golden orb of the sun descended slowly, as if it was in no rush to go, finally disappearing over the horizon.

Sandra put the photo on their Insta account with the caption:

Another thing ticked off the bucket list.

They'd put several photos up while they were away, and they'd attracted lots of comments. She also sent the photo to Kit.

Mary sent her photo to Keith. A few minutes later a message pinged into her phone. She opened it up to see a picture of the sunset from the terrace.

KEITH

Snap

Was his reply.

'I think he's telling me that I don't have to go to the ocean to see the sunset, but I'm glad I did,' she said.

Kit replied.

KIT

Oh, Gran, that's totally gorgeous. Lucky you! xx

'I think I'll send it to Don,' Sandra said. 'Show him what a good time I'm having so that he stops worrying. I'll write "Having a great time. Currently watching the sun go down over the sea. Isn't it beautiful?"' She looked pleased as she sent it.

The reply shot back. Sandra opened it and frowned. 'Well, that didn't work. He's replied "Mum, you shouldn't be out so late. It isn't safe". It's only 8pm in the UK, for heaven's sake!'

'I'm sorry to say it, but I really don't think you should move near your son if he doesn't want you out after nine pm! You'll have no life,' Mary said. And under her breath she muttered, 'Like me.'

She desperately wanted the old, fun-loving Keith back. She missed his company. She was bored and lonely, and if it wasn't for Leo, she'd have gone out of her mind.

30

PATTI

'Want one?' Sandra asked, holding up a mug as Patti padded barefoot into the kitchen of the casita on Sunday morning, yawning and still wearing her nightshirt. Yesterday had been fun but tiring, Patti had zonked out with exhaustion as soon as her head hit the pillow and had only just woken up, whereas Sandra looking bright and breezy in a floral sundress and had obviously been up for a while.

Patti instinctively ran a hand over her cropped hair to flatten it. 'Please.' She perched on the nearest chair. 'Our posts are getting us a lot of interest. Did you see how many comments we got on our Insta this morning? We're getting quite a following now.'

Sandra nodded, her back to Patti as she made the tea. 'I think it turns out there's a lot of people who secretly have a bucket list. Hopefully we're inspiring some of them to have a go at doing the things on it.'

'It seems that we've inspired Kit too, in a way. I woke up to a message from her telling me that she and Carly have decided they're going to take a gap year when they get their degrees and do some voluntary work.' She stretched her arms lazily. 'I'm so pleased.'

'The girls today have got more about them than we had,' Sandra said as she added milk to both mugs. 'We were brought up to think that we had to marry, and we had to do what our husbands wanted. Thankfully it's different now.'

'Do you regret marrying so young?' Patti asked. She knew that Sandra had been barely out of her teens when she married Brian, whereas Patti had been in her mid-twenties when she and Adrian married. 'You both seemed happy together.'

'We were – mostly. And no, I don't regret it. It's what we did back then. But I am glad that things have changed and it's accepted for girls to have a life before settling down, or even to not get married at all.' She put a mug of steaming tea on the table in front of Patti. 'And I'm really pleased that my granddaughters will have the chance to travel, and to have a career, even if they do get married.'

Patti nodded. 'I agree. The world's the oyster for them now, isn't it? I'm afraid that most of the load still seems to fall on the women when they get married and have a family though. My poor Amanda is run off her feet, Jake helps out around the house, but it still seems to me that Amanda's expected to do the most.' She picked up her mug and blew softly across the surface to cool the tea down then took a long gulp. 'Oh I needed that. Thank you.'

'You're welcome. I think I'm going to take mine outside. It's such a lovely morning.'

'I'll join you... unless you want a bit of alone time?'

'Goodness no. I have plenty of that at home.'

They both carried their mugs outside and sat chatting, enjoying the warm sunshine and the gorgeous view.

'This is just what I needed,' Patti said, lifting her head up to the sky so she could feel the morning sun on her face.

'Me too,' Sandra agreed. 'I think we're both going to go back feeling very relaxed.'

A little while later Mary appeared, once again in shorts but this time with a vest top. 'Want to join us for breakfast?' she called. 'We've got fresh orange juice and croissants.'

Patti and Sandra both looked at each other and nodded.

'Sounds great! Thanks,' Patti replied. 'Just give me chance to shower and get dressed.'

'Half an hour?'

'Perfect!'

* * *

They all sat outside on the terrace, eating butter croissants and jam – Keith had his dry – and drinking freshly squeezed orange juice.

'It's a beautiful day,' Sandra said. 'I can understand why you've both moved over here to live. It would be wonderful to have such gorgeous weather and spectacular views.'

Mary dipped her finger in a blob of jam that had escaped from her croissant onto her plate and licked it before replying. 'It is, but after a while it gets a bit samey when you're in all day. And you miss your family and friends.'

Keith shot a look at her but didn't say anything.

'I get that. I vid-chat to my daughter in Australia regularly but it's not the same as a chat over a cuppa, is it?'

'How long has your daughter been living in Australia?'

'Over twenty years. Brian and I were so looking forward to visiting her...'

Mary placed her hand on Sandra's comfortingly. 'I'm sorry, love. Would it have been your first visit?'

Sandra nodded. 'We meant to go before but something always came up. They've visited us a few times though, when Becky worked as cabin crew. She could have got us cheap flights too back then.'

'Life has a habit at throwing curveballs at you. Perhaps, when you feel a bit stronger, you'll go by yourself?' Mary suggested.

'I will. It's top of my bucket list and I'm determined to do it,' Sandra told her.

After breakfast they sat out on the terrace chatting. Then Mary suggested going for a walk. 'We can go along the track by the mountains, nothing strenuous.' She glanced at Keith. 'Want to join us? Walking is good for you,' she added. 'And we can take Rags.'

Keith hesitated.

'Come on, we can have a chat as we talk,' Patti coaxed.

He nodded. 'Okay, but only a little stroll.'

Mary went inside for Rags' lead and when he saw it, the little terrier started barking and running around happily.

They all changed into their trainers, put on sun cream and sunglasses and set off, turning left outside the gates and walking along a dirt track with mountains in the distance. After a few minutes Mary let Rags off the lead and he bounded off joyously.

When they came to a row of detached houses Mary called Rags to her and fastened the lead onto his collar again. A man came out of the second house, walking a crossbreed on a lead. He was about their age but had a full head of silver hair and was ruggedly handsome, Patti noticed. His face lit up when he saw Mary and Keith, the smile reaching his warm brown eyes. He looks nice, Patti thought.

'*Buenos, Keith, Mary ¿Qué tal?*' He pronounced their names 'Keeth' and 'Maree'. He kissed first Keith then Mary on both cheeks. Patti was getting used to that custom now.

'*Bien, Leo. Es tú?*' Keith replied.

'It's our friend Leo, He's asking Keith how he is,' Mary whispered.

Leo's gaze swept to Patti, then to Sandra, then back to Patti.

'This is Patti, my sister, and her friend, Sandra.' Patti wasn't sure whether Keith had exhausted his knowledge of Spanish or was speaking English for their benefit.

'*Encantada, señoras.*' Leo kissed Sandra on both cheeks then Patti. She felt a little flutter as his lips brushed her cheek, his eyes holding hers for a second before stepping back. 'You are here on holiday?' he asked in a thick Spanish accent.

Phew! He could speak English, Patti thought in relief. 'Yes, for two weeks.'

'Then hopefully we will meet again. Coco has missed her walk with Rags.'

'I usually take Rags for a walk every morning, we often meet up with Leo and walk along together,' Mary explained.

'And you've missed the walks because we've been here?' Patti felt really guilty. 'Please don't let us stop you going about your normal life.'

'It's not a big deal. Our garden is plenty big enough for Rags to have a run around. Besides, Keith has taken him while we've been out, so at least it's got him out of the house a bit. Although I suspect that he hasn't walked far.'

'You must pop around for a *cerveza* and a chat, Leo. We're in most evenings. In fact, why don't you come around this afternoon,' Mary said. 'Come for dinner.'

'Thank you, that would be wonderful,' Leo replied. Coco tugged at his lead. 'I must go, Coco is eager for her walk. *Luego*.'

'He seems a nice man,' Sandra said as Leo walked off, Coco trotting by his side. Rags barked and pulled at his lead, as if protesting that he wanted to go with them. Patti wondered if Leo's eyes had lingered on Sandra when he'd pulled away from the hug, as they seemed to do when he hugged her. You're making too much of this, kissing someone on both cheeks is the Spanish custom, she told herself.

'He is. His wife, Elena, died a few years ago and he's lived on his own since. He sometimes pops around. He and Keith like to put the world to rights over a cold *cerveza* – beer. Although it's been a while.'

Patti turned to Keith. 'Well, at least you won't be surrounded by women tonight, Keith. You'll have another man to talk to.'

'I don't mind. It's nice for Mary to have company.' Rags pulled at the lead again, urging Keith to keep walking. 'Let's head back now. I could do with a cool drink.'

'Me too, it's getting warm, isn't it? I think it's going to be a hot afternoon,' Sandra said, taking a tissue out of her pocket and wiping the sweat off her forehead.

'Just the right weather to spend by the pool,' Mary said.

They had crusty rolls and salad for lunch, on the back terrace, then changed, putting their swimsuits underneath their shorts, and did a bit of sunbathing. Patti kept a thin cotton shirt over her swimsuit and wore a big sun hat. The cancer had gone but she still had to be careful.

'I think I'll go for a dip, anyone want to join me?' Mary said after a while.

'I will,' Sandra said. 'I need to keep practising.'

They both slipped off their shorts and jumped into the pool.

'You don't fancy joining them?' Keith asked.

'I will in a while, I have to limit my time in the sun,' Patti told him.

'Yes, of course.' Keith glanced over at the pool where Sandra and Mary were racing across to the other side, Sandra doing the breaststroke and Mary the crawl. 'Sandra's nice, easy to get on with,' he said.

Patti nodded. 'She is. I'm so pleased that I met up with her again. I was starting to feel a bit lonely and wondering if I'd done the right thing moving back to Worcester but then I bumped into Sandra and she's been such a support.' She pushed her sunglasses back up on her nose a little. 'Actually, we've supported each other. Her husband's death really devastated her and her son is rather dominating. I know it's with the best of intentions, he's trying to look out for her, but she's anxious enough without him flapping around her putting doubts in her mind.'

Squeals of laughter floated through the air as Sandra and Mary both stood on the side of the pool then jumped in.

'I'm going for a swim. Coming?'

'Sure. Race you to the pool!'

As they ran over to the pool and dived in, Keith in the lead by a few seconds, Patti thought how much happier he looked than when they first arrived. He'd gone into a shell, she realised, like she had when she'd first been diagnosed with cancer, and Sandra had when she lost Brian. And now he was scared to come out of that shell and start living.

Well Keith might not have a bucket list, but she had added one more to hers. She was going to help her brother live his life again.

31

'Time to blow up the toys,' Patti said, they'd all come out of the pool for a drink and to top up their sun cream. 'Shall I fetch your donut ring, Sandra?'

'Yes please, it's on the chest of drawers in my bedroom.' Sandra poured some sun cream onto her hands and rubbed it onto her face and neck.

Mary disappeared into the house to get her Pegasus.

'I'd better get my electric air pump to blow those up,' Keith said, looking amused when they returned with their inflatables.

He soon had them all pumped up. The unicorn and Pegasus were huge. 'I can't wait to see you all trying to get on those!'

'I'd forgotten quite how big they were,' Mary said.

'Who's going in first?' Patti asked.

'Me!' Sandra threw the big pink donut into the pool then jumped in with a huge splash. She reached out for the donut and scrambled into it, perching herself across the hole in the middle, her head on one side and legs dangling on the other. 'Come on you two!' she called.

Patti and Mary picked up their inflatables and carried them over to the pool, placing them on the water where they immediately floated off. They both jumped in, swam over to the inflatables and tried to climb on. After several unsuccessful attempts where they ended up falling off into the water, they finally managed it.

'Let's have a race!' Patti shouted. 'You too, Sandra!'

Sandra paddled with her hands to move the ring across the pool whilst Mary and Patti paddled furiously with their feet. The huge blow-ups glided majestically over the water, with Patti and Mary clinging to their necks.

'You're going to crash into me!' Mary shouted. 'Change direction!'

Patti paddled faster but her unicorn refused to turn and continued heading towards the Pegasus. 'I can't!' she shouted.

She reached out to push the Pegasus away but toppled off into the water, the unicorn on top of her, swallowing a mouthful of water in the process.

A roar of laughter erupted from the side of the pool. Keith had obviously been watching – well at least she'd made him laugh. Patti managed to swim underneath the unicorn and bobbed up, 'Glad you think it's funny!' She laughed, water dripping from her hair all over her face, she wiped it away to see that Keith wasn't alone, standing beside him was Leo, they both had their heads thrown back and were howling with laughter.

Way to make an impression, Patti! Thank goodness her body was submerged in the water up to her shoulders. She wasn't going to get out until Leo had turned his back! The swimming lessons had given her and Sandra more confidence about their bodies, but she still felt awkward with someone like Leo. She could see that Sandra was a bit embarrassed too, but Mary didn't seem bothered. She was obviously quite at ease with Leo.

'Perhaps I should have brought my swim shorts.' Leo chuckled.

'Borrow a pair of Keith's and you can both join us,' Mary suggested.

Patti was relieved when Leo declined and he and Keith went into the kitchen to start on dinner.

* * *

Mary had cooked a huge paella for dinner, with more crusty bread, followed by a tiramisu, and they all chatted away as they ate, with the conversation mainly in English, although Leo resorted to Spanish when he couldn't think of the word he wanted and then they all tried to translate for him. Patti turned her head as Mary laughed, tears streaming down her face, at something Leo said. She hadn't seen Mary laugh like that all the time they'd been here. Her sister-in-law seemed to have come alive in Leo's company. Patti remembered Mary saying that she and Rags often joined Leo and Coco for a walk. A little fear crept into her mind. Keith and Mary seemed distant with each other, could Mary be attracted to Leo? No, surely not. But that's what had happened to her in her own marriage, wasn't it? They'd both been busy working, become more like ships in the night, then Adrian had met Sally who'd given him the attention he craved.

Is that why Mary had invited Leo over tonight, because she was missing him?

'Are you all right, Patti? You seem a bit troubled.' Sandra's voice dragged her out of her thoughts. They were both sitting next to each other at the far end of the table.

'Yes, I'm fine.' She gave Sandra a reassuring smile. 'I think all that fun in the pool has tired me out a bit.'

Leo glanced over at them both and smiled 'Are you enjoying your stay in my country, *seňoras*?'

'We are, Keith and Mary are wonderful hosts,' Sandra replied.

'They certainly are. They're really looking after us,' Patti agreed.

'They've been out gallivanting every other day,' Keith said, taking a long sip of his beer. 'It's been nice and peaceful for me.'

'Where have you been?' Leo asked.

Mary filled him in. 'And tomorrow we're going jet skiing.'

'Jet skiing! You're all mad. Those things aren't safe,' Keith retorted.

Leo looked surprised too. 'It is many years since I went jet skiing. Do you *seňoras* go often?'

'It's going to be our first time,' Patti told him.

'You have... How do you say...?' he paused. 'Spirit. Spirit of adventure.'

Was that admiration in his voice?

'I think they've lost the plot!' Keith exploded. 'They're much too old to be cavorting about like this.'

'Usually it is something you do when you're younger, but it is a pleasurable experience and safe if you are sensible,' Leo said reassuringly.

'Of course it is. We'll check them all out and make sure we go on an approved one.' Mary looked annoyed and Patti didn't blame her. Keith didn't have to be so scathing.

'Why don't you at least come for the ride, Keith?' Patti suggested. 'You can just sit on the beach and relax. You might have fun watching us. And you probably won't worry so much about us if you're there.'

'You're crazy. The last thing I want to see is my wife, sister and her friend careering across the sea, strapped to a contraption that could tip them into the water any minute, or crash into a boat.'

Mary raised her eyebrows. 'We'll check that the water is clear, and only go for a short ride. Thousands of people jet ski every year quite safely.' She picked up her phone and started tapping the screen. 'Look, it's perfectly safe. We'll have a tutorial and a lifejacket, an instructor will be with us, they ride in a boat nearby, and we'll only go for the short run, twenty minutes max.'

'I don't want you to go,' Keith stated.

'Well, I'm going. Remember – not so long ago – we both said we'd try it one day. We were both going to do a lot of things! Just because you no longer want to doesn't mean that I should give up my dreams too.'

Sandra held her breath as Keith and Mary locked gazes. She hoped this wasn't going to lead to a big row. Then Keith got up from the table and stormed out.

'I think it is time I go too.' Leo stood up. 'Goodnight, *señoras.* I hope tomorrow, it goes well.'

They all said goodbye and Mary walked with Leo to the gate. Patti watched as they stood, huddled together, heads almost touching as they talked. They looked so close.

'I can't help feeling guilty that Keith and Mary had words, it was our talk of fulfilling our bucket list that started all this off.' Sandra sounded worried.

'I think things haven't been right between Keith and Mary for a while.' Patti told her. 'I just hope that it's a blip and they'll get over it.'

Just then Mary came back. 'I'm sorry about that but Keith has to realise that he might want to sit and rot all day, but I've got a life to live and I'm going to live it.'

'It's the heart attack. It's left him feeling vulnerable...'

'I know, Patti. And I don't mean to sound harsh but – whilst I understand his fear – I don't think it's wise to pander to it any longer. Maybe if I start getting out and doing things, Keith will want to join in. It's worth a try. Besides, I'm not going to let you two sit around the pool every day. I want to show you some of Spain while you're here. Leo agrees with me too. He said Keith isn't the man he used to be.'

She picked up her phone again. 'Now let's book us in for our jet ski ride; 11.30 tomorrow okay?'

'Great!' Patti agreed but Sandra hesitated before nodding. Patti could see that her friend was a bit reluctant.

'Okay, they only have double or single jet ski so I guess we had better book one each.' Mary looked up from the screen. 'Unless you two prefer to go together and I'll go by myself. I don't mind at all.'

Patti thought it was a shame that Keith wasn't joining them then they could all pair up. She didn't like to go with Sandra and leave Mary to go alone. 'What do you think?' she asked Sandra.

'How about you two go together? I'm not bothered about going jet skiing to be honest.'

Patti could see that she was nervous. She didn't want to push her into doing something she didn't want to do but was sure that Sandra would regret not joining in when she saw how much fun it was. 'It could be fun to have one each. We can race each other.'

'But we're the three musketeers! We have to all do it,' Mary protested. She looked so disappointed. She really was enjoying the comradeship, Patti realised.

Sandra must have realised the same thing because she nodded. 'You're right. I'll be brave and do it.'

'It'll be three jet skis then. And don't worry, it's all perfectly safe and an instructor will be with us.' She tapped a few keys then Patti thrust her credit card in front of her.

'This is my treat because it's on my bucket list,' she insisted.

She couldn't wait until tomorrow!

32

SANDRA

They'd just finished booking for the jet ski when Don phoned Sandra.

'What have you been up to over there?' he asked curiously. 'I hope you're keeping out of the sun. Sunstroke can be dangerous, you know?'

'I know, dear, I always use sun cream, sunglasses and a sun hat. You should know that! You're the one who had to be badgered to wear it.' She laughed as she remembered the battle she had trying to get Don to put on sunscreen and wear a sun hat when he was a child. He hated it and was always trying to lose his sun hat, leaving it on the beach, in cafés, but she knew what he was up to and he never succeeded in leaving it behind.

He chuckled. 'Rana is as bad now, Laila has to nag like mad to get her to wear sun cream and she absolutely refuses to wear a sun hat!'

'Karma,' she teased, delighted that they were having such a relaxed conversation. She told him about their shopping trip yesterday and that today they had stayed in around the pool. 'I jumped in and I swam three lengths,' she said proudly.

'Well done, Mum. What are you up to tomorrow?' He sounded genuinely interested.

She took a deep breath and braced herself for his reaction. 'We're going jet skiing.'

'You're what? Are you totally mad? Have you forgotten what happened to Martin?'

That stung. How could she ever forget how her adventurous, fun-loving older son had died? Realising this was going to be a difficult call, she got up and walked down towards the pool so she could talk in private.

'Of course not, how could I?' she replied. 'But we're going on the sea not up in the air. And we'll be wearing life jackets and be with an instructor.'

'Listen to yourself, Mum. You're over seventy! I don't know what's got into you just lately. Dad would turn in his grave if he knew what you were up to!'

'What a terrible thing to say!' she snapped. 'I think your dad would be pleased that I'm getting on with my life, Don. He wouldn't want me to grieve forever over him. If I was the one who had gone first, I wouldn't like to think that your dad would shut himself away grieving. I would want him to have the strength to carry on living. To get some pleasure out of his days.' She sounded more angry than she had intended to, but Don really was insufferable sometimes.

There was silence on the other side of the phone. Then Don said slowly. 'I want you to be happy, Mum. I don't want you to be shut away grieving, as you were. But I want you to be safe too. I don't want to lose my mum as well as my dad. That's why I want you to move with us, Mum. So we can help you and look after you.'

She sighed, her anger leaving her. 'I know, love.'

After their call ended she stood there for a moment, looking at the moon shimmering on the surface of the pool and scattering of stars sparkling in the inky night sky. Don's words played on her mind. What should she do? It wasn't a bad thing that Don wanted her to move by him, was it? A lot of parents complain that they hardly see their grown-up children, and here was Don wanting her to still live nearby. She should be grateful.

Except she didn't want him to worry about her like that. And there was Laila too, surely she didn't want Sandra there all the time? It was time Don concentrated on his own family, not feeling like he had to keep looking out for her too. And if she moved to Cambridge, they would be the only people she knew and the truth was, they would be too busy working to see that much of her. She would likely be lonely. Isolated in a strange area.

Patti and Mary both gave her sympathetic looks when she returned to her seat on the terrace. 'I take it Don doesn't approve of us going jet skiing either?' Patti said.

Sandra rolled her eyes. 'He doesn't approve of me doing anything! And he's still pressuring me to move with them. I really don't know what to do. What if I move to Cambridge and I'm not happy there?'

'If your son hadn't mentioned you moving with them, how would you feel? Would you be wishing that you could go with them?' Mary asked.

Sandra thought about this. 'No. I probably would be wishing that they weren't moving away, but it wouldn't even have occurred to me to go with them. I love my home. I want to stay where I am.'

'There's your answer then.' Mary looked up from stroking Rags who was lying on her lap. 'Don't let anyone else talk you into moving if you don't want to. You might regret it and then you're stuck.' She put Rags down. 'Come on, boy, let's get you fed.'

Sandra noticed that Patti was watching Mary thoughtfully as she went into the house. 'Do you think your sister-in-law regrets moving to Spain?' she asked.

'I don't know. They seemed really happy here at first but now that Keith won't go anywhere it's probably just pretty lonely for her.'

Mary looked a lot more cheerful when she came back out. 'Well, ladies, are you all ready to go jet skiing tomorrow?'

'You bet,' Patti said. 'I can't wait!'

No, I'm dreading it, Sandra thought but she kept her feelings to herself. She didn't want to spoil this for Patti. Besides, she would be fine, people went jet skiing all the time. There was absolutely nothing to worry about.

33

Patti and Sandra were sitting outside, sipping orange juice, the next morning when Mary came along, her face like thunder. Oh dear, it looks like she and Keith had had another argument, Sandra thought. And she could guess what about. Their jet skiing adventure. She half wished that Keith had managed to talk Mary out of going, she was dreading it herself. Patti really wants to do this, she reminded herself.

'Want some?' Patti held up the jug.

'Please.' Mary sat down beside them. 'I know I'm a bit early, but I had to get out before me and Keith have a barney. He's still trying to talk me out of jet skiing.'

'I hope we aren't causing trouble between you both,' Sandra said worriedly. 'Maybe we should cancel.'

'Absolutely not! I want to do it, and I love you two being here. You're both like a breath of fresh air. Honestly, I'd almost forgotten what it was like to have fun. I'm so pleased that you came to visit.'

'Keith will come around,' Patti said comfortingly. 'The more things you do and come home safe, the more he'll relax.'

'I perishing well hope so!' Mary picked up the glass of iced orange juice that Patti had just poured for her. 'Right, let's knock these back and get on the road. Before we lose our bottle.'

'Are you driving?' Mary asked with a grin as Patti opened the door to the driver seat.

'Oops, I can't get used to driving on the other side of the road!' Patti said as she went around the car and got into the other side.

'Me neither.' Sandra sat behind Mary at the back, so that Patti could half-turn in her seat and talk to her. 'Did it take you long to get used to it?'

'Not really. All you have to remember is whatever country you drive in the driver is seated by the white line in the middle of the road,' Mary told her.

'I never thought of that!' Patti replied. 'Shall we put some music on? Get us in the holiday mood?'

'Sure. I can only seem to get Spanish radio but there's some CDs in the dashboard.'

Patti pulled down the dashboard cover and took out a few CDs. 'Beatles, Abba or Party Selection?' she asked.

'You two are the guests, you choose,' Mary replied.

Patti spread three out on her lap, the CD cases face down. 'Left, middle or right, Sandra?'

'Right,' Sandra said.

'Beatles it is then.' Mary put the CD in the slot and 'Can't Buy Me Love' blasted out a couple of seconds later.

'I love the Beatles! They were my favourite group back in the day,' Sandra said. They all joined in, singing away as Mary drove along.

Mary parked the car at the meeting point and they all got out.

Sandra looked over at the row of jet skis and her stomach plummeted. What on earth was she thinking? She could barely swim and she was going to ride on of those contraptions on the open sea!

'I can't do this,' she stammered. 'You two go ahead. You can share a jet ski. I'll watch and take photos.'

'Oh, love, it's just an attack of nerves. You'll be fine once you get on,' Mary told her.

Sandra shook her head vehemently. 'No I won't. I can't do it!'

'Of course you can! Remember, feel the fear and do it anyway!' Patti told her. 'Come on, San have a bit of backbone. Don't wimp out on us now.'

'I am not "San"! and I am not "wimping out"!' Sandra retorted crossly, her hands on her hips. 'I don't have to do everything you want to do! You need to stop being so damn pushy!'

'Wow! Keep your hair on!' Patti retorted, glaring at her.

Mary looked worriedly from one to the other. Then Patti's face broke out into a grin. 'Well, you can tick "standing up to people more" off your bucket list now!'

They all collapsed into a fit of giggles.

'Seriously, you're right. I shouldn't try and talk you into it if you don't want to. Sorry. I just didn't want you to miss out on the fun,' Patti apologised.

Sandra took a deep breath. 'I know. I'm sorry too, I didn't mean to snap. I will join you, but for me. Because *I* want to,' she said determinedly.

'Good for you!' Patti grinned. 'Let's do this!'

Rob, the instructor, gave them life jackets to put on, briefed on how to use them, and safety precautions for using the jet skis.

'What if we bump into each other?' Sandra asked, still nervous.

'The jet ski automatically turns off if you get too near another jet ski, or are about to leave the zone you were meant to be in,' Rob told her. 'And I'll be riding alongside you.'

'It all sounds pretty safe to me,' Sandra said, relieved.

'Let's take a photo for Insta,' Patti said. 'We'll post it now and let our followers know that we're about to tick something else off our bucket list. Shame we won't be able to post one of us actually riding them on the sea!'

'We'll be taking a few photos so you can choose one from those. And let me take a shot of the three of you now,' the instructor offered. 'Tag me in on your Instagram account and we'll share any photos you put up.'

* * *

Sandra gulped as Mary and Patti mounted their jet skis. Whatever had possessed her to agree to do this? She should have let Mary and Patti share a jet ski, whilst she sat in a café sipping a cocktail and waited for them to come back. Instead, she had to get on this contraption and try to stay afloat. And the sea was far too wavy right now for her liking.

You've had a safety lesson, you're wearing a life jacket and Rob is accompanying you, she reminded herself. *Just get on it!*

'Come on, Sandra!' Patti called. 'You can do it.'

Sandra took a deep breath. 'Coming!'

Rob waited alongside her as she got on the jet ski, put in the tether key and started it up. 'Now take your time, go really slow until you get used to it,' he shouted.

He didn't need to worry, she had no intention of going fast! Patti and Mary were soon ahead but she took her time, scared of crashing or falling off.

I must be mad! I can barely swim!

'Come on, slowcoach!' Patti shouted as she raced past Sandra on her jet ski, the wind blowing through her short hair, making it stick up like hedgehog's prickles.

'Catch us if you can!' Mary followed, her head thrown back with laughter, leaving a spray of foam in her wake.

Adrenaline suddenly flooded through Sandra. She'd show them! She increased her speed and shot through the waves, her hands clenched on the handlebars of the jet ski, exhaling the salty air, excited at the sheer wonder of what she was doing.

'Steady on ladies!' Rob called.

She was actually enjoying it! The wind in her hair, the sun on her face, laughing as she caught up with Patti and Mary.

'Isn't this brilliant?' Patti called.

'Yes, yes it is!' she replied. 'It's wonderful!' She wished Brian could see her now, he would have been pleased for her, she was sure of it.

'Hey, look!' Patti shouted and pointed in front of them to a couple of dolphins who were jumping out of the foamy water. It was spectacular.

This is living, Sandra thought. She was so glad that Patti had come back into her life, and asked her to join her on her visit to Spain. She was starting to live again.

34

PATTI

The organisers had taken a few photos of Patti, Sandra and Mary riding the jet skis, some individual ones and some showing the three of them. The friends gathered around, laughing as they looked at them.

'I've got to have this one. It will be a fantastic souvenir,' Patti said.

Sandra and Mary agreed. It was a photo of them, almost head-to-head, the wind blowing their hair behind them (upwards in Patti's case as her hair was so short), a look of exhilaration on their faces as they sped across the ocean on their jet skis.

'I'm going to buy a frame for this and hang it on the wall,' Patti announced. 'That was the best experience ever!'

'Me too. I can't believe that I finally did it!' Mary agreed. 'I'll take a snap of this photo and send it to Keith to let him know that we've survived! I bet he's pacing the floor.'

'Good idea. I'll send a photo to Kit. She'll love it,' Patti said.

'I'll send it to Becky. She, Honey and Zac will love to see it, and I'll message Don and tell him that I've survived. He'll be pacing the floor too,' Sandra said.

They all sat down on a wall in the shade and snapped the jet ski photo, sending it to their respective family members.

'Shall I put it on our Insta too and let our followers know that we've struck another thing off our bucket list?'

Sandra nodded. 'Go for it.'

Patti uploaded the photo and added some smiley face emojis with the caption:

Another one off the bucket list!

'Still here, ladies,' Rob walked over to them, smiling.

'We're updating our Insta account.' Patti turned her screen towards him so he could see.

'Hey, that's brilliant!' He cocked his head to one side. 'I don't suppose going for a spin on a speedboat is on your list, is it?'

'It's definitely on mine!' Mary said. 'Why?'

'Seeing as you're influencers, you could take one of our motor boats out for a quick spin. It's a bit quiet today and we might get more customers if they see you three whizzing around. Especially if you put the photo on Insta and tag us in.'

Patti laughed. 'You mean they might think "if those old gals can do it, so can we"?'

Rob grinned. 'Something like that. And there'd be no charge, you'll be doing us a favour.'

'You know, I've always fancied going on one of those,' Patti said.

'Don't you need a licence or something?' Sandra asked nervously. Those boats go fast!

'Not for those,' Rob told them. 'What do you say? I'll take a snap for your Insta?'

They all looked at each other then said, 'Yes!' in unison.

* * *

'Well done, you attracted a lot of attention,' Rob told them when they returned. 'And I took some fabulous shots. Shall I send them to the email used to book the jet skis?'

'That's fine, I'll share them with these two,' Mary replied.

Rob sent the photos over and waved goodbye, saying he had another jet ski group to take out now.

The friends crowded around to look through the photos.

'You two are amazing,' Mary said. 'I feel like I'm going to be famous, being in some of your Instagram photos!'

'I've told you, you should start your own Instagram account? It'll be fun. Keith might even join in too,' Patti suggested.

'Huh! We don't go anywhere interesting enough!'

'Nonsense, you live in such a beautiful place. There are so many photo opportunities. The mountains, the sky, the pool, the gorgeous fruit trees,' Sandra told her. 'I think people will enjoy seeing snapshots of your life in Spain.'

'Maybe you're right. I'll have a think about it,' Mary agreed.

She glanced at her phone as a text came in. 'It's from Keith. He said well done and have a nice day. Leo has popped around again and they're sitting outside having a beer.' Her face lit up. 'Well, that's a big improvement.'

'I don't know about anyone else but I'm starving. Shall we go and get some lunch? There's a new restaurant a few minutes' drive away I've been dying to try,' Mary suggested.

'Lead the way, my stomach is growling,' Patti replied.

So they all got back into the car and a few minutes later Mary pulled up in a side street. 'The restaurant is just around the corner,' she said. 'Hopefully it won't be booked up this time of day, but I know you have to reserve a table in the evening.'

They were lucky, there were quite a few empty tables. They chose one outside, overlooking the sea.

A waiter came over to them, 'Can I get you something to drink, *señoras*,' he asked.

'I'll have a soft drink as I'm driving, but you ladies treat yourself to some wine if you want,' Mary said.

Sandra and Patti both ordered a glass of white wine and a big bottle of sparkling water for them all to share.

Whilst the waiter went off to get the drinks, the women studied the menu.

'How about we all be adventurous and try something on the menu that we've never eaten before?' Patti grinned impishly. 'I'm going to have octopus. That will be another thing off my bucket list.'

'Oh yuk!' Mary looked horrified.

Patti grinned. 'It doesn't have to be octopus, it can be a different salad, or curry. Anything you like as long as you haven't had it before. What do you all think?'

'Yes, I like the idea of trying something we haven't eaten before. But I'll leave the octopus to you,' Sandra said. 'Although I might go for fried calamari – squid – I've always fancied trying that.' She skimmed the menu. 'Ah, here it is with caramelised onions and baby potatoes. That sounds tasty.'

'Tuna, cod, salmon or prawns are the only fish I like to eat,' Mary declared as she studied the menu. After much deliberation she decided on black spaghetti with prawn and gulas melted with aioli piquillo pepper.

The waiter returned with the drinks and took their orders.

'I think you might need more than one glass of wine to swill that octopus down,' Sandra said with a grin when their meals were placed in front of them.

Patti was wondering the same but to her surprise the octopus was tender and had a smoky flavour whilst Sandra declared that the squid was light and tasty with a surprisingly sweet texture.

'Today has been amazing! I can't remember the last time I had so much fun,' Sandra said. 'I was nervous about going on the jet ski – and that speedboat! – but I'm glad I did it.'

'Me too,' Mary agreed.

'So was I,' Patti admitted. 'But we did it! Feel the fear and do it anyway!'

They all held up their glasses – Sparkling water for Mary as she was driving – and clinked them. 'All for one and one for all!'

* * *

When they got back Keith was strimming one of the bushes and there was no sign of Leo.

'You've been busy,' Mary said.

'Yeah, it needed doing. Did you all have a good time?' he asked.

'Wonderful,' Patti told him. 'It was such fun. You should try it sometime, you'd enjoy it.'

Keith shook his head. 'Not for me. Anyone fancy some sangria? I've made a fresh jug. I've cooked some pasta and got some strawberries and cream too.'

Mary looked surprised. 'You went to the shop?' she asked.

Keith shrugged. 'Yeah, I decided to get a couple of things in, as you women were out for the day. I also thought I'd do a barbecue tomorrow. Anyone fancy it?'

'Yes!' they all said in unison.

'We could invite Leo,' Keith suggested. 'You just missed him actually, he's meeting a friend. It's been good to catch up with him the last couple of days.'

'Yes, we must invite Leo!' Mary exclaimed. Patti glanced at her, she's sounded very enthusiastic about that!

'How about inviting Thelma and Doug over too?' Mary continued. 'We haven't seen them for ages and it would be lovely to catch up with them. They keep messaging us.' She turned to Patti and Sandra. 'You'd both get on well with them.'

Keith hesitated then nodded. 'Sure. I've bought plenty. Although it might be too short notice for them.'

'I'll find out, shall I?' Mary took out her phone and dialled.

A few minutes later she ended the call, her face wreathed in smiles. 'They said they'd love to come.'

Patti looked thoughtfully at her brother. Was he starting to relax a bit and live his life again? It would be fantastic if he was. And it seemed like this couple who were coming tomorrow were good friends so that was a big step forward. And Leo was coming too. She was looking forward to seeing him again, he was good company. Mary had looked really pleased too. Almost too pleased. Were they just friends or was something else going on?

35
SANDRA

Don phoned early the next morning. 'We asked the estate agent to give us a quick quote for your house, Mum, just so you know what sort of money you've potentially got to play around with. He went around yesterday to value it,' He sounded as if he expected her to be pleased.

'What? You've got the estate agent looking around my house!' She was appalled. How dare he! Don had gone too far this time.

'Of course he hasn't seen inside, Mum. I wouldn't do that. He did a "drive by valuation" but he said you'd easily get three hundred and fifty thousand for it. And – some other exciting news is that another apartment has come up at Orchard House, a downstairs one this time right by the communal gardens, and Marilyn has said she'll give you first refusal if you get back to her today.' Don's voice was persuasive, almost pleading. 'Please say you'll think about it. This is too good an offer to refuse. You'd have some money left over for emergencies too.'

She was annoyed that Don had asked someone to value the house, even if it had only been from the outside. And that he was still trying to push her into buying one of those bloody apartments despite her repeatedly telling him that she wasn't interested in them.

'This is completely out of order, Don. I am not moving into an apartment and if I want my house valued, I'll arrange it. Will you please stop trying to control my life!' She ended the call, pulled on her kimono and went into the kitchen where Patti was sitting at the table, eating a bowl of cornflakes and talking to Kit on Facetime.

'It looks amazing, Nan. And you've got so many followers on Insta now. You "Old Gals" are famous!'

Patti chuckled. 'Infamous more like. Anyway, you get off to uni. I'll speak to you later.' Patti ended the call and glanced at Sandra. 'You've got that "I've just been talking to Don" look on your face.'

'Oh dear, is it that obvious?' She repeated the phone call to Patti who raised her eyebrows. 'It's a bit controlling, don't you think?'

'I do. And I told him so in no uncertain terms!' Sandra flicked the kettle on and took a bag of muesli out of the cupboard. 'Did Keith mention what time he's doing the barbecue?'

'About two. So don't worry, you've got plenty of time.' She looked up at Sandra. 'I'm so pleased that Keith has organised this barbecue, Mary said they haven't had one for ages.'

'It's a good sign, isn't it? Maybe he might even come out with us one of the days. Especially if we go somewhere he would like,' Sandra replied.

'I hope so. I'll talk to Mary and see if she can come up with anything. Although she did say that they'd both planned on going jet skiing. And on the boat trip, and he didn't even come on that, did he? Even though it wasn't even slightly strenuous.' She sighed. 'I'm worried about him, Sandra. This isn't like him at all. He's always been very outgoing.'

'I guess it was a shock when he had the heart attack. Things like that make you aware of your own vulnerability, don't they?'

'I know, but it's not healthy. I wish I'd known how much he was struggling. I was so wrapped up in my own recovery.'

'Which is perfectly natural. And he was probably embarrassed about it and didn't want you to know. Also, I would imagine he thought you had enough to cope with so wouldn't want to worry you.'

'Poor Mary, these past few months must have been so hard for her.' Patti picked up her mug and walked over to the window to look out into the garden. 'Well, at least Keith's doing bits around the garden now and has invited friends around for a barbecue today. That's progress.'

'It is. I'll just eat this and then get ready.' Sandra took her mug of tea and bowl of muesli into her room.

She enjoyed Patti's company, but her friend tended to chat a bit, and right now Sandra wanted to be quiet. Her mind was in a bit of turmoil after the conversation with Don. He really was determined to persuade her to move to Cambridge with him, but as the days passed she could feel herself becoming more independent. She still missed Brian desperately but she'd started to enjoy her life again, and to build up a friendship group. Several members of the swimming group had commented on their Instagram posts, and Beryl and Mabel had both messaged to ask how they were enjoying their holiday and that they were looking forward to meeting up again. She didn't want to start all over again in Cambridge.

She didn't want to live so far away from Don, Laila and the children either.

* * *

They had a swim in the pool then helped Mary and Keith get things ready for the barbecue. Doug and Thelma arrived first, they were a larger-than-life couple, full of bonhomie, and it was evident they were delighted to be invited.

'We've missed you, mate,' Doug said, patting Keith on the back. 'We were a winning team us four, when are you coming back to play Bridge?'

Keith grinned. 'We've got visitors at the moment, but when they've returned home we'll come back,' he said.

Mary shot him a look of surprise.

'Perfect!' Doug clapped him on the back again. Then turned his attention to Patti and Sandra. 'Now which one of you two is Keith's sister?'

Patti raised a hand. 'I'm relieved to know that I don't look much like him,' she jested. There was a roar of laughter at this.

Then Leo arrived, carrying a bag from which she could see a couple of leeks peeping out, and half a dozen eggs perched on the top, and a bottle of red wine. Mary went to greet him and they stood chatting for a while, before joining everyone. Patti watched them thoughtfully.

'Caught your eye, has he? Well, I'm not surprised he is quite a dish,' Sandra said.

'What? God no! I don't fancy him!' Patti denied a little too quickly.

'Really? I wouldn't blame you and you were staring at him...'

'Not at him, at *them*.' Patti frowned. 'Do they seem a bit... close to you?'

Sandra's eyebrows shot up to her hairline. 'You don't mean—?'

'Yes. No. I don't know. Mary always seems so pleased to see him, and they go on dog walks together, and they're always huddled together chatting.' She bit her lip. 'I hate thinking like this but surely if I've noticed then Keith must have done.'

Sandra glanced over at Keith and saw that he was busy talking to Doug and Thelma, his back to the gate so wouldn't have noticed Mary and Leo talking. 'I think they're all just very good friends and that you're jumping to the wrong conclusion, maybe because Keith and Mary are going through a bit of a rocky patch.'

'And because Adrian cheated on me. I didn't see the signs then, so maybe I look out for them more now.'

Mary and Leo were now walking back up the path to join everyone, Mary carrying the bag. She took it into the kitchen while Leo greeted everyone.

'Buenos,' Leo said cheerily, kissing each of them on both cheeks. Patti made sure not to meet his eyes this time, but the brief kiss was still a bit unsettling.

'Leo, old boy, good to see you again!' Doug shook Leo's hand vigorously and slapped him on the back. Thelma leaned in for her cheek kisses. They obviously knew him well, Patti thought.

'It's a good job you two women have come for a visit, this one has turned into a bit of a recluse,' Doug said. 'We've been trying to drag him back into the land of living for ages.'

Keith reached out and put his arm around Patti's shoulder, pulling her into him. 'Well, I guess if my little sis can beat cancer and overcome her fear of going on a plane to come and visit me, then maybe I can start getting out a bit too. You should hear all the other things they've been up to as well.'

Mary came back out and the conversation turned to their bucket list – with Leo asking, 'Bucket list? What is that?' and the others realising that they hadn't mentioned it to him before, explained. Mary showed them the photos of the jet skiing yesterday, and on the speedboat.

'You're a gutsy trio, I'll say that for you,' Doug said. 'Now what's next on the list?'

'A hot air balloon ride, going to a music festival, walking the Caminito del Rey.' Seeing a flamenco dance, Mary related. She grinned at Sandra and

Patti. 'I've just added that because I'm sure you two will love to see one. And you said you fancied learning a new dance, Patti.'

'Ah, I might be able to help you with that. My friend has a restaurant in Estepona and sometimes he books two flamenco dancers at the weekend. I can check if they're here this weekend, book us a table, and give you a lift there so that you can enjoy a glass of sangria, if you wish.'

'Leo, you are a hero,' Mary kissed him on the cheek and he smiled affectionately at her.

Sandra saw a frown cross Patti's face as she watched Leo and Mary. They looked close, yes, but surely nothing more than that. And it was nice of Leo to arrange this for them. This was turning out to be quite a holiday.

36

PATTI

'Oh goodness, I don't know which one to choose!' Patti said, looking at the display of delicious looking cakes laid out on the counter in front of them. They'd spent the morning looking around the local town of Coín and had now stopped for a snack.

Mary and Sandra were having a similar problem choosing, luckily there wasn't a queue behind them and the lady serving was obviously used to her customers being indecisive and patiently waited until they made up their minds. Iced coffees and a cake ordered, they headed for a vacant table in the corner and sat down, putting their bags down on the floor by their feet. Patti had treated herself to a delicate red shawl embroidered with silver to put over her shoulders when the evenings got chilly, and Sandra had fallen in love with a pale green handbag.

'Are you going to be able to fit that into your case?' Mary asked as they sat down. 'If not you might have to leave it with me.' She grinned.

'She has a point, your case was already pretty full, and so was your hand luggage,' Patti said. 'Thank goodness I only bought a scarf.'

'Oh, it's fine. I can pack it flat and slip it in. I've done that many a time when Brian and I used to travel. I never could resist a nice bag.'

'I can't believe that we've been here a week already,' Patti said as the assistant brought their order over and placed their respective cakes, coffees and three glasses of ice in front of them.

'*Gracias*,' they all chorused.

'*De nada*,' the woman replied. Patti had heard that phrase a few times this week and now knew that it meant 'You're welcome'.

'Me neither. It's been a wonderful break. Thank you so much for your hospitality,' Sandra said as Mary poured her coffee into the glass of ice. She and Patti did the same.

'*De nada*!' Mary grinned. 'Seriously, it's been a pleasure. I've loved having you both here.'

Patti dug her fork into her cake and scooped up a mouthful. 'It's not over yet though. We have another week to go. So what adventure are we going on next?'

'Well there's the flamenco dance hopefully, thanks to Leo. Keith's agreed to come too,' Mary reminded her. 'We can have a drive out tomorrow. And don't forget we have the Caminito del Rey on Tuesday.'

Patti was so glad she'd come to visit them. And it was good that Keith was going to join them. He'd perked up a bit and really seemed to enjoy the barbecue. And she was worrying too much about Leo and Mary, they were clearly only good friends.

'Most of the shops are closed now but there's still plenty to see, I'll take you for a tour after we've eaten. And then shall we go back and have cocktails by the pool?'

'That sounds perfect,' Sandra said.

'Why don't we have a go at making cocktails?' Patti suggested. 'That's on Sandra's bucket list.'

'Great idea!' Mary agreed.

They spent the afternoon exploring Coín. As Mary had said the smaller shops were closed for siesta but cafés and restaurants were open. Mary took them to the big square with a picturesque church where Mary explained the religious icons were carried out for the Easter parades. 'It's a shame that you didn't come for Easter, they're quite spectacular. Maybe next year.' And where everyone gathered in fancy dress on New Year's Eve. 'That's such fun and you'd be amazed at the variety of costumes. Maybe you could come over for that, Patti? You too, Sandra, if you're not spending New Year with your family.'

'I'd like that. Thank you,' Patti said. She turned to Sandra. 'What about you?'

'It's very kind of you to include me and I really appreciate the invitation but I'm not sure what I'll be doing yet. I'm really hoping I can pluck up the courage to go to Australia and see Becky and her family.'

'That would be wonderful. No rush to make a decision, there's plenty of time. You can let us know later,' Patti told her. She had an idea that Sandra didn't want them to think that they had to invite her along every time Patti came to visit. Not that she minded, Sandra was good company. Patti was definitely going to come over again. Now she'd flown over once, she could do it again. And by herself, if necessary. It would be good to see more of Keith and Mary.

And Leo.

She thrust the thought away. Where had that come from? She wasn't interested in Leo.

Especially if he was hooking up with her sister-in-law behind her brother's back.

37

When they got back, Keith's car was missing. Mary looked puzzled. 'I wonder where he's gone? He never goes out – unless he's gone to the shops again.'

'He's coming around a bit, I think,' Patti said. 'He was really enjoying the barbecue yesterday. Maybe he's popped over to see your friends.'

Before they could speculate any further, Keith drove in. He opened the car door. 'Afternoon, I thought I might be back before you three got home. I know what you're like when you get out together.'

'Where have you been?' Mary asked curiously.

'You mentioned having cocktails by the pool tonight, so I went out to get some ingredients for the cocktails. And some snacky things.' He paused. 'You didn't stop to get them on the way home, did you?'

'No, I was going to the shop later so you've saved me the journey. Thanks, love.' Mary gave Keith a peck on the cheek and he smiled at her.

Patti's spirits lifted as she watched them. Keith was unwinding, and Mary adored him, that was evident. She was worrying over nothing.

'I've invited Leo too,' Keith said. 'He popped over this afternoon to say that there are some flamenco dancers at his friend's restaurant on Saturday night so he wanted to check if that was okay with us. He's provisionally booked a table as the restaurant gets busy. It's really decent of him, isn't it?'

'Yes it is. He's a good friend.' Mary turned to Patti and Sandra. 'Did you hear that, girls? Leo has managed to arrange for us to see some flamenco dancers. Honestly, nothing is too much for that man. He's a dream.'

'He certainly is! I can't wait!' Patti said eagerly.

'Neither can I. I can't wait to try your cocktails either, Keith,' Sandra added.

'Maybe you can show Sandra, she wants to make her own cocktail,' Mary said. She turned to Sandra. 'Keith's quite an expert. We used to have friends around a lot and Keith always made cocktails whilst I did special desserts for everyone. We had such fun.' Mary sounded wistful and Patti's heart went out to her. She obviously missed those fun times. Well, hopefully Keith was ready to start socialising again.

Patti and Sandra went over to the casita to get changed. Patti chose a brightly patterned maxi dress with a lacy bolero top whilst Sandra put on some white cropped trousers and a lilac short-sleeved blouse.

'We better not forget the mosquito spray,' Sandra said, picking up the can from the worktop. 'They'll make a meal of us otherwise.'

'Tell me about it, pesky things. The smell of the spray overrides my perfume though so I prefer to use the mosquito bands Mary gave us.' She had one on each wrist and one on each ankle.

'I'm wearing those too, but a mosquito sneaked down my top the other day and bit me right in the middle of my boobs, so I'm not chancing it.' Sandra sprayed herself liberally with the mosquito repellent.

Patti hesitated then followed suit. It was stupid to risk getting a couple of mosquito bites because the smell overpowered her perfume. Who would notice?

When they went back to the terrace Leo was there, looking quite dashing in long beige shorts and a green and white patterned short-sleeved shirt, talking to Mary. Again.

They both sprung apart when they saw them coming. They looked a bit uneasy, Patti thought. She hung back, letting Sandra carry on.

'Hello, what are you two all in a huddle about?' she asked.

Mary flushed and glanced over her shoulder. 'Oh dear, is it that obvious?'

Patti swallowed. Had she been right?

'You do seem to be whispering together a lot.'

Leo and Patti exchanged glances. He nodded slowly.

'Okay, I'll tell you but please don't breathe a word to Keith,' Mary said.

Oh God, she'd been right. Suddenly she didn't want Mary to confess. She didn't want to know. How could she keep this from her brother?

'Maybe you're best not to tell me. It's not fair to ask me to keep it from Keith,' she stammered.

'Goodness, Patti, you look horrified. What on earth do you think I'm going to confess?'

Patti looked from Mary to Leo then back to Mary again. 'I... er...'

Mary's eyes widened. 'Heck! You think we're having an affair, don't you?'

Patti felt her cheeks heat and couldn't even bring herself to look at Leo. 'Well...' Her voice trailed away.

'We're planning a surprise for Keith. Leo is sorting it out for me.' She shook her head. 'I can't believe you jumped to that conclusion. I hope Keith hasn't as well!' She turned abruptly and walked off into the house.

'Oh dear. I'm so sorry. It's just that Keith and Mary are at loggerheads a bit, and you seemed very attentive...' She couldn't look him in the eye.

Leo smiled. '*De nada*. It is nothing. You are right that things are a little... not quite right... with Keith and Mary, which is why we are planning this surprise.' He thrust his hands in his pockets his eyes meeting hers, unwavering. 'I would not do that to a friend. To cheat like that. I am not that kind of person.'

Now she felt even worse. 'I really am sorry.' How stupid was she to jump to that conclusion just because Leo spent a lot of time here, and she'd caught him and Mary talking together. Now she'd embarrassed herself and everyone else.

'Besides, there is someone else that I like. Someone who is free. And I was asking Mary's advice about that, also.'

'Oh, I see.' She guessed it must be one of the neighbours. She could understand that Leo was a bit hesitant and wanted advice. It was hard to get back into the dating game when you'd been out of it for a while. She should know! She'd made a few attempts with Tinder and other dating apps since she and Adrian split up but there had been so many disasters she'd given up. She was better off on her own. 'I hope it works out for you.'

He nodded solemnly. 'Me too. But this *señora*, she doesn't live in Spain.'

His eyes rested on her face, as if he was watching her reaction. He couldn't mean... No... That would be stupid.

'I see.' She was repeating herself but she didn't know what else to say. She'd already made a fool of herself once and she wasn't going to say anything to make things worse. He must have met someone on the internet, lots of people did nowadays. 'That's difficult.'

He nodded again. 'But not impossible.'

Time to end this conversation and go and make her apologies to Mary. 'There's always a way if you look for it, I guess.' She hurried off to the kitchen to find Mary.

Mary was putting the last touch to the meal and Keith was opening a bottle of wine.

Patti looked at them both. 'Sorry.'

Keith raised an eyebrow. 'What for?'

'She thought I was having an affair with Leo,' Mary told him.

Keith threw back his head and laughed. 'You're way off the mark there, Patti. Leo has his eye on someone else.'

'I know, he's just told me. I think it's someone he met on the internet.'

'What?' Mary and Keith exclaimed in unison.

'He said it was someone who didn't live in Spain.'

Keith shook his head and Mary put down the knife she was chopping the tomatoes with.

'You really have no idea, do you?'

Patti looked from one to the other. 'What do you mean?'

'Patti. The lady Leo is interested in is *you*.'

38

They all tucked into the goat cheese salad and crusty bread, followed by strawberries and ice cream, and Patti tried to act natural, tried not to stare at Leo. Could Mary and Keith be right? She was definitely attracted to him, he was kind, and handsome, but what future was there when she would be going home next week?

Sandra and Keith had disappeared into the kitchen to make cocktails, so Mary, Leo and Patti sat chatting on the terrace.

'Now let us tell you the secret we've been planning for Keith,' Mary said. 'You know how he loves the old Cadillacs and has always wanted one.'

'How could I forget? He was always going on about it when we were younger. He used to watch those Humphrey Bogart films over and over again. He even had a trench coat, didn't he? And a fedora.'

'We still have them in a box in the spare bedroom.' Mary leaned forward and lowered her voice. 'Well Leo has a friend who owns a Caddy. He's been away but he's back tomorrow and Leo is going to ask him if he can take us all for a spin in it on Friday.'

'Really? Oh, Keith will love that! That's amazing,' Patti exclaimed. She glanced at Leo. 'It's a big ask though. These cars don't come cheap. You must be VERY good friends.'

'We are.' Leo smiled at her. 'It might be the push Keith needs to get out and about. We are keeping it a surprise until we know for sure but we hope that you ladies will join in too.'

'Oh, I'd love to. It sounds amazing!' Patti said. 'And more Insta pics too!'

'And we're all going to dress up in forties style,' Mary added. 'I'm thinking of channelling Audrey Hepburn. Scarf, sunglasses, red lipstick. Sandra would make a good Marilyn Monroe with her hair and full lips.'

'And you would be a perfect Shirley MacLaine, Patti, with those amazing cheekbones,' Leo said.

Patti felt her cheeks flush at the compliment. 'It sounds exciting. And Keith's got his Humphrey Bogart trench coat and hat. But what will you wear, Leo?'

'I can be Cary Grant. I have a trilby and a trench coat too.'

'Mary!' Keith shouted from the kitchen.

'I'd better go and see what he wants.' Mary got up and went into the kitchen, leaving just Patti and Leo outside. She felt awkward, after what Keith and Mary had told her. It couldn't true. Leo barely knew her.

'It's very kind of you to organise this for Keith,' she told him.

'Keith and Mary, they are good friends. I would like to help.' He smiled at her, his eyes meeting hers. 'It will be a nice day out for you *señoras* too, yes?'

'It definitely will!'

'Panic over, they couldn't find the cocktail glasses,' Mary came back out, followed by Sandra holding a tray containing five fancy cocktails. She indicated the glasses with a flourish as Sandra put them down on the table. 'Let me introduce you to a Sandra Surprise!'

Patti looked at the glasses filled with a strawberry-coloured drink, garnished with a strawberry and a slice of lemon. 'They look great. Let me take a photo for Instagram – it's another thing off your bucket list.' She snapped the tray of cocktails. 'I'll upload it later.'

'Can we ask what's in them?'

Sandra tapped the side of her nose. 'Top secret!'

'See if you can guess,' Keith suggested.

They all took a sip of the drinks and Patti took a swig and almost choked. 'This is strong!'

Sandra grinned. 'That's the surprise!'

'I can taste Cointreau,' Mary said.

'And vodka, I think, a double shot by the taste of it,' Patti added.

'I think I detect a taste of honey.' This was from Leo.

Sandra giggled and chinked glasses with Keith. 'There's a secret ingredient that only we know.'

'I've made a Keith Special too. So drink those up and I'll bring out round two!'

'We should play some games,' Patti suggested. 'How about charades? Do you know how to play that, Leo?'

'Charades?' He frowned then his eyes lit up. 'Ah, cha-ra-das! *Si*, I know it.'

They had a fun evening, drinking cocktails and playing charades, which included lots of amusing photos for their Instagram account.

When Leo had, left Patti and Sandra helped Mary clear up. Patti followed Mary into the kitchen with a tray of snacks.

'It's so kind of Leo to organise this surprise for Keith. How stupid of me to think you were having an affair I'm so sorry. I didn't mean to insult you.'

'Goodness, it's a compliment that you think someone like Leo would be interested in me. He's quite dishy, isn't he? But my heart belongs to Keith, even if I do want to wring his neck sometimes.' She put a tablet in the dishwasher and closed the door. 'I asked Leo if he would come around more often while you and Sandra were here as I thought if another man was here Keith would join in, instead of leaving us women to it. He always gets on with Leo.'

'I should have known.'

'How could you? You're right, things are a bit strained between me and Keith but we'll sort it out.' She gave Patti a hug. 'Now stop stressing about it. It's late, let's all turn in for the night. I've got a feeling we're all going to wake up with headaches tomorrow.'

39

SANDRA

She'd had such a marvellous time, she didn't want to go home, Sandra thought on Thursday morning as she relaxed on the sunbed feeling the warmth of the sun on her skin. It was still morning, so it wasn't burning hot yet, just warm and pleasant. She didn't want to go back and face real life. Didn't want to have to make the decision whether she moved to Cambridge or not. The clock was ticking. Don told her that both parties had already booked surveys and were expecting to exchange within the next few weeks, looking to complete before the summer holidays.

This break had done her good. Done them all good. Patti looked so relaxed now. And Keith and Mary seemed closer. Yesterday evening had been fun.

Mary was taking them to a pretty white village up in the mountains later – Mijas Pueblo – so they were chilling out before the journey.

Then, tomorrow, all being well, Leo was taking them to Marbella for a ride in his friend's Cadillac. Patti had told her about it when they returned to the casita last night, saying it was a secret from Keith until Leo had the go ahead from his friend. And they were all dressing forties style. Apparently, that's what they'd been whispering about, and Patti said she felt mortified thinking that her sister-in-law was having an affair.

Saturday was the flamenco night and Mary had booked them in for the Caminito del Rey on Tuesday. Then it was home on Wednesday and back to real life. It had been such a marvellous time. And such a shame they didn't have longer because anyone could see the growing attraction between Patti and Leo. They had really hit it off. Perhaps that might encourage Patti to visit again.

She opened her eyes as her phone buzzed in, reaching for it from under the sunbed where she'd put it so that it didn't get hot. She sighed when she glanced at the screen and saw that it was Don again. This time with the link to a small, detached bungalow for sale in Cambridge. He'd sent her at least two properties a day for the last few days. She sighed again as she put her phone back down on the coffee table.

Patti glanced over enquiringly. 'Let me guess… another property for sale?'

'Yep.'

'When does he go? Is there any more movement on his house sale?'

Sandra filled her in.

'A month or so then. Are you any nearer to making a decision?'

'It's difficult to decide while I'm here. We've had such an amazing time. Your brother and sister-in-law are wonderful hosts and it's so kind of Mary to run us around like this.'

'It is, but she's enjoyed it too.' Patti edged herself into a sitting up position, sensing Sandra was keen to change the subject. 'I'm so glad we came, Keith and Mary seem in a happier place now. Maybe he'll even start going out with Mary again, once we return home. Doug and Thelma will encourage him, I'm sure. As will Leo.'

'They're all lovely people, aren't they? And how kind of Leo to ask his friend if he can borrow his car tomorrow.'

'Yes, I'm really looking forward to that. We've ticked so many things off our bucket list, haven't we?' Patti sat up, hugging her knees, pulling her kimono down over them. 'I do feel a bit awful that Mary is doing the Caminito del Rey walk with us though, when it was something she and Keith had always planned on doing together. I wish he would join us.'

'Maybe he will later on. I'm sure she won't mind doing it again.'

'I guess you're right. After all, look how long it took me to pluck up the courage to get on a plane!'

'And me to learn to swim. Sometimes things take time.'

'Yahoo! Lunch is ready!' Mary was waving to them from the terrace.

'Coming!' Sandra stood and grabbed her maxi dress from the back of the chair, pulling it over her head. Then they both slipped their feet into their sandals and went over to join Keith and Mary who were sitting at the table outside.

'I can't believe we've been here more than a week already! I shall miss it so much,' Sandra said as she sat down. 'You two have been very good to us both. I really appreciate it.'

'It's a pleasure,' Mary told her.

After lunch they got changed then climbed into Mary's car and headed off for the hillside village of Mijas Pueblo. Sandra sat in the back, as usual, knowing that Patti always felt nauseous in the back, and off they set. They'd tried to talk Keith into coming with them, but he'd replied that he'd been there loads of times, and Leo was coming around later for a beer. 'Well, at least Keith's socialising again, I'm so glad,' Mary said as they set off.

Sandra looked out of the window, admiring the view, as Patti and Mary chatted in the front. Sometimes Patti turned and said something to her, but she was mostly content to leave them to it.

'I can't get over how the mountains are literally sliced through to make way for the roads,' Patti observed. 'And how some of the places are so remote, high on top of the hills, I wouldn't like to live that far away from everything.'

'Me neither, but some people like the solitude.'

'You said this village was up the mountains?' Patti said.

'Yes we're about to turn off to go up to it.'

At first the road was quite wide but the higher up they went the narrower it got. The mountain wall was on Sandra and Mary's side but Patti was sitting in the front passenger seat, on the side of the drop, and she was getting more and more nervous.

'Oh shit, Mary!' she screamed, clinging onto the edges of her seat. 'It's a sheer drop on this side! And there's no barriers along this bit!'

'We're nowhere near the edge. And holding on to your seat won't help!' Mary told her with a chuckle. 'There will be barriers again in a minute.'

'I'm going to have to shut my eyes,' Patti squeaked. 'Let me know when we're there.'

She'd feel the same if she was on the side facing the drop, Sandra thought. She'd make sure that she sat behind Patti on the way back so she'd be against the mountain again.

It was a bit of a hair-raising journey, but once they'd parked up they had a great time looking around. It was such a pretty little town, with lots of little shops and restaurants. Sandra had to stop herself buying another handbag, because there was no way she could fit it in her case, so she settled instead for an elegant black beret – she'd taken to wearing them a lot now back at home. Patti bought a colourful scarf and Mary treated herself to a soft beige leather jacket and a plaid cap for Keith. They stopped for lunch, sharing a paella with salad and garlic bread, had a wander over up to the fortress walls and beautiful gardens, stopping to look at the breathtaking view below before visiting the historic chapel of the Virgin of the Rock.

'This is a beautiful place,' Patti said. 'It's a shame it's such a scary route up here.'

'You'll be okay going down, you'll be on the mountain side, I'll be the one with the drop on my side,' Mary reminded her.

'Aren't you scared, Mary?' Sandra asked. 'I'm going to sit behind Patti this time. I don't think I can handle looking down.'

'It was a bit nerve-wracking the first couple of times we came here, but I'm used to it now.'

* * *

When they arrived back at home Keith and Leo had just returned from taking both dogs for a walk.

'Did you have a good time?' Keith asked.

'It was beautiful, but you could have warned us about that mountain road!' Patti told him.

He grinned. 'If I had, you wouldn't have gone and it's well worth the visit, isn't it?'

'It certainly was,' Sandra agreed.

'Will you stop for a coffee – or a beer, Leo?' Mary asked.

'A *cerveza* would be good, *gracias*,' Leo said. 'I'll give you a hand.'

'I'll give the dogs some water.' Keith went off, the two dogs trotting behind him, to refill the water bowls and Leo followed Mary into the kitchen.

'I wonder if he's heard whether he can borrow the Cadillac tomorrow,' Patti whispered, crossing her fingers.

They both returned with a tray of coffees, two bottles of beer and a bowl of crisps just as Keith came back and sat down by Patti and Sandra. 'Well, ladies, what plans do you have for tomorrow?' he asked cheerily.

'I have a good day planned.' Leo pulled out a chair and sat down, opening the beer and taking a sip before continuing. 'My friend in Marbella, he has a vintage Cadillac and he is allowing me to borrow it tomorrow to take some friends out for a drive.'

Keith's eyes widened. 'A Caddy! Wow! Lucky friends.'

'Do you think they will like it, to ride in such an old car?' Leo asked.

'Are you kidding! It's a classic. Who wouldn't want a ride in one?'

'Ah, I am pleased you think it. So, you will come with us?' Leo took another swig of his beer.

Keith looked taken aback. 'Me? Join your friends? But I don't know them...'

'Oh, but you do. It is all of you.' Leo held out his arms to encompass the group. 'You are the friends I'm taking.'

Keith looked stunned. Mary reached over and squeezed his hand. 'We planned it for you as a surprise. You've always wanted to go in one. Will you come?'

'You bet I will!' Keith exclaimed, his eyes dancing.

'That's great. And we're all dressing up forties style,' Patti told him.

'Brilliant! I've got a fedora and a trench coat. I'll go and get them.'

Mary looked amused as he hurried out of the room. 'I've spent the last few months trying to coax Keith to go out and all it's taken is the promise of a ride in a classic car. Leo, you're a genius!'

40

MARY

Mary was so pleased to see that Keith had a spring in his step the next morning as they all got ready for the trip to Marbella for the ride in the vintage Cadillac. It had been awful to see him so down, not wanting to go out or do anything but now she felt like she was getting her husband back.

He put on his fedora and beige trench coat. 'How do I look?'

'Perfect, Humphrey!' She wrapped her arms around him and gave him a hug. 'I think you might be hot though.'

'Yeah, me too.' He kissed her forehead. 'It's going to be a scorcher today. But it will be cooler this morning, and Leo said it will only be a short ride. Can't blame his friend for that, if I had a Caddy, I wouldn't want to lend it out to anyone. He must think a lot of Leo.'

'He's a good chap, Leo. Salt of the earth. Have you noticed how friendly he and Patti are getting?' Mary asked, stepping out of the hug to grab her red lipstick off her dressing table. 'It's a shame she isn't stopping longer. I think they'd be good together.'

'Yes, me too. It's a bit weird though, my sister and my mate fancying each other – just like when we were teenagers.'

'Do you think they'll keep in touch? It would be so nice for Patti to find love again. She's been on her own for so long.'

'I don't think she's that interested in a relationship. She's very independent.'

'You can still be independent and have a relationship. Leo has been on his own for a long time too and he's very independent. I think they'd be a perfect match.' Mary applied the lipstick and blotted her lips with a tissue. 'Now I just need my sunglasses and scarf.'

'Very sexy!' Keith said in approval as she tied the silk scarf Audrey Hepburn style over her head and knotted it loosely under her chin then slipped on her sunglasses. He pulled her into another hug. 'Thanks for arranging this, love.'

'You've very welcome, but it was Leo's idea.' And what a brilliant idea it was, Keith looked more cheerful than she'd seen him for a long time. And they hadn't even had a ride in the Cadillac yet.

* * *

Leo arrived a little later and they all got into his large estate car and set off for Marbella.

Rupert lived in a luxurious large villa on the outskirts of Marbella.

'Wow, this must be worth over a million,' Mary said as the electric gates opened and Leo drove inside.

Rupert came out to greet them, and was amused to see them all dressed up as forties' film stars. 'That's brilliant! I must take a photo of you all.'

'Talking of photos, would you mind if we posted one of us all in your car on our Instagram account later?' Patti asked.

'Oh yes! You can say it's one of the things on Keith's bucket list,' Mary suggested.

'What bucket list?' Keith asked, in surprise.

'The one you've just started!' Mary grinned.

'Of course. Leo told me about your bucket list, and I checked out your account. You're certainly living your life. Good for you!'

The Cadillac was parked in the drive. Shiny maroon with a black fabric convertible top, that Rupert had already put down, it looked like something out of an old movie. The Cadillac crest was on the front, and the trademark silver bird on the bonnet.

They all posed in front of the car for a couple of photos, which Rupert said he'd send to Leo, then Rupert opened the doors to show them inside.

Keith whistled at the chrome with wood veneer steering wheel, the polished wooden dashboard with chrome dials, the beige leather bench seats in the front and back. 'This is amazing!'

'I'm rather proud of it. It was my father's. I've kept it in pristine condition,' Rupert said.

'Do you often hire it out?' Keith asked.

'Yes, hiring out vintage cars is my business. I have a Mercedes Benz too and an MG. They make me a tidy income. Not that I'll be charging you. I owe Leo a favour, he saved my life.'

'It was only what anyone would have done,' Leo told him. 'I was in the right place at the right time.'

'What happened?' Patti asked.

'A bunch of us were sailing on my yacht and it was a bit rocky. I got up in the middle of the night to check the sails, got knocked out and fell overboard. Luckily Leo couldn't sleep and came on the deck, saw what happened and rescued me. That was ten years ago.'

Leo had never mentioned this and they'd been good friends for a few years now, Mary thought, but then he wasn't one to talk about himself much. She could believe it of him though, he was that sort of man.

They all got inside the car, Leo and Keith sitting on the bench seat at the front and Patti, Sandra and Mary in the back.

Sandra looked for her seat belt to fasten. 'Oh, of course there's no seat belts!' she said.

'It's not a problem, I won't be driving fast,' Leo told them. 'And it's perfectly legal in a classic car.'

'Enjoy your trip!' Rupert waved as Leo started up the engine.

'*Gracias,* we will only be an hour or so,' Leo promised. He drove smoothly out of the drive and along the road.

'You've obviously driven this a few times,' Patti said.

'Yes, I help Rupert out sometimes if he needs a driver.' Leo turned onto the coast road, the views were spectacular. It was breathtaking. Driving along, the warm breeze on their skin, the ocean sparkling in the sun, Mary felt a flood of happiness. Life was good.

* * *

When they'd returned the Cadillac, Leo offered to take them to Puerto Banús. 'Unless you're in a rush to get back.'

'Absolutely not! These two are only here for a few more days, and Puerto Banús is definitely worth seeing,' Mary said.

So, they piled into Leo's car and he drove them into Puerto Banús, parking in the underground car park by the marina there. It was getting hot now so Leo and Keith left their trench coats in the car. Then they headed off to walk around the marina.

'Look at that yellow Lamborghini,' Patti exclaimed. 'Imagine driving along in *that*.'

'Unfortunately, I don't know the owner of this one, so can't take you for a ride,' Leo told her.

'Well at least I can have my photo taken by it. Come on, ladies!'

Keith took photos of Patti, Sandra and Mary posing in front of the Lamborghini, and some of the luxury yachts. Then they splashed out on lunch in a bar overlooking the marina – with Sandra insisting on treating everyone as a thank you – and that had gone on their Insta page too.

Later, as Leo drove them home Mary thought she had never felt happier. Thank goodness that Patti – and Sandra – had come to visit. Between them, and Leo, she was getting the old Keith back.

41

SANDRA

Don video called later that evening. 'I saw your latest post on IG, Mum. That Cadillac looked amazing. It sounds like you're having a wonderful time over there.'

She was taken aback, and pleased, by his positive response. 'I am. Keith and Mary have made us so welcome, and so have their friends. It's been wonderful and relaxing for me. Just what I needed.'

'I can see that, and I'm glad that you went. I guess I worried a bit too much, but it's only because I don't want anything to happen to you. I don't want to lose you too.'

'I know, darling. I understand.' She was so relieved that she and Don were back on track. 'How are you enjoying it in Cambridge? Have you settled in yet?'

'The job's great, but I'll be glad when the house sale has gone through then Laila and the kids can join me permanently. I miss them.' Laila and the children had been staying with him in the flat but now they'd gone to London to see their other grandparents.

'I'm sure you do. It won't be much longer now though. How is the sale going?'

'We should be exchanging in a couple of weeks. You'll love the house. There's a little bungalow for sale nearby too. It would be ideal for you.'

Here he goes again. 'I must go now, darling, we're about to have supper on the terrace. Speak to you soon.'

'Bye, Mum. Love you.'

'Love you too.' Then the screen flickered and went blank.

Don had looked tired, and a bit sad, she thought. It must be difficult for him living in the flat, away from his family. They'd been with him for the weekend, but that must have been difficult too, the children sharing a room and no garden to play in. Hopefully they'd soon all be living together again.

Then another video call came in, it was Laila and the children.

'Nanny, we're in London!' Kali shouted.

Rana popped her head in front of Kali's. 'We're staying with our Nani and Nana.'

'That's wonderful. Are you having a good time? There's lots to see in London.'

Kali pushed herself back into view. 'We saw the palace where the King lives but he wasn't at home.'

The children talked over each other in their eagerness to tell her what they'd seen and done.

'And we walked across London Bridge.'

'And we had a ride in a bus with no roof all around London.'

'That all sounds marvellous!' She told them. It was lovely to see them so excited, and Laila's parents must be enjoying having them to stay.

'We saw you and your friends in that funny old car on Insta,' Kali said.

'It looked good fun,' Laila called off-screen.

'It really was,' Sandra replied.

'Where are you going tomorrow, Nanny?' Rana asked.

'We're going to watch some people do a special dance called The Flamenco. I'll put a photo of it on my Instagram.'

Rana's face popped onto the screen again. 'When are you coming home, Nanny? We miss you!'

'A few more days. I miss you all too, but we'll have lots to talk about when we see each other again,' she said.

'Okay, girls, off you go and play and let me speak to your nan for a bit,' Laila said, coming into view.

The two children obediently said goodbye and ran off.

'How are you, Sandra. Are you enjoying yourself?' Laila asked.

'Yes. I really am. I hear that you should be in your new house soon.'

She nodded. 'I can't wait. The house is lovely, just a few minutes' walk from the children's school and it has a big back garden.'

'I can't wait to see it.'

'You must come over and stay when we move in.'

'I will. I'd love that.'

They chatted a little longer, then Laila's mother called her, and she said she had to go.

Sandra sat thinking for a while after the call. Laila hadn't asked her if she'd decided to move. Was that because she didn't want to pressure her, or because she was starting to enjoy not having Sandra in their lives so much, glad that she was free to spend time with her own parents now?

42

PATTI

Patti woke up on Saturday feeling a bit restless. It had been a warm night and even with the aircon on it had been difficult to sleep. She went over to the window, opened the blinds and looked out into the little garden. She was having such a marvellous time here. She didn't want to go home. She would miss Mary and Keith and this gorgeous house. And Leo.

She was falling for him which was ridiculous as she barely knew him. But he'd been so kind and was such fun. And the way he looked at her with those rich, brown eyes made her heart flutter.

Don't be silly, he's being friendly because you're Keith's sister.

But Keith and Mary had said that he was interested in her.

What if he was? Nothing would come of it. She and Sandra were going home on Wednesday.

The thought made her feel sad.

She went into the kitchen, there was no sign of Sandra so she must be still asleep. Patti had been pleased to see how her friend had relaxed over the holiday. And how much she'd joined in. She smiled to herself as she recalled their little spat because Sandra had got cold feet about going on the jet ski, but she'd totally rocked it. It was good to see her friend enjoying her life again.

She poured herself a glass of orange and went out into the garden to drink it, savouring the smells of citrus mingled with various floral scents, the sounds of the birds and the early sun shimmering on the pool. Time was ticking. She was looking forward to the flamenco dancing tonight and then tomorrow Mary was taking them for a ride out.

There were no plans for Monday, as yet, but they were doing the Caminito del Rey walk on Tuesday. She really, really wanted to do this. And she was really, really terrified. When she'd looked at the images, the pathway was so high up she'd felt faint. She couldn't look at them any more or she would back out. And she didn't intend to do that. No way. She would keep to the cliffside and not even glance at the huge drop below, she told herself.

'Morning, you're an early bird.' Sandra came out, yawning and stretching. 'What a beautiful day!'

'Isn't it? Keith and Mary are so lucky to be living here.' Patti sighed.

'Oh dear, do I take it that you aren't looking forward to going home?' Sandra pulled out the chair opposite Patti and sat down.

'It's just such a different life, isn't it? The sun, the pool, all the lovely places to go and visit.'

'Not forgetting the very handsome Leo.'

Patti shot a glance at Sandra who was smiling teasingly at her. 'Is it that obvious?'

'It's clear that you both like each other.'

Both like each other. Was it really possible that Leo was attracted to her, like she was to him?

She shrugged. 'I'm too old in the tooth for a holiday romance.'

'I'm amazed to hear that you consider yourself too old for anything!' Sandra replied. 'What about "grabbing life by the horns"?'

'"Life" not "love". And we live in different countries, remember?' She got up. 'I'm going for a swim in the pool. It's a shame to waste such a lovely day.'

She'd just got out of the pool and was sitting on the side drying her hair when Leo came by with Coco. For a moment Patti felt awkward at being in her swimming costume then she thought, damn it, I am what I am and pasted a big smile on her face.

'*Buenos*, Patti. You like an early swim?' he said.

'Morning, Leo. Yes, I do, it livens me up for the day.' She wrapped the towel around her hips and stood up. 'Are you off to walk Coco?'

'Yes, I wondered if anyone wanted to join us?' he asked.

Mary came out of the big house. 'Morning, Leo. I'm afraid me and Keith are a bit busy at the moment. Perhaps you could take Rags for a walk with Leo, Patti? Would you mind? He could do with some exercise as we'll be out later and he'll be home alone.'

Talk about perishing obvious! Patti felt a little awkward at Mary's attempt to push her and Leo together but Leo's smile had widened.

'That would be delightful. If you would like to, Patti.'

So of course she agreed. 'Give me a few minutes to get changed,' she said.

'I'm wondering what to wear for the flamenco dancing tonight,' Patti said as they walked along with the little dogs. 'We only came with a small case each so no space for party dresses.'

'There is no need to worry, it is – how do you say? Smartly casual. Only the dancers will be dressed up.'

'Yes, I've seen the outfits, they're very showy, aren't they?' Patti replied. 'You know, I'd love to be able to do a dance like that. It's one of the things on my bucket list, to learn a new dance.'

'And what else is left on your bucket list?' Leo asked, stopping to let Coco off the lead so she could run free now they were out of the residential area.

Patti let Rags off the lead too. 'To get over my fear of heights,' she said. 'That's why we're going on the Caminito del Rey on Tuesday. I admit I'm terrified.'

'The thought is scary, I can see that. But I have walked it a few times and I assure you that it is safe.'

'I'll take your word for it,' she said.

'You will be okay, you are very brave. I admire you,' Leo said softly.

Patti raised her eyes to his and swallowed. He was looking at her so tenderly.

He's being friendly, kind. Don't read more into it.

'Brave? I'm guessing Mary and Keith have told you about my cancer?'

He nodded. 'It is a lot to go through.'

'It is, but that doesn't make me brave. I survived – kicking, screaming and protesting about the unfairness of it all. And now I'm picking up the pieces and trying to rebuild my life.'

'I think you are more than rebuilding it. You are embracing it,' Leo told her. 'And that is a wonderful thing to do.'

'Thank you.' Patti felt her cheeks burn and tore her gaze away and looked over at Rags who was now rolling in the grass so that Leo wouldn't see her flaming face. *God, she was acting like a teenager on her first date. It was ridiculous. Get a grip, Patti!*

* * *

'Do you think I'll be okay to wear this?' Sandra asked, holding up a white, floaty maxi dress.

'I think it's perfect. Leo said that it's casual smart. I'm going to wear this,' Patti held up a calf-length orange and red flared dress with a zig zag hem. 'I've got some orange sandals to match.'

They had both just finished applying their make-up when Mary, dressed in a pair of smart white linen trousers and a floral top, knocked to say that Leo had arrived.

'We're ready!' Patti said. She and Sandra picked up their bags and headed over to the house where Leo and Keith were chatting on the terrace.

'You look *muy hermosas señoras*,' Leo said, standing up and kissing first Sandra, then Patti on both cheeks, his kiss lingering just a little longer on Patti's. He said we all look very beautiful, don't take it personally, she told herself.

* * *

Patti couldn't take her eyes off the dancers. They were fantastic. The woman was dressed in a red dress that hugged her waist and draped over her hips into a tiered, ruffled skirt. The sleeves also had ruffles at the wrists and she wore shiny, red patent shoes. She was holding a small pair of black castanets in one hand. A man in black flared trousers, white frilled shirt, red cummerbund and black patent shoes was sitting down on a stool, playing a guitar while the woman danced, her hips moving seductively, her hands moving in fluid, circular movements as she clicked the castanets, twisting and turning, her skirt swirling around her as she tapped her feet in time to the music.

Then the owner of the restaurant beckoned Leo forward and Patti's mouth almost dropped open as the man on the stool handed Leo the guitar. Leo sat down and started playing amazingly while the man and woman danced together. The man's hand movements stronger and more energetic than the woman's with controlled hip movement, a perfect display of both masculinity and femininity. Patti watched entranced. The dance ended to enthusiastic applause.

'Did you know Leo could play the guitar like that?' Patti whispered to Mary.

She nodded, her eyes shining with fun. 'He planned it as a surprise for you. He knows the dancers.'

Did Leo know everyone?

'That was wonderful,' she said as Leo took his seat again.

'*Gracias*. My mother, she was a flamenco dancer,' he told her. 'My father used to play the guitar while she danced and he taught me.'

'I would love to be able to dance like that. It's a beautiful, sensual dance,' she said. 'Do you have any photos of your mother doing the flamenco?'

'In my house, yes. Perhaps you would like to see them?'

Was he inviting her to his house or offering to bring the photos over to Keith and Mary's?

'I'd love to,' she replied.

43

MARY

Leo had suggested a trip to Nerja on Sunday and offered to do the driving, 'It's only an hour away and it makes sense to all go in one car,' he said. 'You'll join us won't you, Keith? Don't leave me alone with these mad women. Who knows what they'll be getting up to?' His eyes twinkled.

'I guess I'd better,' Keith said, to Mary's delight. She was so glad she'd confided in Leo about her worries about Keith, and he had offered to organise the ride in the Cadillac, and come out with them a few times in the hope that Keith would join in. Their plan was working nicely. And a bonus was that Patti and Leo seemed to be getting on really well. Mary was sure that Patti was as attracted to him as he was to her. Which could mean that they would be able to coax Patti over for a visit more easily in future. Sandra seemed to be having a good time too, she had really relaxed since she'd arrived. She was a nice woman, hopefully she would return home stronger and more sure of what she wanted. It was good that her son cared about her, but he had to listen to what Sandra wanted too, not just decide for her.

They had all piled into his car on Sunday morning and set off. It was a glorious day, and cool in the car with the aircon on. As before, the three women sat chatting in the back with Keith in the front next to Leo. They'd left Rags in the garden with plenty of water, he had the cool shade of his large kennel to go into and Leo had brought Coco around so that the two little dogs could keep each other company.

Nerja was one of Mary's favourite places. She loved the Andalucian old town with its pebbled streets, whitewashed houses, colourful terraces and quaint shops selling a variety of goods from homemade honey to souvenirs and clothes. Patti and Sandra were fascinated with it too, not being able to resist popping into the shops and buying a couple of souvenirs to squeeze into their cases.

'Wait until you see the Balcón de Europa,' Mary told them, leading the way to the famous tourist spot in the centre of the town. The three women were leading the way, with Keith and Leo walking behind, chatting. They stopped to admire the beautiful tall white arches, decorated with blue flowerpots, taking it in turns to take a photo of themselves standing in the arches that perfectly framed the sea below. She heard Patti gasp. 'This is wonderful! No wonder you love it.'

Patti and Sandra both gazed around them at the amazing views as they walked along the promenade, stopping to look at the various monuments. They sat together on one of the benches and got Leo to take photos of them. Then they walked onto the balcony itself, the spectacular views taking their breath away, as it always did for Mary. She and Keith had come here for their anniversary every year, until he'd had his heart attack last year.

'Oh goodness, this is totally gorgeous!' Patti said as they all stood on the left side, looking down at golden sands of the beach below.

'Isn't it? And look at that cute little house. I wonder if anyone lives there.' Sandra pointed to a little white house with a blue door that was nestled under the rocks against the cliff. 'It looks like it's actually been carved into the cliff.'

'I think it used to be a fisherman's house. I'm not sure if anyone lives in it now but someone definitely looks after it. Look at the plants in the pots, there's a little vegetable garden too.'

They then walked onto the viewing platform and gazed down at the sparkling waters of the Mediterranean Sea below. It really was spectacular. Keith stood next to Mary and put his arm around her waist, Mary smiled up at him, leaning her head against his shoulder. Leo and Patti were standing side by side, gazing out at the sea then Leo turned to Patti and said something and she threw her head back and laughed. Sandra quickly snapped a photo.

They took a selection of photos, Patti and Sandra standing in one of the white archways, gazing out at the sea and mountains; standing each side of the monument of Alfonso XII as well as several of the scenery and group photos. Then they went down the steps to the beach for a closer look at the little cottage cut into the cliff, took a few photos of it, then had a paddle in the sea before going back up the steps to have lunch in a bakery that had a balcony overlooking the beach. It was a wonderful day.

'Only two more days left,' Patti said wistfully when they were all back at home again. 'I've had such a lovely time.'

'I thought that you might want a chill day tomorrow seeing as we're doing the Caminito del Rey on Tuesday so I'm quite happy to stay in and relax around the pool tomorrow. If everyone else is?' Sandra said.

'Sounds good to me,' Patti agreed. 'Although I might take Rags for a walk, have a bit of an explore around, if you don't mind. Don't think you have to come with me. Company accepted but not expected.'

'Coco could do with a walk too, we could join you,' Leo offered. 'Then you can pop in and see the picture of my mother doing the flamenco. That is, if you wish.'

Patti flashed him a smile. 'That sounds perfect. I'm sure these two will enjoy the run together.'

'Let me give you Leo's number, Patti, so that you can message each other when you're ready to go,' Mary said, wanting to give her sister-in-law the option of contacting Leo or not.

'Thank you, if that's okay with you?' Patti looked questioningly at Leo and he nodded.

'Of course.'

Mary sent the number via WhatsApp and Patti immediately sent a message to it. 'Best for you to have my number too,' Patti said.

Mary was pleased that they were going on a walk together tomorrow, hopefully they would decide to keep in touch. It was a shame that Patti was going home the day after tomorrow, but her connection with Leo might make her come over again. She hoped so. Leo was a close friend, he would be good for Patti, and she for him.

44

PATTI

'You have enjoyed your stay?' Leo asked as he and Patti took Rags and Coco for a walk the next morning.

'Very much. I wish we were here longer,' she told him. She didn't feel ready to go back to her normal life yet. She loved it here, the wildness of the countryside, the sun, the fruit trees everywhere, the smell of citrus mingled with oleander and jasmine, the little white house and sparkling blue pools. And Leo. She would miss seeing him almost every day. They got on so well, and she sensed that he liked her, but they were always with the others, so it was hard to tell if it was anything more than friendliness he felt. And maybe it was only friendliness that *she* felt. It had been a while since she'd been close to a man, and she was on holiday. She was probably reading more into her feelings, and the smiles he gave her, than he meant.

'Spain is a beautiful country, will you come over and visit Keith and Mary again?'

She nodded. 'I certainly will now that I've conquered my fear of flying.'

'You were afraid to go in an aeroplane?' He looked so surprised. 'I thought nothing would fear you. You are so strong and,' he paused for a moment, obviously trying to think of the word he wanted, 'fearful… no fear-less, yes that is the word. As if you look life in the eye and take it on.'

He said the words with feeling. She turned her head to look at him. His dark eyes were rested on her and their gazes locked. Her heart did a somersault and her throat felt dry, she moistened her lips with her tongue. 'Thank you. I wouldn't say that I'm fearless, but I am determined to live my life and not let fear *stop* me from doing anything.' She pointed to the tattoo at the top of her right arm 'That's why I had this!'

'Tell me about yourself. You have children, yes?' he said quietly. So, as they walked she told him about her marriage to Adrian, Amanda, her divorce, the cancer. She talked and he listened and then she asked him about his life and he told her about his wife, Elena, and children, Sophia, Pablo and Carlos, how Elena's death had devastated him. 'One moment your life is full, your house is busy and there is no time. Then, in a flash, it is all gone. And all you have left is time. Endless days and long nights.' His expression was solemn, his eyes sad as he gazed over at the two dogs running around. 'I miss Elena every day but she has gone and I am here.'

'Sandra is struggling to get over the death of her husband too,' she said softly. 'I am lucky, I guess, my ex-husband is still alive. A divorce is easier to handle than a death.'

'Surely a divorce is like a death. Your marriage has died.'

'It died long before we got divorced so in a way the divorce was a relief.'

They talked about everything. Their lives, their hopes for the future, their likes and dislikes. Patti thought she had never felt so close to anyone before. How she wished she wasn't going home on Wednesday and could get to know this man more, spend more time walking and talking to him. You're far too old to go all swoony-eyed over someone you've met on holiday, she told herself.

They were on their way back now, the dogs back on their leads. Soon they came to Leo's house, which like Keith and Mary's house, was surrounded by a wall and a high gate.

'Please come in. We will get a cold drink and you can see the picture of my mother,' he said as he unlocked the gate and pushed it open, standing back to allow Patti to go first. She gasped as she stepped inside. There was a large flat area where his car was parked, then the garden was graduated downwards, with colourful plants and cacti growing on different levels. The path led to a pretty pale lemon painted house, with dark brown shutters. There was a pool to the side, set on a crazy paved terrace, surrounded by orange and lemon trees.

'You can let Rags off the lead now,' Leo said, slipping Coco off her lead. 'He knows where to find his bowl of water.'

As soon as she let the little dog off the lead Rags and Coco ran around to the side of the house. Leo and Patti followed them. She saw a large kennel on a platform, two bowls of water by the side. Both dogs ran over and started drinking.

Suddenly, she was aware of a clucking sound from the left. Chickens? She glanced around and saw a wired pen with half a dozen chickens strutting about. A hen house on stilts was in the furthest corner.

'Do they lay eggs?' she asked.

'Yes, I have fresh eggs every day. Sometimes there are too many and I share them with my friends and neighbours.'

Then she remembered the fresh vegetables and eggs he'd given Mary the other night. 'Where is your vegetable patch?' she asked.

'It is down here.' He led her to some steps. Looking down she saw rows of cabbages, lettuces and other vegetables. He stood by her, hands in his pockets, gazing proudly at the vegetable patch.

'This must keep you busy,' she said.

'It does. It is good to have something to fill the time. Shall we have a drink? A *cerveza*? Sangria? Water or perhaps fresh orange or pomegranate juice. It is from my own trees.'

'You have pomegranates growing too?'

'*Si*.' Leo pointed over to a tree where she could see large pomegranates hanging from the branches. 'Fresh pomegranate juice sounds delicious! Thank you.'

They walked back to his house and she paused, wondering whether to wait outside while Leo fetched the drinks, but he beckoned her in. 'Come, I will show you my home.'

Inside, it was very traditional. A big lounge with dark wooden furniture, tiled floors, a wood burner for heating, a huge coffee table, comfy sofa and chairs and a large TV. The far wall was covered in photos. Leo's wife and children, she guessed. On another wall was a large painting of a woman in a red and white dotted flamenco dress, poised mid-dance, a man on a stool beside her playing the guitar.

'My mother and father,' Leo said proudly.

'It's a wonderful painting,' she told him. 'Who was the artist?'

'My father. He used a black and white photo of them both as a guide.'

'That's amazing. What a talented family.'

Her gaze rested on a certificate on the wall, Leonardo Sanchez. She read through, picking up the word *dentista*. 'You were a dentist?' she asked. Then added. 'Oh, you trained in London. So that is why your English is so good.'

'*Si*, I retired a few years ago.'

'Leonardo, it's a nice name. But you prefer Leo?'

'It is easier to say.'

She nodded. 'My name is Patricia, but I prefer Patti.'

'Patreecia,' he said slowly. 'It is pretty.'

Their eyes held for a moment then Leo turned. 'Come, let us get those drinks.'

The kitchen was huge too, again with dark wooden cupboards, a gas stove and a wooden table and six chairs.

'It's very spacious.' Patti gazed around, imagining Leo, Elena and their children gathered around the table eating and chatting.

'Too big now, but when the children were little we needed the space.' He opened the fridge and took out a jug of pomegranate juice, put ice in two glasses and poured the drink over it. 'Would you like tapas? Bread and cheese?' he asked.

'No, thank you. I'm fine.'

He took out two bowls and filled one with olives and the other with a mix of nibbles anyway, then placed it all on a tray. 'Let us sit outside and enjoy the sunshine.'

Both dogs were lying in the shade when they went back out. Leo put the tray down on the table on the terrace, taking the glasses and dishes off and placing them out.

'Please, sit down, help yourself.'

Patti sat down on the nearest chair, picked up one of the drinks and took a long sip. 'This is delicious. Just what I needed.' She gazed around in admiration. 'It must be wonderful to live here and drink juice from your own trees. And eat fresh vegetables and eggs.'

'It is, yes.' Leo sat down beside her. 'Life is good.'

They sat and talked more, Leo told her about Elena who had died in a car accident almost ten years ago. 'The bends here, they are so dangerous.' And his son and daughter who now lived in Barcelona and Madrid. 'They need to be where the work is. I don't see them often now, but we keep in touch.'

'Have you thought of moving nearer to them?' she asked.

He took a long sip of his juice before replying. 'They have asked me, but my life is here.'

She thought about Sandra, and Don trying to persuade her to move to Cambridge. She told Leo about it. 'So you are glad that you didn't move to be by one of your children?'

He leaned back, gazing out over to the mountains. 'The city is not for me. When you are young you are always chasing things, but when you are older it is different. You want a slower life. It is good to go out, to do things, but it is also good to come home to peace and quiet.'

Patti reached for a handful of the nibbles then leaned back to enjoy the view too. There weren't many places more peaceful than this. She didn't blame Leo for wanting to stay here. She wished she could stay here, with him.

The thought took her by surprise and she blinked. Wow, talk about getting carried away.

'Will you be sad to go back and leave all this?' Leo asked quietly. His eyes were fixed on her face, as if her answer was important to him.

She bit her lip as she considered this. 'I will miss it. And Keith and Mary and...' she stopped herself from adding 'and you' but as if he knew what she was going to say he reached out and placed his hand softly on hers. 'And I will miss you. You are...' he paused as if searching for the right word. '*Una luz* – a light in the room.'

Was he saying that she lit up the room? She stared at him, wondering what to say.

'Maybe you will come again to visit your brother very soon?' His voice was soft and his eyes were still on her face.

She nodded. 'Yes, definitely.'

He sat back and smiled. 'I will look forward to that.'

45

SANDRA

Sandra sat outside the casita, enjoying the peace and quiet. Patti had taken Rags for a walk with Leo and Coco, and Mary had invited her over to the house; but she wanted to give her and Keith some time alone. It seemed that their rocky period was over and they were back in tune with each other. She and Patti had walked in on them smooching in the kitchen yesterday, which was endearing but she didn't want to invade their privacy again. And it had been obvious that Patti and Leo were getting close too. Although both couples were going out of their way to include her, Sandra was beginning to feel like a spare part. What was it Honey called it – 'a third wheel'. She'd had a lovely time, and was glad that she'd come with Patti, but she was ready to go back now.

Go back to what though? She'd enjoyed the company whilst she'd been over here, and having places to go, but now she had to go back to an empty house and make a decision on what she did next.

She picked up her phone to check the Old Gals Insta account and noticed that she had a WhatsApp message – she hadn't heard that come in. She opened it up and saw that it was the swimming group chat and there was a string of messages – she'd muted the chat while she was away. She scrolled through the messages; sharing news and asking if they were having a good time, Beryl said it was her birthday on Thursday and she was inviting everyone to her house for a little party after the swimming lessons.

They would be back home by then so it was something to look forward to. Sid had a glut of cabbages and asked if anyone wanted some. Sandra sent a quick text apologising for not reading the messages earlier, replying that they were having a wonderful time, and she'd love a cabbage please She added that she'd be at Beryl's party and was sure Patti would too, but she was out at the moment, and that they'd both catch up with them all on Thursday. Thank goodness for the swimming club, the messages had cheered her up a bit, reminding her that she had friends back at home.

She checked the Insta account, they had over 5,000 followers now and there were several comments about the photos, with people sharing their own photos too. That lifted her spirits as well.

She had no idea what she was going to do when she got back but she did know that she had to keep busy. There was no point in moping around.

What she needed was something to look forward to. Like going to Australia to see Becky. That was the thing she wanted to do most, top of her bucket list. She'd achieved so much in the past couple of months, she'd had a tattoo, had her ears pierced, learnt to swim, gone on a jet ski – and what an experience that was! – a speedboat and with Patti at the helm! Surely, she could catch a plane and go on a flight to Australia. What was stopping her?

She looked at the tattoo just above her wrist. 'Embrace change, live life.'

She could do this.

She picked up her phone and started checking flights. Twenty-two hours it took to get to Australia. She could take something to read, and Hogan had told her that there was plenty of legroom on the long-haul flights. They'd saved the money for the trip, it was still in the bank, although she'd be going by herself not with Brian, as planned.

She was going to do it. She was determined to.

She went inside the casita, poured herself a cold lemonade, grabbed a book and started reading to pass the time.

A couple of hours later she heard Rags barking. Patti was back. That was a long walk. She waited where she was, giving Patti chance to talk to Keith and Mary. A little later Patti came over to casita. 'Hello, have you had a restful morning? Mary said you were having some "me" time.'

Sandra looked up from the book. 'It's been very relaxing. How did your walk go? You must have covered some distance.'

Patti flushed and sat down on the chair next to her. 'Leo invited me back for a drink and to see the picture of his mother – it's a painting actually of both his parents and is really stunning. I can see where he gets his good looks from.' She gushed. 'His house is lovely, and he's such good company. He used to be a dentist, you know. And his wife died in a car accident and he's got three kids but they live in Northern Spain. You should see his garden, he's got chickens and all sorts of veg growing there. Even pomegranates.' She paused for breath.

'You two have really hit it off, haven't you?' Sandra asked. 'Will you keep in touch when you go back home?'

Patti sighed and leant on the table, resting her chin on her hands. 'We haven't talked about it. To be honest, I'd love to keep in touch, but what would be the point? Leo's home is here and mine is in the UK. Although he did say he'd miss me and asked me if I would come back again.'

'And will you miss him?'

'He's good company and really interesting to talk to.' Patti glanced at her watch. 'Goodness, is that the time. Sorry. I didn't mean to leave you alone for so long.'

'I don't mind at all. I've had a lovely time sitting here reading. This holiday has been wonderful, but I never expected you to spend every minute with me.'

'Are you sure? I was a bit worried that you might be feeling left out.' Patti poured herself a glass of lemonade. 'Now, what's been happening?'

'Have you checked the WhatsApp swimming group chat?' Sandra filled her in.

'No to cabbages but yes to the party. We've got ourselves a great little bunch of friends there, haven't we?'

'We have. I'm quite looking forward to going back and seeing everyone again.' She'd had a really great time, but she'd be glad to be back in her own house, and to see Kali and Rana and Don and Laila, of course. They'd all be leaving soon, she wanted to make the most of the time they'd got left together.

'Me too,' Patti said, but Sandra had the feeling that her friend was much fonder of Leo than she was letting on, and wasn't looking forward to going home as much as Sandra was.

46

PATTI

'I almost wish I was going on the walk too. We always said we'd do it together,' Keith said as they got ready to go to the Caminito del Rey the next morning.

'I did ask you to come with us. You didn't want to,' Mary reminded him.

'I know. Well, maybe we can both do it another time.'

Mary folded her arms and cocked her head on to one side. 'Are you serious? If we could get you a ticket, you'd come with us…?'

'I would but don't worry, I know it was my fault and you're not likely to get a spare ticket at this short notice.'

'Actually, I've got one. I bought an extra ticket in the hope that you might change your mind.'

Keith looked really taken aback. 'You did?'

'I did,' Mary told him. 'So go and get yourself ready. We'll be leaving in ten minutes.'

For a moment it looked like Keith was going to say no, but then he nodded. 'Okay, I will.'

'Well, that was a turn up for the books!' Patti exclaimed. 'Good for you getting an extra ticket. What if Keith had turned it down though?'

Mary shrugged. 'Then I'd have wasted my money but I thought it was worth taking the chance. We've been saying for years that we'll go on that walk so I hoped he might come with us at the last minute. Especially as he's been out and about the past few days. And he's stopped taking his blood pressure every morning,' she confided. 'That show's he's relaxing a bit now.'

'I don't know about relaxing, I'm freaking out!' Patti said.

'You'll be okay. You saw the photos, it's all been reconstructed and looks perfectly safe,' Sandra replied. 'There are barriers everywhere, and everyone has to wear a hard hat.'

'Which indicates that there's a need to wear one.'

'Look, if you really feel that you don't want to do it when we get there, we'll sit it out. There's a café we can sit in it and wait for Mary and Keith to come back.'

Patti wondered if they should do that anyway, Mary and Keith were growing closer and it might be nice to let them do the walk together.

'You'll be waiting a couple of hours.' Mary told her. 'Besides I really think you'll regret it if you don't do it, Patti. We'll look after you. You can walk close to the cliff wall, then you won't be looking down.'

'I'm really nervous but I do want to do it. Especially as I've told Kit – she's jealous as she says she'd love to do that walk – and the swimming group gang.' She nodded firmly. 'I'm going to do it.' She had to. She would regret it if she didn't.

***

The Caminito del Rey really was spectacular. Patti had a bit of a wobbly moment when she saw the narrow paths running along the side of the cliffs of the El Chorro gorge, but once she was walking along it – keeping near the cliff side at first, clutching onto the rope handrail – she started to relax. There were a lot of other people doing the walk, some older children too, and many of them were peering over the side looking down into the blue waters of the gorge a hundred metres below. Keith and Mary were fascinated by it all, but Patti kept back a little.

Sandra did too. 'It's a bit hairy but I'm glad we're doing it,' she whispered.

They even plucked up the courage to stand on the glass platform for a photo. Crossing the suspension bridge over to the other side was the scariest. Keith went first, then Mary, then Sandra and Patti last. Patti gripped the sides of the bridge and kept her gaze focused on her friends ahead. Keith with his arm around Mary and Sandra urging her on. Finally, she stepped off, relieved to have firm ground underneath her feet again.

Mary took a photo. 'You've both done great! I've got some amazing photos for your Insta!'

* * *

Leo came around later that evening to say goodbye. They had supper out on the terrace, with wine. Leo was sitting opposite Patti and she could feel his eyes upon her. She raised her eyes to meet his for a moment and was taken aback by the intensity she saw in them.

'Have you both achieved everything on your bucket list?' he asked.

'Not yet, the list keeps growing!' Patti replied. 'We keep thinking of other things we want to do.'

'Top of my list is to see my daughter and family in Australia,' Sandra said. 'I've decided that I'm going this Christmas, as me and Brian planned. I can do it. Becky wants me to spend a couple of months with them. I've even started looking into flights!'

'Good for you,' Patti told her.

Their flight home wasn't until mid-morning, so they sat outside talking until fairly late that evening. Patti didn't want to go back but resolved that she was definitely going to come again. It had been good to see Keith and Mary, and their gorgeous home. Now when they were talking to her about the places they'd been, she could imagine them.

And it had been lovely to meet Leo. They had bonded immediately and it felt so right being with him. She wished that they'd had more time to talk, to develop their relationship a bit. Apart from when they walked the two dogs they hadn't had much time just the two of them, because they'd all gone out together. Besides, Sandra had come to Spain to support Patti so Patti wasn't about to ditch her for a man she'd only recently met, no matter how much she liked him.

She went into the kitchen to get a cold drink. Opening the fridge, she took out the home-made lemonade, not wanting to drink any more alcohol as they were flying tomorrow. Suddenly, she was aware that someone was behind her and turning around she saw Leo watching her.

'I'm sorry, I didn't hear you come in. Did you want a drink? Or more snacks? Or are you going?' The words came tumbling out because she didn't know how she was going to say goodbye to him.

'I am leaving now, yes, because I want to give you some time with your family and friend.'

'Oh.' Her heart sank.

He moved a little closer. 'It has been good to meet you, Patti. You are fun —' She was suddenly aware that his eyes were looking into hers and she felt a flutter in the pit of her stomach. 'And brave, and beautiful.'

Beautiful! She was sixty-eight for goodness' sake, with a lined face and wrinkly skin. 'Thanks, I'll take the fun and brave but...'

'No buts, you are beautiful.' He paused, his dark eyes searching her face. 'I would like us to keep in touch. If you would like that too?'

Would she ever! 'Facetime you mean? Message each other?'

'Yes,' he said solemnly. 'And maybe we can visit each other too? England is not too far away. A couple of hours on the plane.'

He wanted to see her again. He would even come and visit! She swallowed. 'I would. Yes. That would be good. Really good.'

His face creased into a smile. 'You will let me know when you arrive home?'

'Of course.' What happened now? Was he talking about them being friends? Or something more? *Just ask him, for goodness' sake, Patti!*

'I will. It's good that we can remain friends.'

'Friends?' He raised his hand and lightly caressed her cheek. 'I am hoping we can be more than friends. Is that all you want, to be friends?'

I want you to kiss me.

He'd moved a little closer. 'I was hoping we might kiss before you go.'

'That sounds good to me!' *Gosh, she hadn't meant to sound that enthusiastic!*

She didn't know who made the first move, but they were in each other's arms, kissing, when suddenly someone coughed behind them. It was Mary.

'About time! I thought you two were going to pussyfoot around each other forever.' Her face broke into a wide grin. 'Does this mean you'll come back and visit us again very soon, Patti?'

Leo kept his arm around Patti as they turned to face her. 'I think we can visit each other. Maybe, as Patti's friend is going to Australia for Christmas, Patti might come to Spain then.'

Mary's grin spread even wider. 'That's a wonderful idea.'

Patti walked to the gate with Leo and they kissed goodbye again, lingering with their arms around each other for a while, as if they were both reluctant to let go.

'Shall I call you tomorrow night or is that too soon?' he asked, softly.

'I'd really like that.' She caressed his cheek with her hand. '*Adiós.*'

He shook his head. 'Not *adiós. Hasta luego* – see you soon.'

'*Hasta luego*,' she repeated softly.

Sandra's eyes were wide with surprise when Patti returned to the terrace.

'Are you two—?'

'We're going to keep in touch.'

'That's brilliant. I'm delighted for you both.' Sandra grinned. 'I can't believe that you've got yourself a Spanish boyfriend.' She cocked her head to one side. 'Is that going on our Insta page? It might remind other older women that they're not too old for love.'

Patti picked up an apple from the bowl on the table and took a bite. 'It's not love. Yet.' She said with a twinkle in her eye.

Sandra gave her a hug. 'I'm so pleased for you. You make a great couple.'

'It's like being teens all over again, my sister and my best mate!' Keith said with a grin. 'Good on ya, Patti!'

47

SANDRA

It was nice to be home, Sandra thought as she wheeled her suitcase into the hall. The house felt quiet, empty after the past two weeks with constant company. She had really enjoyed herself but now it was time to get back to normal, and also to decide what she was going to do with her life.

Tomorrow they had the swimming group and Beryl's party, then she would see Don, Laila and the children, and she was going to tell them that she'd definitely decided that she wasn't going to move to Cambridge. She was no longer scared of change, Mary and Keith had made a new life in Spain and she could make a new life in Cambridge if she wanted, it would be an adventure. The thing is, right now she was having plenty of adventures where she was, she'd realised. She'd leant on Don, Laila and the children while she'd got over her grief for Brian, and she was very grateful for their support, but now she had to stand on her own two feet and leave them to live their lives. She had friends here, not just Patti, but the swimming club gang. She could do some volunteering, that would keep her busy, and when Don and Laila moved, she could find a little B&B near them and stay for weekends. That way she could get to know the area, and if she fell in love with it, *then* she would consider moving there. But that was for the future.

One thing she was definitely going to do though was visit Becky. She was longing to see them all again, it had been so long. She and Brian had saved hard for the trip and he would want her to go – for both of them.

And to make sure she didn't change her mind, she would message Becky right now and let her know. They'd all be in bed, asleep, but it'd be a nice message for them to wake up to.

When she came back, she might get a little dog, she thought. Rags was so cute, and it would be good to have a dog to take for a walk. She always felt odd walking by herself, but with a little dog it was fine. Dogs were an ice breaker too, they opened the doors to a new community and she could always find a nice kennel or dog minder for when she went away. As for going to Cambridge for the weekend, she was sure that there were some B&Bs that welcomed well-behaved little dogs.

She went over to the photo of Brian that stood on the sideboard and picked it up, her fingers touching his face. 'I'm going to be all right, darling. I'll never stop loving you and missing you, but I'm strong enough to build a life without you now.'

His eyes twinkled back at her and she knew that wherever he was he understood.

* * *

Beryl's party was great fun. They all brought something with them. Sandwiches, sausage rolls, quiche, Sid bought lettuce and tomatoes from his garden and Bill brought some home-made wine. Madge had told them all to bring a CD of their favourite music – 'I don't have one of those Alexa thingies,' she said. Patti had taken a Tina Turner CD and Sandra a Beatles one. Madge was a Queen fan, Beryl was mad about Elvis, Sid came with some Jazz music and Bill had brought a Beatles CD too – luckily a different one to Sandra.

'Are they your favourite group too?' he asked.

'You bet,' she replied.

'Well how do you fancy going to a Beatle's Tribute night tomorrow? My mate Ray was supposed to be coming with me, but something's come up at the last minute, so his ticket is going spare.'

Sandra hesitated. Go for it, she told herself, it would be a good night out. What have you got to lose? 'I'd love to,' she said.

* * *

Don looked surprised when he popped in with the girls on Sunday to find Beatles music blaring out the CD player.

'I didn't know you still had that!'

'I found it in Dad's shed along with a pile of CDs. I went to see a Beatles Tribute act with someone from the swimming group last night. It was good fun. Reminded me how much I loved the music so I found all my old CDs and thought I'd play some of them.'

'You and Dad were mad on them, weren't you?' Don said with a smile.

'We were. George was always my favourite but your dad favoured Paul.'

'Nanny, we saw your Insta pics of Spain. That cliff walk was scary,' Rana told her. 'Were you frightened?'

'A bit, but it was very safe. And I'm pleased I did it,' Sandra said.

'And we saw you on a jet ski. I want to go on a jet ski,' Kali said.

'Now that was even scarier. I almost didn't do it.' Sandra chuckled at the memory of the spat she had with Patti over it.

'You do look like you had a lot of fun. I think it did you good to go away, Mum. Did your friend enjoy it too?' Don asked.

'She did. And her brother and sister-in-law were wonderful hosts. They looked after us really well and took us out and about.' Sandra went over to the cupboard. 'I have presents for you all.' She took out the T-shirts and yo-yos she'd bought Kali and Rana and they shouted their thanks and immediately took the yo-yos out in the garden to play with. Then she handed some Spanish coasters to Don. 'I only had a small suitcase so couldn't bring much, but I thought you might like these for your new home.'

'They're great, thanks, Mum.' He looked at her. 'Now, are you going to sell your house and come with us? We all missed you when you were away in Spain.'

She patted his hand. 'Sorry, love, but I'm staying here. I've got a great bunch of friends, so you don't have to worry about me being lonely. And I'm going to start decluttering the house, which will keep me busy for a while.' She pointed to the two big plastic storage boxes she'd started packing some of Martin's things into.

Don's forehead puckered into a frown. 'Mum, are you sure about this? What if you need help with anything? It will take me a while to get to you.'

'If I need help then I'll ask one of my friends. I'm not alone, Don. I have people I can turn to.'

Don was silent for a moment then he nodded. 'Well, it sounds like you've got it all figured out, Mum, and I feel like you're in a good place now. I don't feel so concerned about leaving you.'

'I am, darling. I was floundering for a while, but I've found my feet again. There's no need to worry about me, I'm going to be absolutely fine. In fact, I've decided to visit Becky for Christmas, like me and Dad planned.'

Don's eyes widened with shock. She braced herself for him to tell her that it was much too far for her to go alone. It took him a moment to compose himself then he smiled. 'That's great, Mum. You'll have a fantastic time. Maybe we could come too, just for a couple of weeks.'

'Really? That would be fantastic. And Becky would be over the moon!'

'Let's see, once we're settled into our house. This job is a higher wage, we might be able to do it.'

Things really were looking up, Sandra thought happily. She would go alone if she had to but it would be wonderful if Don, Laila and the children came too.

48

SANDRA

December

Life had changed so much in the last few months. Although they no longer attended the swimming class, the group met up regularly for a swim, and for lunch, or to go to the cinema. They all shared skills to help each other, with Sid and Madge – who were both a dab hand with a drill – offering their services to put up shelves, do general repairs or mow the lawn, Bill making cakes, Beryl doing clothes repairs and turning up curtains. Patti loved decorating and Sandra was always happy to offer help in the garden or with spring cleaning. She loved the companionship of the group. She'd been to a few Beatles tributes with Bill, he had encouraged her to join the Beatles fan club, which was great fun and they had become good friends, both agreeing that they weren't looking for romance, but enjoyed each other's company.

Patti and Leo had become very close, he'd been over to visit Patti twice and she was flying over to spend Christmas and New Year with him, Keith and Mary.

Both their bucket lists were ever growing. Sandra and Patti had both started going to Zumba classes, which was great fun and helped them keep fit. They'd both been to London to see *Chicago* on stage, Sandra had bought a gorgeous pair of dangly diamante earrings for the occasion, and Patti had actually grown her nails long enough to paint them silver and decorate them with gems. She was so proud of that. They'd taken photos of course, and uploaded them to their Instagram page with the caption:

> Two more things off our bucket list. And well done, Patti for growing your nails!

They hadn't got around to going in an air balloon yet, but she would soon. It was on her list to do in Australia. She was excited about going. Don, Laila and the children were travelling with her, but coming back after two weeks whereas she was staying for two months. It would be good to have company on the way there. And in a way, Brian was coming too. It had been Becky's idea. 'Bring Dad's ashes, Mum,' she'd said. 'You can scatter them over here. He might not have been able to visit us when he was alive, but he can be with us in spirit.'

Sandra thought it was a lovely idea. Don had too. They were all going to scatter the ashes together and share memories of Brian. They'd looked up the procedure, got the necessary paperwork and were all set to go.

When Brian had died, Sandra thought that her world had ended, and she would never find enjoyment in life again. But, thanks to her family and friends, she'd come through. And yes, she still missed Brian, always would, but she was living her life again. And enjoying it too.

The beep of a horn told her Don had arrived. She was travelling to the airport with him, Laila and the children, leaving her car in the garage here. Kit was going to check on Patti's house whilst she was away in Spain, and Bill had promised to check on Sandra's.

She was excited about the trip and looking forward to seeing Becky, Hogan, Zac and Honey again. She pulled up her sleeve and looked at the words tattooed there. 'Embrace change, love life.' Well, she was doing that.

She smiled as she thought of Patti's tattoo. 'Grab life by the horns.' Patti was certainly doing that. She loved jetting between Spain and England, she said it was the best of both worlds and it meant she and Leo didn't get bored with each other.

'You know, I had a secret thing on my bucket list, that was to fall in love again,' Patti had confessed to Sandra, 'but I didn't write it down as I thought it would never happen at my age. But I was wrong. You're never too old for love.'

'You should add that to our Insta, it will give others hope,' Sandra had told her. 'Not that I'm looking for love, but I'm very happy for you and Leo.'

The horn sounded again. Time to go. Sandra picked up her suitcase and set off down the stairs. Don was waiting by the car, he took the suitcase off her and put it in the boot.

'Ready, Mum?'

'Yes, love.' She slid into the back of the car, next to Kali. She'd just fastened her seat belt when a text pinged in. Then another. And another. She took her phone out of her pocket and opened it. It was the swimming group. Everyone was wishing her and Patti fabulous trips. 'See you when you get back.'

'You've got lots of friends, Nanny,' Kali said.

'I have, haven't I? Sandra smiled. How her life had changed since she bumped into Patti again. And it had all started with the Old Gals' Bucket List.

49

PATTI

New Year's Eve

'Are you ready?' Leo asked, coming into the bedroom. 'We need to leave soon.'

'Coming!' Patti took a final look at herself in the mirror. The red and black flamenco dress fitted her perfectly. She slipped her feet into a pair of black patent shoes and picked up the castanets, then turned to Leo. 'How do I look?'

'Stunning,' he told her.

'So do you,' she said with a smile. He did too. He was wearing high-waisted black flared trousers, a gold cummerbund, a black bolero embroidered with gold over a white, frilled shirt and black patent shoes.

He took her hand and looked at her bright red nails, decorated with a single black gem in the middle. 'These are beautiful.'

She smiled. 'Thank you. Are you taking your guitar?'

He shook his head. 'There will be a crowd and I might lose it, or it could get damaged.' He crooked his arm. 'Shall we go? Keith and Mary will be waiting.'

When Keith and Mary had told them they were joining in the local tradition of gathering in the square by the church, wearing fancy dress, to see the New Year in, Patti had wanted to join in. She'd spotted the flamenco dress in a charity shop and immediately bought it, suggesting that Leo wear his flamenco outfit too.

She thought of Sandra over in Australia, ticking the big thing from her bucket list. They'd both achieved such a lot over the last few months and had so much fun.

Leo was driving then leaving the car in one of the car parks on the outskirts of the town. They beeped their horn at the gate and Mary and Keith came out, dressed in 1920's outfits. Mary in a fringed Charleston dress, complete with a string of pearls, headband and a cigarette holder, Keith in a black suit, with a white shirt, braces, trilby, black shoes and a pair of spats. They looked amazing, and happy. They'd started an Instagram page themselves, sharing photos of their life in Spain.

Patti couldn't believe how many people turned up in fancy dress, throngs of people in a wide assortment of costumes filled the streets, all piling into the square just before midnight. It was an amazing scene and a real festive atmosphere. People were gathered on the surrounding balconies, eager to join in the celebrations.

'Do you have your grapes?' Mary asked. She'd bought each of them a small tin of twelve grapes, explaining to Patti that when the clock chimed midnight it was the custom to eat a grape on every chime.

'They are in my pocket.' Leo took them out and handed a small tin to Patti.

'Thank you.' She pulled the silver foil lid of the tin, relieved to see that they were small seedless grapes and would be easy to swallow.

There was a chorus of cheers as the clock started to chime and everyone began to count in Spanish, popping a grape into their mouth at every chime. Midnight was greeted with even louder cheers and bottles of fizz were uncorked, spraying everywhere, showering the crowd. Everyone was kissing, hugging, wishing each other happy new year.

'*¡Feliz año nuevo*!' 'Happy New Year!' The shout went out in Spanish and English.

Mary hugged Patti. 'I'm so glad you plucked up the courage to visit us. It changed everything.'

It certainly did.

'Happy New Year, sis.' Keith kissed her on the cheek.

'Happy New Year!' she replied.

A hand wound around her waist and Leo turned her towards him. '*¡Feliz año nuevo*!' he said softly. He lowered his lips to hers. '*Te amo, cariño.*'

For a moment she was stunned. He said that he loved her. His eyes were searching hers, waiting.

What the hell, 'Grab life by the horns, Patti!' She kissed him back. 'I love you too.'

And that was the last thing off her bucket list.

For now.

EPILOGUE

SANDRA

'Oh my goodness, look at Don!' Laila exclaimed, pointing out to the sea.

Sandra followed her gaze and saw Don standing on the surfboard, riding a wave. He held the pose for a moment then wobbled and fell off into the sea. Laila got to her feet, shielding her eyes with her hand, then breathed out a sigh of relief as Don surfaced, laughing.

'He's really taken to it, hasn't he? Who knew?' Sandra remarked.

Rana and Kali had both begged for surfing lessons and to their astonishment Don had not only agreed but joined them. She was sure that was mainly so he could keep an eye on the kids, but he seemed to be actually enjoying it.

'You've been a good influence on him, Sandra. He's seen how you've been determined to pick yourself up and live your life to the fullest and it's encouraged him to do the same.'

Sandra smiled. 'I'm pleased to hear it. Now he's stopped worrying about me he can relax and get on with his life instead.'

'We've all decided to go on the air balloon with you this afternoon,' Laila told her. 'It will be an adventure for the girls.'

Well, that was another turn up for the books. Don had been aghast when she'd first mentioned going up in an air balloon but Becky, Hogan. Zac and Honey were all going too. Don must have decided he didn't want to miss out. Kali was now seven which meant both girls met the age and height restrictions so Don and Laila had agreed they could go with them on the half an hour flight. They were all so excited.

* * *

'I can't believe I'm doing this,' Sandra said as the air balloon floated serenely through the almost cloudless sky over the scenic valley below. She felt overwhelmed with happiness at taking this flight with her family, all together, enjoying the experience. For a long time she thought she would never be happy again but now she was looking forward to the future.

'That's the last thing off your bucket list, isn't it Mum?' Becky asked when they had landed, collected their photo that the organisers had taken and were having lunch before they went home. 'Has Patti completed hers?'

Sandra opened up The Old Gals' Instagram page, uploaded the photo of them all in the air balloon, ticked it off the list and added something to the bottom of the list. Then she turned her phone around so that Becky could see the screen.

Patti

- ☑ Get over my fear of flying and go to Spain
- ☑ Get a tattoo
- ☑ Get over my fear of heights
- ☑ Stop biting my nails
- ☑ Grow my nails and wear nail gems
- ☑ Eat some exotic food
- ☑ Learn a new dance
- ☑ Go on a jet ski
- ☑ Sit on the beach drinking fizz as I watch the sun go down
- ☑ See a musical on stage in London
- ☑ Secret wish - to fall in love again

Sandra

- ☑ Visit Becky in Australia
- ☑ Get a tattoo
- ☑ Learn to swim
- ☑ Have my ears pierced
- ☑ Wear a hat
- ☑ Start decluttering
- ☑ Create a new cocktail
- ☑ Sail across the sea in a motor yacht
- ☑ Go up in a hot air balloon
- ☑ Sit on the beach drinking fizz as I watch the sun go down
- ☑ See a musical on stage in London
- ☑ Secret wish - to be able to look forward to the future again

'For now. But I'm sure we'll both be adding a lot more to the list in the future.'

* * *

MORE FROM KAREN KING

Another book from Karen King, *Growing Old Disgracefully*, is available to order now here:

https://mybook.to/GrowOldDisgracefully

ACKNOWLEDGEMENTS

Huge thanks to my amazing editor Isobel Akenhead for your eagle eye in spotting inconsistencies, absurdities and the occasional howlers in my early drafts. I am always grateful for your expertise and insight. You are so fantastic at grasping the story I'm trying to write, helping me bring it out and making it better.

It takes a whole team to turn a manuscript into a book, including editors, proofreaders, cover designers, sales and marketing people, so huge thanks to everyone at Boldwood Books for their input. Thanks also to the bloggers, readers and other authors who support me, share my posts, review my books and host me on their blogs. I appreciate you all. Also thanks to the members of the Savvy Writer's Snug and the Boldwood Authors Facebook groups for their support, encouragement and advice.

As always, a massive thanks to my Dave and my family and friends who all support me so much. I love you all. A special mention to my granddaughters Kit and Honey who are the inspiration for their namesakes in this book. You are both amazing!

Patti's story was inspired by the real-life Cancer Queens that I know, women – both close family and friends – who have gone through this terrible disease with such courage and strength and come out the other end determined to make the most of their lives. You know who you are, and I'm in awe of you. Sandra's story was inspired by all the women who have lost their partners and have somehow found the courage to pick themselves up, carry on with their lives and make every day count. And we all know a woman like Mary whose marriage suddenly takes a detour from the path she expected and who holds on trying to steer it back on course. This is a story of sisterhood, of women helping and supporting each other to live their best lives. To all my 'sisters' thank you for being there for me.

Final thanks to The Troopers, for sharing your bucket lists with me and for being a constant inspiration. I hope you all manage to tick everything off your lists. Keep on 'grabbing life by the horns'!

ABOUT THE AUTHOR

Karen King is the internationally bestselling author of romance, psychological thrillers and women's fiction.

Download your exclusive bonus content from Karen King here:

Visit Karen's website: www.karenkingauthor.com

Follow Karen on social media here:

facebook.com/KarenKingAuthor
x.com/karen_king
instagram.com/karenkingauthor
bookbub.com/profile/karen-king

ALSO BY KAREN KING

The Runaway Wives

The Old Gals' Bucket List

Growing Old Disgracefully

www.ingramcontent.com/pod-product-compliance
Lightning Source LLC
LaVergne TN
LVHW030914080826
845145LV00012B/2892